A WICKED WAGER

AVENGING LORDS - BOOKS 2

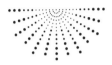

ADELE CLEE

This is a work of fiction. All names, characters, places and incidents are products of the author's imagination. All characters are fictitious and any resemblance to real persons, living or dead, is purely coincidental.

No part of this book may be copied or reproduced in any manner without the author's permission.

CHAPTER ONE

BROOKS' GENTLEMEN'S CLUB, LONDON,
OCTOBER 1820

The ivory dice rattled in the wooden cup. Three shakes and they flew out onto the pristine green cloth covering the hazard table. Ten men stood stiffly and watched with bated breath as the white cubes rolled to a stop.

No one moved.

No one spoke.

No one dared blink.

"Ten," the setter called in his monotone voice. "You roll again, Lord Criddle."

The room erupted in a chorus of frustrated grumbles and whoops of pleasure. Men dabbed their brows with their handkerchiefs, others snatched glasses of port from the tray of a waiting footman and downed the contents without pause.

Devlin Drake weighed the odds of Criddle rolling his third *chance*. Winning at hazard had as much to do with understanding probability as it did with luck, and Devlin was exceptionally skilled when it came to mathematical equations.

Of course, there were always those desperate to steer the game in their favour.

Here, in this private room at Brooks', the house took every

1

precaution to guard against cheats and chancers. New dice were inspected for shaved edges and bristles. The tapping of dice was strictly forbidden lest one wished to find themselves accused of dishonesty and issued with a challenge to meet on the common.

"A thousand pounds on Lord Criddle rolling a throw out," one eager gentleman called.

Devlin needed to lose to the house once more, perhaps twice if he hoped to lure his quarry into his trap. He did not need to lock eyes with Baron Bromfield to know that the arrogant lord watched his every move. The man's beady stare felt like hot rays searing Devlin's skin.

A warm wave of satisfaction rippled through Devlin's chest. Before the evening was out, he would have the bastard on his knees, begging and pleading for clemency.

The setter—a thin man with spectacles and long, bony fingers —scanned those crowded around the table. "Any more bets, gentlemen?"

Devlin cleared his throat. "A thousand pounds in favour of Criddle rolling another *chance*."

Stunned gasps replaced the mumbled chatter.

Devlin moved to the side table, took a slip of paper, dipped the nib of the quill in ink and scrawled his wager. After dusting the note, he returned and handed it to the setter.

Other gentlemen followed suit, taking advantage of the brief respite to whisper and stare in Devlin's direction.

No one cared how much Lord Criddle won or lost. No one cared for the sotted fools willing to stake everything they owned, hoping for a stroke of luck.

Everyone wanted to know what had brought Devlin home from India after five long years. Everyone wanted to know when he would issue Baron Bromfield with a challenge after learning of the spiteful gossip spread by the lord's daughter.

Valentine appeared at Devlin's shoulder and drew him away from the gaming table. "I trust you know what you're about,

Drake," his friend whispered before taking a sip of port. "Despite numerous attempts, Criddle has yet to roll three in a row."

Devlin turned to the viscount and raised a brow. "You've seen me play enough over the years to have faith in both my judgement and my ability."

Along with Greystone and Lockhart, Valentine had been Devlin's constant companion during their time abroad. The four men were closer than brothers.

"Bromfield is no imbecile. He knows you're seeking an opportunity to settle the score."

"Settle the score?" Devlin's hatred ran deeper than a game of tit for tat. Satisfaction would take more than an apology or a call for first blood.

Devlin had come to win something more valuable than money.

He had come to win a wife.

Indeed, he would spend the rest of his life making Miss Bromfield pay for the evil lies she had spread about his brother, Ambrose.

"Miss Bromfield's vicious snipes played some part in my brother's death," Devlin said, frustrated at having to keep his voice low. "I plan to make that spoilt harpy rue the day she crossed my family."

All boisterous talk in the room suddenly dissolved into an uneasy silence.

Devlin turned back to the gaming table to watch Lord Criddle roll a two.

"Throw out," called the setter and Devlin cursed at his loss as did those who had followed suit.

And so the evening went on.

Devlin ensured he lost more than he won. When it was his turn to cast, his usual stern expression heightened the nervous tension thrumming in the air about the table. Towering above most men, and with a chest twice as broad, few people were brave enough to bet against him.

Valentine wagered two thousand pounds on Devlin to win—a measly amount for a man of Valentine's wealth, which was why Devlin felt no remorse when he deliberately lost.

Other than the fact Mr Danes had to be escorted home for fear the man's losses might lend him to swallow the muzzle of his pistol, the game passed without incident.

Notes were tallied. The house made calls for the settlement of all debts.

While watching anyone win or lose in a high-stakes game proved exciting, it was the private wagers made after the event that sent hot blood rushing through a man's veins. Indeed, Devlin stepped forward as planned when Edwin Harridan-Jones—Greystone's illegitimate wastrel of a brother—pleaded for more time to settle his account.

"You know the rules, sir," the setter said in a tone that gave no room for negotiation. "In placing your bets, you agreed to the terms."

"I'm not saying I cannot pay. I am simply asking for more time."

"Perhaps I might offer a suggestion," Devlin called out from the crowd, eager to deal with this matter so he might focus on his own cunning plan. The crowd parted as he pushed closer to the gaming table and addressed the setter. "I will cover the gentleman's debts in exchange for his vowel."

Mr Harridan-Jones' lips trembled as he craned his neck to look at Devlin. "Wh-what so you may give the vowel to Greystone? I would rather take a trip to the morgue than let him hold me to ransom."

Devlin fixed him with a hard stare, the vicious look that caused men to stumble backwards wide-eyed and ready to run. "Trust me. That can be arranged. Indeed, I would take great pleasure in seeing to the matter personally."

"I—I suppose Greystone suggested that, too," his friend's scrawny brother said.

If Greystone wanted the dolt dead, he would not be breathing.

"Lord Greystone has more important matters on his mind." At this hour, the lord would be in bed entertaining his new bride. "What say you? Shall we let the dice decide your fate?"

The desperate fool searched the curious faces in the crowd. "Will anyone else stand good for me until I can secure the necessary funds?"

Baron Bromfield snorted, unable to resist the urge to intervene. "Take your chances, that's what I say. Roll the damn dice. Drake has his brother's luck, and we all know how that ended."

Anger ignited in Devlin's chest—a hot fiery rage capable of tearing through the room and causing carnage. How dare the bastard mention his brother. Devlin grabbed a goblet of port off the table and downed the contents to douse the flames. Oh, he wanted to beat the baron to a pulp. But revenge hurt best when delivered from unexpected quarters.

Devlin scooped up the wooden cup and thrust it into Mr Harridan-Jones' hand. "You win, I pay your debt. I win, I pay the house and take your vowel. Agreed?"

No serious gambler could refuse such a generous offer.

Mr Harridan-Jones took a few seconds to reach a decision and then he nodded to the setter. With his free hand, he scribbled his vowel on the paper slip, then rattled the cup and after some hesitation threw an eight.

Hushed whispers breezed through the room.

Devlin captured the cup and shook a ten.

Gentlemen snorted, others chuntered.

Mr Harridan-Jones gripped the table. Bony white knuckles looked ready to burst through the skin as he tried to remain upright. "Damn you to hell," he snarled between gritted teeth.

The setter waved to the door of the private room. "You're free to leave, sir. Mr Drake will settle your account and take possession of your vowel."

It took a moment for Mr Harridan-Jones to regain his composure. Even so, he stumbled from the room like a man deep in his cups, barged shoulders with those standing in his way and knocked over chairs to release his pent-up aggression.

"You were wrong about me having my brother's luck, Bromfield." Devlin fixed his gaze on the baron, the comment being his first move in the next game of wits.

The lord was of slender proportion—one punch would take him clean off his feet. Blonde locks gave Bromfield the appearance of a much younger man for it was almost impossible to note the fine streaks of grey at his temples. But it was the baron's arrogant countenance and air of superiority that brought bile bubbling up to Devlin's throat.

"Beating Greystone's pathetic brother is hardly something to boast about." The baron's tone brimmed with contempt as he stared down his aquiline nose. "Next time seek a worthy opponent."

Devlin resisted the urge to fold his arms across his chest for the circumference of his muscular arms often gave men pause. "That sounds like a challenge." His hands throbbed to knock the smirk off Bromfield's face. "Are you suggesting we make a wager?"

All noise in the room ceased.

The atmosphere grew heavy and oppressive.

Men froze, glasses half raised to their mouths, awaiting the baron's reply.

The baron's cold gaze drifted over Devlin, hard and assessing. "I would hate to relieve you of your measly winnings."

Devlin caught Valentine's inconspicuous smirk. The baron knew nothing of their triumphs abroad, and Devlin preferred to keep it that way.

"I understand," Devlin began in a tone full of mockery. "The gentlemen here can see through your bravado. You fear I might beat you. Is that it?"

Devlin had the baron cornered. Should the lord retreat now, he would only look craven.

The lord muttered a curse. The muscle in his jaw twitched. "And on what shall we wager?" he said, taking the bait. "How long it will be before you're found dead on the common? Whether there is a woman alive who doesn't tremble when you enter a room?"

The last comment found a chink in Devlin's armour. Towering above most men, he was a veritable giant compared to those petite ladies of the ton. His raven-black hair and obsidian eyes accentuated his menacing aura. The baron was right. Most women found his powerful countenance unsettling.

The sudden urge to end the game came upon him. A lead ball between Bromfield's brows would atone for the spiteful gossip, would ease the ache in Devlin's chest, appease his need for revenge. But it would shed no light on the circumstances surrounding Ambrose's mysterious death. Only one person had an intimate knowledge of his brother's final days. Only one person had lied, had made up stories about his brother's nefarious activities—Miss Bromfield.

"Let us wager on something more substantial," Devlin said, pushing aside all doubts to the contrary. "Something more precious than money or reputation."

An excited hum burst through the room.

Everyone shuffled closer to the gaming table.

"And what is more precious than money or reputation?" The baron gave a mocking chuckle as he baited the crowd, but uncertainty flashed in the man's frosty blue eyes.

Devlin was about to answer but paused.

An image of Greystone and his wife, Lydia, burst into his mind. Devlin had stood witness at their wedding, had seen the look of love and devotion in their eyes as they exchanged vows, as they shared a passionate kiss regardless of the onlookers. The thought that he would never feel the same abiding affection had stabbed his heart, drawn blood. But that pain was nothing compared to the crippling sense of loneliness that followed.

"Well?" Bromfield's amused tone drew Devlin from his reverie. "For what shall we wager?"

Devlin cleared his throat and took comfort from Valentine's reassuring smile. "For the hand of your daughter in marriage."

A collective gasp tore through the room.

Shock turned into amusement when Lord Marshborough chuckled, slapped Devlin on the back and said, "Mighty good show, Drake. You had Bromfield quaking in his boots for a moment there."

From the rigid set of Devlin's jaw, it took but a few seconds before someone in the crowd said, "By God, it's no jest."

"Indeed." Devlin shot Bromfield a hard stare. "If you're brave enough to bet, we'll wager for the hand of your daughter."

Bromfield jerked his head back and scoffed. "You expect me to risk such a valuable treasure?"

"Is she a treasure?" The insult sliced through the volatile atmosphere. "Some might disagree." Miss Bromfield lashed out with her vile tongue as a man did a sharp blade—with menace, with deadly intent.

"You have spent too much time abroad, Drake." Bromfield brushed a lock of hair from his brow, and Devlin noted the slight tremble in his fingers. The baron was no fool. He knew he had his back pressed to the wall. "You have spent too much time bartering with heathens if you think I would gamble with my own daughter's happiness."

Devlin arched an arrogant brow. "You have yet to hear what I offer in exchange."

"I doubt you have anything of equal worth or status."

Were it not for her connection to Ambrose, Miss Bromfield wasn't worth the scrapings off his boots.

"I don't?" Devlin paused. "What about the deeds to Blackwater?"

This time, the crowd looked too stunned to utter a sound. With wide eyes, they exchanged puzzled glances. Some shook their heads. Some edged closer, not wanting to miss a word.

With his usual aristocratic grace, Valentine stepped forward ready to play his part in the game. "Don't be a fool, Drake," he pleaded. "Good God, that house has been in your family for five generations."

"Six generations," Devlin corrected.

He watched the baron's eyes flicker to life. But the glint of pleasure stemmed from more than the value of the prize. Baron Bromfield had visited Blackwater after Ambrose's death under the guise that his daughter wished for the return of all private correspondence. In light of the scandal, the lady was eager to preserve her reputation.

The housekeeper, Mrs Barbary, refused. Citing that only written permission from the master would prevail her to allow such an intrusion. Days later, an intruder ransacked Ambrose's room, stole a silver shaving pot and brush—took nothing else.

So, what had Miss Bromfield written in those letters?

Was it all a ruse, the letters an excuse for the baron to gain access to the house?

And if so why?

Valentine appeared at Devlin's shoulder. He bent down, giving the impression of whispering in Devlin's ear but spoke loud enough for everyone to hear.

"Although you took Harridan-Jones' vowel, luck has not been your friend tonight. God damn, Drake, you'll lose your home."

Oh, Valentine was good. The usually suave, sophisticated lord did indeed seem ruffled.

Devlin shrugged. "I have the townhouse in Wimpole Street. What need have I for a draughty old mansion?" He focused his gaze on the baron. "Well? Do you doubt me enough to wager your daughter against Blackwater?"

The ugly green vein in the baron's temple swelled and pulsed. Everyone could see he was tempted. The beads of sweat forming on his brow confirmed as much. He fiddled with the seal ring on his little finger, twisting it back and forth. A gentleman to his left leant down and advised caution, called for prudence, but the baron dismissed him with an irate flick of the wrist.

The thought of possessing Blackwater proved too enticing.

"Highest roll wins." The words burst from the baron's lips, though from the deep lines on his brow it had not been an easy task.

"Agreed." Devlin inclined his head though wanted to jump up and punch the air. "We should remove our coats."

"Our coats?" The baron's mouth drew thin. "I am a gentleman who plays by the rules, Mr Drake, though I doubt the same could be said for you."

"Which is why I shall remove my coat." Devlin shrugged out of his black coat and handed the garment to Valentine. "Should there be any accusations of cheating, I would have to call that gentleman out. Having spent five years abroad, I would rather refrain from fleeing the country again so soon."

All eyes in the room settled on Devlin. It was not the relaxed sight of a man in his shirtsleeves that drew their attention, but rather the bulging muscles straining against the fine lawn.

Bromfield removed his coat. His scrawny physique failed to draw the crowd's attention. But anyone with the baron's cunning was considered a worthy adversary.

A thick, clawing silence surrounded the table.

Bromfield reached for the polished wooden cup. "We will shake to see who rolls first." Without pausing for thought, the baron rolled a nine.

Devlin used the opportunity to test his sleight of hand. For three years, he'd been perfecting the skill of knowing exactly how to claim the dice off the table, how to drop them into the cup in precisely the right way to achieve the desired result. Yes, he had made his fortune with Lord Greystone and their friends, buying and selling commodities. But he had doubled his wealth at the gaming tables.

Devlin shook the cup and cast the dice, pleased when he rolled a seven as planned.

The baron snorted. "When I claim Blackwater, I intend to raze the place to the ground."

"When I claim your only daughter, I plan to treat her with the same kindness and respect she showed my brother."

The baron cast icy daggers Devlin's way. He grabbed the cup again, muttered to himself and shook the vessel too vigorously, too many times for there to be any skill involved. He released the dice, and they flew across the table, rolling and rolling until coming to a stop an inch from the edge.

"Ten," someone shouted.

Bromfield's lips curled into a sardonic grin. "Your turn to roll, Mr Drake, though it's clear to see that the odds are against you. Oh, I can almost smell a Blackwater bonfire."

"Only frightened men boast," Devlin countered. "Confident men have nothing to prove."

Devlin joked about there being nothing to do abroad other than gamble. The distraction gave him an opportunity to scoop the ivory cubes into his hand, shuffle them into the required position before dropping them into the cup.

Three short, sharp shakes and he emptied the vessel knowing that they would roll twice, no more.

Devlin did not look at the dice but kept his gaze focused on the baron. The shocked gasps from the crowd confirmed his success. Bromfield's grin slipped, replaced by a look of horror. The baron gulped and tugged on the knot in his cravat.

"By God, Drake rolled a twelve," Lord Criddle said, amazed.

Valentine stepped closer. "Never have I met a man with more luck than you. It seems you have won a wife, my friend."

The sudden rush of elation was fleeting. Luck did not wrap its lithe legs around a man's waist and promise to keep him warm at night. Luck did not profess love, did not rub the aches from one's shoulders. Luck did not make a man feel glad to be alive.

"I demand someone inspects the dice," the baron snapped.

"You have used the house dice," Lord Criddle countered. "There is no trickery here. You lost, Bromfield, and must pay the debt."

"You cannot expect a girl to marry a beast." The baron dragged his hand down his face.

"Some consider me a devil," Devlin countered. "Where your daughter is concerned, I shall strive to live up to my reputation."

Bromfield growled and thumped the table. "But she will never agree."

"Then her father will give me satisfaction some other way."

"Failure to pay the debt will damage your reputation," Valentine reminded the baron. Elegant fingers straightened the diamond pin in his cravat, brushed imagined dust from his coat sleeves. "I for one would not entertain a gentleman who is considered dishonourable."

Devlin had heard enough. It was time to bring the night's proceedings to an end. He had an appointment to empty the port decanter for it was the only way he would sleep tonight. Moving to scrawl a few particulars onto a slip of paper, including a signed statement declaring no impediments to the marriage, he returned to the gaming table and threw it down.

"I expect to meet my bride tomorrow at noon. Bring her to Wimpole Street. You will arrange a special licence, or common if the archbishop refuses. You have proof of my consent."

While it was usual for the groom to make the application, no man of God would grant a devil a licence to procreate. Despite his daughter's failings, the baron commanded respect amongst his peers. Besides, Devlin refused to wait, refused to give Miss Bromfield an opportunity to flee.

"You expect me to force the girl?" the baron said, insolence abandoned.

"I expect you to honour the wager." Devlin shrugged into his coat. "Do not attempt to make things difficult. Do not force me to do something you might live to regret. Your daughter will be my wife, or I shall ruin her name for good."

CHAPTER TWO

"The master didn't ring for more tea," Nora panted as she raced into the kitchen, her cheeks glowing berry-red. "Lord knows what's happened between them this time, but Miss Bromfield threw a plate of eggs at the wall."

Nora hurried off to the broom cupboard and returned with a brush and scuttle.

Juliet Duval slipped the dinner menus back between the pages of her ledger and closed the leather-bound book. "No doubt the baron has refused to increase her clothing allowance. We should be grateful it is only eggs. Last time it was the port decanter."

"Oh, they're not arguing about money but about some devil of a gentleman. Miss Bromfield thumped the table and shouted so loud it shook the chandelier." The maid glanced back over her shoulder. "I'd best hurry as there's no telling what she'll do next."

Juliet watched the maid scurry away, relieved she'd taken sanctuary in the kitchen. No one could control Hannah Bromfield when the lady was in a temper. And as the baron's illegitimate daughter, Juliet often took the brunt of her half-sister's rage and knew when to make herself scarce.

Scooping up the ledger and hugging it to her chest, Juliet went in search of Mrs Wendell. She found the housekeeper upstairs, hands clasped behind her back as she inspected the new maid's ability to sweep and clean the grate.

Noticing Juliet waiting on the landing, Mrs Wendell instructed the maid to continue with her chores.

"I have the amendments to this week's menus." Juliet withdrew the list from her ledger and handed it to the housekeeper. "Miss Bromfield insists on celery sauce with her glazed lamb and refuses to entertain the guinea fowl."

Mrs Wendell scanned the notes. "Is that what all the noise was about? I feared you might be in the midst of it again." She patted Juliet's upper arm with genuine affection.

The staff cared not that Juliet was born on the wrong side of the blanket and treated her more like family than Hannah or the baron ever had.

Baron Bromfield considered Juliet a useful inconvenience and had given her the task of assisting the housekeeper in the running of his home. She slept in the servants' quarters. Ate in the kitchen. Wore the garb of the lower classes. The only time she left the house was to accompany Hannah on her endless shopping trips—someone had to help the footman carry the boxes.

"Oh, Miss Bromfield did more than shout when she demanded damson tart," Juliet said with amusement for her sister often behaved like a spoilt child. "She jabbed her finger as if it were a blade." Juliet sighed. "I have no idea what they're arguing about this time, and for my own sanity wish to keep it that way."

Pity flashed in Mrs Wendell's brown eyes. "You do well to remain so calm when they provoke you as they do."

"*Come not between the dragon and his wrath.* Or so my mother used to say."

"And never were wiser words spoken."

Juliet's chest swelled when she thought of the dainty lady with a huge heart. She was like her mother in so many ways—in frame, in height, had the same vibrant red colouring and sprinkling of freckles on her nose.

"My mother received her education on the stage. An education in life and Shakespeare."

A sudden thud on the stairs captured their attention. Nora appeared, still flushed and breathless.

"How many times must I tell you?" Mrs Wendell chided in an authoritative tone. "No running on the stairs. You're liable to twist an ankle and then where will we be?"

Nora nodded. "I'm sorry, Mrs Wendell, it's just his lordship wants to see Miss Duval in the dining room, right away."

Juliet resisted the urge to close her eyes and groan. Whenever Hannah was in danger of losing an argument, she sought to deflect their father's wrath.

"I shall be right down, Nora."

Mrs Wendell waited for Nora to leave before placing her hand on Juliet's arm. "With any luck, Miss Bromfield will soon marry, and then we shall all find peace."

"Peace?" Juliet smiled though inside she was closing down the hatches, darting about to reinforce the gates. No one could hurt her once she'd bolstered her defences. "Knowing of Miss Bromfield's predilection for cruelty, she will insist I go with her."

A heavy stillness hung in the air outside the dining room. Juliet lingered in the hall and tried to gauge the mood beyond the door. The argument had dissolved into a disturbing silence.

It did not bode well.

Gathering her courage, Juliet rapped on the door twice and awaited her father's reply.

"Come."

With trepidation, Juliet entered the dining room.

Her father sat at the head of the long mahogany table. Rather than take her place at the baron's right, Hannah sat at the opposite end for she insisted she had earned the privilege. The baron agreed merely as a ploy to keep the girl out of arm's reach.

"Come in, Juliet, and close the door." Her father waited for her to obey and then beckoned her forward. "I'll not bandy words," he said, looking her squarely in the eye. "I know you're a girl who likes straight talking."

"Indeed, my lord." Juliet never called him Papa. Many times, she had whispered the word silently in her mind but was not permitted to let it escape her lips.

"I fear I have been remiss in my duties to you as a father," the baron said, although his indifferent tone conveyed a complete lack of remorse. "The circumstances of your birth made it somewhat difficult. But the time has come to make amends."

A mild sense of panic sprung to life in Juliet's chest.

Six years she had lived in the baron's household, and not once had he openly acknowledged his parental responsibilities. Yes, during the time she lived with her mother, he had paid for her governess, for music lessons but not dancing for what need had she to see the inside of a ballroom? He had provided food and shelter after her mother's death had left her destitute. But this sudden interest in her well-being had flown over Juliet's defensive wall like a fireball from a trebuchet.

"I need nothing from you but the simple things," she replied calmly but imagined crouching and covering her head while waiting for the impact of this unexpected attack.

The simple things?

The impoverished found nothing simple about securing food and a warm bed for the night.

Hannah scanned Juliet's plain brown dress and sniggered. "How can anyone possibly be content to wear that old rag? Would you not like to dress in fine gowns, have rubies gracing your throat, diamonds dangling from your earlobes?"

Juliet considered her sister's elegant appearance. Every strand of hair was swept up in an immaculate coiffure—for Hannah refused to wear a cap regardless of the time of day. Her skin was a pure creamy-white, unblemished by the sun's rays. Her pale pink dress spoke of sophistication rather than the simplicity other ladies required from their morning wear. Hannah did not waste her time reading or writing letters, and so comfort was not a requirement.

"Why would I wish for fripperies when I spend my days below stairs?" Juliet said though it was not a complaint.

"Well, your circumstances are about to change." Hannah's smug grin stretched from ear to ear. "You can say goodbye to dear Mrs Wendell for you will no longer serve us in this house."

The blood drained from Juliet's face.

Surely they were not planning to throw her out.

But then had her father not said he wished to compensate for his lack of attention? Was he to elevate her from the status of servant to daughter? Lord, no. The thought of spending her days in Hannah's company sent an icy shiver from her neck to her navel.

"Why must things change? I am more than happy with my current situation." Juliet swallowed down her apprehension. She loved her small room in the basement. She could read until the early hours, sing to her heart's content, and Hannah never ventured below stairs.

"You're to be married," the baron blurted. "To a … to a gentleman with distinguished bloodlines. There. Let it be known that I do consider your welfare."

The words hit Juliet like the slash of a whip though shock prevented her from feeling the sting straightaway.

"M-married?" It was the only word she could form.

"Indeed," her father replied, "that is what most young girls aspire to."

Hannah brought her napkin to her mouth and tittered. "Well, those girls without fortune. Some of us can afford to be choosy."

While Juliet stood there dumbfounded, the baron sipped his coffee and Hannah slathered butter on her toast as if neither had a care in the world.

Juliet cleared her throat. "Do I not get a say in the matter?"

"A say?" Her father frowned. "A say! As your legal guardian, I am well within my rights to decide for you."

Suspicion flared.

The baron was so ashamed of his extramarital liaison he refused to acknowledge Juliet publicly. So why arrange a marriage to a gentleman when clearly he would have to explain the nature of his relationship to the bride?

"May I ask whom I am to marry?"

"Have I not already told you?" the baron snapped. "The gentleman is more than an acceptable match for you, my dear."

"Even if he is an odious beast." Hannah snorted.

"A beast?" Juliet prayed Hannah was teasing. No doubt her sister had a hand in picking the suitor. "Is he old and grouchy, then?"

Not that it mattered. She would have to dissuade her father from such a ridiculous notion. Perhaps she could run away. But where would she go? If they had paid her for her domestic services, then she might have ferreted away a few shillings.

"I believe the gentleman is twenty-five or thereabouts." The baron pushed aside his plate, steepled his fingers in front of his chest and studied her with a level of scrutiny that almost made her knees buckle. "Though I will not lie, he is rather a huge fellow, and the match will look frightfully odd."

Huge? No doubt he had a paunch large enough to act as a tea tray.

"Oh, I wouldn't worry," Hannah said with her usual air of superiority. "When he sees you he's bound to change his mind, which is exactly what Papa hopes."

"Not necessarily," the baron corrected. A sly grin graced his thin mouth. "It would serve me well to have an ally in Drake's household."

"Mr Drake?" Juliet said with some confusion. Was this some sort of game for their amusement? The gentleman had been dead for three years. "But Mr Drake is no longer with us."

No, the poor fellow had been attacked by footpads on Wimbledon Common. And while many questioned why a man of such prominence would wander the wilds at night, a witness had come forward to suggest nefarious motives.

"We are not speaking about that revolting letch," Hannah chided.

Ambrose Drake had not been revolting when Hannah accepted his marriage proposal. He had not been revolting when Juliet spied them sharing a passionate kiss in the garden.

Hannah shivered visibly. "I always knew there was something strange about Ambrose Drake, though I did not expect him to have such a fondness for gentlemen."

"Enough, Hannah. I will not have you speak of such obscenities around the dining table." The baron met Juliet's gaze. "You're marrying his younger brother, Devlin Drake."

Devlin Drake?

Juliet clasped her hands in front of her as she fought the urge to drop to her knees and beg for clemency. They expected her to marry a man whose name bore a striking similarity to Satan's? They expected her to marry a man who must surely hold a grievance against her half-sister. After all, Hannah had sat with her friends in the drawing room and slandered Ambrose Drake in the vilest way possible.

"And Mr Drake has agreed to the match?" Juliet couldn't understand why any man would want to marry the illegitimate daughter with elfin features when they might offer for the legitimate beauty.

The baron shuffled uncomfortably in his chair.

"Mr Drake won you on the throw of the dice," Hannah said in a tone brimming with excited mockery.

"He won me?" Good Lord. The shocking revelation left her aghast. "In a bet?"

"Well, Mr Drake believes he has won *my* hand, but Papa would never permit me to marry such a brute." Hannah clapped her hands. "Oh, isn't it marvellous? I can just picture the disappointment on his face."

The hard lump in Juliet's throat grew to boulder-size proportion. Her chest tightened until she could hardly breathe. Painful knots in her stomach almost brought tears to her eyes, eyes blinded by bright flashing lights.

It wasn't her father's recklessness that hurt—many gentlemen made foolish wagers. It wasn't the thought that Mr Drake would find her inadequate—she lacked everything an aristocratic gentleman required in a wife.

No.

Knowing her family had used her as a pawn in this game cut to the bone. No one cared for her feelings. She was a commodity to discard without thought. Oh, it was foolish to imagine her father might feel some affection for her—but the dream had shone in her breast like the night star, and now a black cloud had swallowed all hope.

"And if I refuse?" Juliet asked, mentally scrambling to maintain her composure.

The baron stared down his nose. "Then I must assume you lack the loyalty I require in a daughter. Your lack of gratitude for taking you in when your mother died will force me to throw you from this house into the gutter." His ice-cold tone sliced through the air between them.

"I see." Juliet ground her teeth together as tears surged to her eyes. But she would be damned before she would give Hannah the pleasure of seeing her cry.

As Juliet stood there, wringing her hands, watching these two strangers plot and scheme with her life, the thought of aligning herself with Devlin Drake didn't seem quite so terrifying. Ambrose had been kind and sincere. And they were brothers after all.

And yet one look at Hannah's beaming grin told Juliet there was fault in her logic.

"I doubt Drake will take you," the baron continued. "Then again, if he suspects I hold you in high regard, he will accept the match."

"Am I permitted to meet him before I am sold like meat at Smithfield Market?"

The baron's gaze turned ominous. "Purely because I know you find the news distressing, I shall allow your disrespect to pass. You will accompany me today while I attempt to secure a licence." He muttered something beneath his breath. "Though I shall have to put forward a compelling case if the archbishop is to deem you worthy of his consideration."

Hannah snorted as she returned her china teacup to the saucer. "Drake won't have her, so I don't know why you're going to so much trouble."

Oddly, the thought that Mr Drake might turn her away roused a faint flicker of regret. This would be the one and only time she might marry, might have a family—children to shower with the same motherly love and devotion she had received as a child.

The stark reality of her situation hit her like a sharp slap. She was trapped in this house with two cold-hearted devils, and Mr Drake afforded the only opportunity for escape.

"I shall come with you, my lord," Juliet said. In truth, she could not refuse, and she was eager to meet this odious beast. If only to sate her curiosity. "Should I find something more suitable to wear?"

The baron scanned the brown garment that did nothing to enhance her colouring. "Hannah will find you a dress."

"For goodness' sake." Hannah huffed. "Look at her. Do you

22

honestly think my expensive muslins will sit well on her dainty frame?"

Dainty? Hannah's preferred words of choice were usually *scrawny* and *gaunt*.

The baron gave an indifferent wave. "Wear whatever you wish. We leave at twelve." When Juliet failed to move, he added, "You are dismissed."

Only when Juliet reached for the doorknob did she notice how violently her fingers shook.

"Oh, Juliet. Have Nora bring fresh tea, won't you?" Hannah couldn't resist barking one last order.

Juliet nodded, slipped out into the hall and closed the door behind her. She remained there for a moment, gathering her breath and her wits. Eventually, she found the strength of will to amble to the kitchen.

"Miss Bromfield is in need of more tea, Nora," Juliet said in a monotone voice for she was still suffering from shock.

Nora frowned as she searched Juliet's face. "What is it, miss? Don't tell me Miss Bromfield has smashed the teapot again?"

"No, Nora. I fear the damage caused this time is far worse than that."

The Bromfields had taken a knife to Juliet's heart, had taken turns to slash and stab at the fragile organ. The robust fortifications had offered no protection. And now, all she could do was side with the devil and pray that Satan's beast might bring her salvation.

CHAPTER THREE

Devlin sat bolt upright in the leather wingback chair, his teeth clenched, his irate gaze fixed on the mantel clock. How long did it take to inform a lady she was to be married? How long did it take to convince the damn bishop of their urgent need to wed? He should have dealt with the matter personally, stomped over to the baron's townhouse and demand he settle the debt immediately.

Devlin tapped his fingers on the arm of the chair, the solemn beat like that of a death knell. Whatever happened within the next few hours, death was the inevitable outcome. Should the baron fail to appear, he would pay the price for his daughter's loose tongue and his own lack of honour. Should they arrive as planned, it meant the end of any hope Devlin had of ever making a love match.

A love match?

The idea was bloody ridiculous for a man of his size and gruff countenance. Even so, the thought of marrying Miss Bromfield made his stomach coil in revulsion.

God damn.

And to think he'd have to bed the spiteful witch. In all likelihood, he'd struggle to rise to the occasion.

The need to banish all thoughts of bedding such a cold and callous harlot forced Devlin from his fireside chair. He tugged the bell pull so hard plaster dust fell from the ceiling rose.

Mere moments later Copeland entered the study. It was the third time Devlin had called for the butler in the last half an hour.

"Well?" Devlin asked. "Have you any news?"

Copeland raised his chin. "Not at present, sir." His indifferent expression bore no sign of frustration. "Your missive was delivered, but the boy is yet to return. And other than to address your immediate concerns, I have not moved from my post."

Damnation.

Darkness would be upon them in a matter of hours. If the baron had procured a special licence, Devlin intended to leave for Blackwater immediately.

The rattle of carriage wheels drew his attention to the window. Four long strides—the benefit of being so tall—and he rounded the desk to peer out onto Wimpole Street.

The canary-yellow chariot rolled to a stop outside Devlin's house. Only one man rode about town in such an ostentatious contraption—Bromfield. A servant dressed in garish yellow livery jumped down from his perch and hurried around to open the door and lower the steps.

Baron Bromfield descended. The lord surveyed the exterior of Devlin's townhouse, his lips curling in contempt. The baron stepped aside, and the servant assisted Miss Bromfield to the pavement.

The sight of the golden-haired beauty sent bile shooting up to burn the back of Devlin's throat.

Evidently, Miss Bromfield had inherited her father's need for extravagance for she wore a ridiculous wide-brimmed bonnet dressed with three large ostrich feathers. Her midnight-blue pelisse flattered both her colouring and slender figure—and still, she was the most abhorrent woman he'd ever laid eyes on.

Devlin's heart thumped hard in his chest—from anger, from the need to wipe the arrogant grin off Miss Bromfield's face. Clearly the lady knew nothing of the wager else the baron would have dragged her from the conveyance, kicking and screaming.

Last of all, the lady's maid clambered out of the chariot. The petite girl with red hair had a more pleasant countenance. Devlin pitied anyone forced to spend a second in Miss Bromfield's company, let alone have to dress and pander to the spoilt chit.

"We have visitors, Copeland. Be sure to show them in, although there is no need to be polite."

"Indeed, sir. I shall greet them in a tone befitting a man of a much lower station."

"Excellent."

Devlin watched the scene from the window. The baron and his daughter strode up to the front door as if neither had a care in the world. The maid looked the most terrified of all. She stood gawking, her teeth sinking into her bottom lip. She hugged her arms and shivered. Perhaps hearing her master talk of the hulking beast set to marry her mistress had sent her nerves skittering.

The baron barked an order, and the maid hurried to his side.

Devlin wasn't sure where he wanted to sit. Eager to convey an air of authority, he chose the chair behind the desk. When Copeland escorted the illustrious guests into the study, Devlin was surprised the maid followed them in, too. Perhaps she came armed with the vinaigrette bottle ready to revive Miss Bromfield once she'd received the distressing news.

"No need for pleasantries," the baron snapped when the butler opened his mouth to announce them. "Drake knows who we are."

The muscles in Devlin's stomach clenched. He couldn't bear to look at Miss Bromfield, couldn't bear to look at the baron and found himself staring at the maid instead. The woman held his gaze with a level of enquiry considered ill-mannered for a servant. A look few aristocratic women dared to bestow.

"That will be all, Copeland. Do not go to the trouble of arranging tea." Devlin's tone was as cold as the ice casing around his heart. "We hope to conclude our business quickly."

This was nothing more than an arrangement, a task, a chore.

"May we at least take a seat?" The baron gestured to the two chairs facing the desk.

Devlin gave a curt nod.

Miss Bromfield made sitting seem like an art form. She examined the seat. With poise and an air of self-possession she straightened her back, gathered her skirts and lowered herself down gracefully. Her movements were so affected even the maid rolled her eyes.

The baron waited for his daughter to sit before taking the seat next to her.

The maid looked at them both, rolled her eyes again and stood stiff and rigid behind the baron's chair.

"Am I to assume you have not broached the subject of our wager with your daughter?" Devlin did not need to glance at Miss Bromfield to know her grin stretched from ear to ear. Indeed, she put her gloved hand to her lips and tittered at the question.

"On the contrary," the baron said with mild condescension. "My daughter is aware of her obligations and will consent to the match."

Shocked, Devlin's head shot to the venomous creature whose mind was riddled with poison.

"Yes, Mr Drake," Miss Bromfield said in a high-pitched voice that grated. "We discussed the matter at length this morning."

"And you're happy with the arrangement?" Devlin stared at Miss Bromfield and tried to find something attractive in her countenance, something that might sweeten the deal, something that might make the next twenty years moderately bearable.

But alas, his search was in vain.

"Oh, I am more than happy with the turn of events." Miss Bromfield smiled in the sly way that persuaded a man to sleep with one eye open.

This was not the reaction he envisioned while waiting patiently these last few hours. Wails and screams, yes. A tantrum to surpass all others, certainly. This sickly sweet sense of acceptance, most definitely not.

Devlin stared at her with a level of disdain he could not hide. Once at Blackwater, he would have his answers. What was the real reason Miss Bromfield ended her betrothal to his brother? Why had she invented the story of Ambrose's fondness for men? What prompted his brother to wander Wimbledon Common in the dead of night? And what was so important about the letters she'd written that her father would demand access to Devlin's home?

"Then I trust you had luck with the bishop," Devlin said in an attempt to focus on the matter at hand.

The baron reached into his coat pocket and retrieved a tightly rolled scroll. "The archbishop refused to grant a special licence." Bromfield leant forward and threw the document onto the desk.

Damnation.

"On what grounds?" Devlin snatched the paper.

"On the grounds that one applicant is of inferior birth," the baron said haughtily.

Miss Bromfield sniggered.

Anger ignited in Devlin's chest. "My bloodline is purer than yours. My grandfather was a viscount." How dare the baron suggest a Drake was an inferior match for his serpent daughter.

"The bishop granted a common licence," the baron said. "With some persuasion, I managed to make him see the urgency of the case."

A brief flutter of relief filled Devlin's chest—until he remembered whom he was marrying. "Then we will marry in the private chapel at Blackwater at ten in the morning."

"So, you have been a resident in the parish for four weeks?"

The baron stared down his nose. Would he use Devlin's absence from Blackwater as an excuse to delay?

"Of course," Devlin lied. "I'm certain the Reverend Fisher will confirm that to be the case." The clergy rarely enforced the rules as long as there were no impediments to the marriage. Devlin unravelled the scroll. The blue tax stamp confirmed the document's legitimacy. "Should we discuss the lady's dowry, any portions or trusts set aside for children?"

Baron Bromfield cleared his throat. "There is no dowry. You won my daughter's hand, nothing more."

The comment drew Devlin's attention away from the document. "A dowry is about protecting Miss Bromfield's future as much as rewarding me for shouldering such a burden." And what a crippling weight it was.

He waited for Miss Bromfield to gasp at the insult, to jump up from her chair and flick her forked tongue in warning. But she sat there demurely as if nothing he could say or do could unsettle her calm composure.

"Miss Bromfield has a sizeable dowry," the baron informed with an arrogant grin. "However, Miss Duval does not."

The maid put a trembling hand to her mouth and sucked in a breath.

Devlin surveyed the scene. It suddenly occurred to him that a man as cunning as the baron or a lady as devious as Miss Bromfield would come out fighting when backed into a corner.

"And who is Miss Duval?" Devlin asked though he had a suspicion he would not like the answer.

"My daughter." The baron gestured to the petite girl behind him. "The lady whose hand you won at the gaming table."

Devlin did not breathe, did not blink.

The baron had attacked his flank, and he had not seen the bastard coming.

Do not show any sign of weakness.

Do not give them the satisfaction.

Using every ounce of willpower he possessed, Devlin kept an impassive expression as he scanned the details of the document. His gaze lingered on the name Juliet Duval. Well, at least the bishop had recorded Blackwater as the place to solemnize the marriage.

Once confident he was not likely to dart across the desk and throttle the baron with his bare hands, Devlin looked up and met Miss Duval's gaze. While she, too, tried to keep her chin high and shoulders square, he could see a wealth of pain hidden behind her vibrant green eyes.

How was he to protest without making the woman feel more worthless than she already did? It was clear from her dress, her name, the way she stood behind her family like the hired help, that the baron cared nothing for Miss Duval's welfare.

Devlin exhaled slowly. "Miss Duval is your illegitimate daughter?" he attempted to clarify.

How the hell had he missed something so vital?

How was it society knew nothing about this lady?

The baron nodded. "The details of her birth are hardly worth mentioning. I have done more for the girl than most would expect under the circumstances. She received a reasonable education. Understands what it takes to run a large household."

Miss Duval pursed her lips.

The longer Devlin sat opposite the arrogant lord, and the longer he had to listen to Miss Bromfield's mocking snorts and chuckles, the more the blood in his veins burned. His heart thumped against his ribcage. His hands throbbed with the need to inflict pain, to punish, to maim.

"One might argue that you deliberately deceived me when making the wager," Devlin said evenly, though he wanted to rant and rave and rip the place apart. "Some might consider your deception enough to warrant a call for satisfaction."

The baron shrugged. "You cannot hold me accountable for your lack of clarity. Should the gentleman who offered the wager not stipulate exactly what is at stake? You won the hand of my daughter, and I have come to pay the debt."

"And you expect me to accept?"

God damn. He'd spent three years dreaming of Miss Bromfield's demise. The only reason he'd settled on marriage was to make the lady's life a misery and discover the truth about Ambrose.

"You are under no obligation to accept payment." Baron Bromfield sat forward. "We can call the matter satisfied, and both agree that we were hasty in our decision to gamble. The slur against my daughter is offset by her inferior bloodline and lack of connections."

Devlin was of a mind to agree.

He'd risk everything—his home, his reputation—if it meant marrying for love. But he had no need to shackle himself to the subdued creature hovering behind her father. No doubt when he rose from the chair, the sight of his large frame would terrify the girl.

But then something unexpected happened.

Miss Duval smiled at him and inclined her head. The look in her eyes spoke of compassion and understanding, and before Devlin knew what he was about, he said, "Before I make my decision may I have a moment alone with your daughter?"

The baron appeared surprised, almost as surprised as Devlin. "Certainly."

Devlin pushed out of the leather chair and straightened to his full height. Miss Duval inhaled sharply as her gaze scanned the breadth of his chest and then climbed higher, higher still. A flash of fear replaced her brief look of shock.

"My butler will attend you in my absence, and you will both remain here while I speak to Miss Duval." Devlin had no intention of leaving the Bromfields alone with his private papers. He turned to Miss Duval. "I trust you are happy to accompany me out into the garden?" Outside, they were in no danger of anyone hearing their conversation.

Miss Duval nodded. "Indeed."

"Very well." Devlin rang for Copeland. He gave the butler strict instructions not to leave the study and then escorted Miss Duval into the drawing room and out through the terrace doors. "Would you care to sit? There's a stone bench at the end of the path, or we may walk if you prefer."

She craned her neck and looked up at him. "For fear of causing myself a permanent injury, I think it is best we sit."

Her voice breezed over him, soft and sweet. Her elocution was faultless, held not a trace of artifice, unlike her sister's. And she seemed less timid than she had in the study.

"Some find my size somewhat overpowering." It was a polite way of saying people thought him a beast.

"I imagine they do," she said, and he found he appreciated her honesty. "While being rather small in stature myself, some think they may ride roughshod over me. My father included."

That had nothing to do with her height and everything to do with the character of the man determined to use her as a pawn.

Devlin led Miss Duval along the gravel path. They walked in silence. He wasn't sure why he'd asked her to step outside, wasn't sure how to phrase his objection without causing offence.

"So, you live with the baron?" he said as they arrived at the bench. He brushed the dead leaves onto the ground and waited for her to sit before dropping into the space next to her.

"I have lived with him ever since my mother died six years ago."

"And your mother was—"

"An actress, sir."

"Of course."

Good Lord, he felt like a giant seated beside her. She seemed so small and fragile as if she might break were he to hold her too close, too tightly. Not that he would be holding her at all.

"One cannot help but notice that there is a distinct lack of affection between you and your family, Miss Duval." Society treated illegitimate children like an inferior breed.

She clasped her tiny hands in her lap. "I'm an inconvenience to them, sir, and I fear my sister is jealous of anyone who might steal her thunder."

Again, the truth fell from her lips with ease.

Devlin resisted the urge to call her sister a malicious crone.

A tense silence ensued.

"Do you want to marry me, Miss Duval?" It was a ridiculous question. Clearly she was at her father's beck and call. "Before you answer, know that I require honesty in this matter." Devlin's harsh tone carried the frustration of having been outwitted by the pompous baron.

She glanced up at him and for a moment said nothing. Her vibrant green gaze drifted over his face, settling on the grim downward turn of his mouth that he knew made his dark features appear more menacing.

"If you want the truth, sir, I would do anything to escape spending another night with those who have the gall to call me family." She sighed. "But they tricked you, and it is clear we are unsuited. I fully understand your reasons for withdrawing your claim."

Did she?

Did she think her inferior status was reason enough for him to retreat? He was not a preened lord of the *ton* who lived and breathed for his mama's good opinion. Why would he permit a horde of gossipmongers to control his life or his destiny?

"What makes you think we are unsuited?"

Miss Duval arched a brow. "You mean besides my illegitimacy and the fact you're twice my size?" she said with a faint hint of amusement.

"Twice your size when standing. Seated here, it is not so obvious."

"No," she agreed. "It is not."

"Do I frighten you?"

"A little."

"Only a little?" Less than most, then.

Once again she fell silent.

"I met your brother, Ambrose, numerous times," she suddenly said, and the mere mention of his brother made Devlin's heart pound hard in his chest. "I found him to be a most kind and generous gentleman. You have the same dark hair, though his eyes were lighter if I remember correctly."

"They were hazel. Mine are almost black."

"Yes."

Devlin clenched his jaw. What the hell was he doing outside with Miss Duval when it was his need to punish Miss Bromfield that led him to make the wager?

"Are you aware of the vicious things your sister has said about my brother?" After death, a man's reputation was his legacy. Miss Bromfield had destroyed that which mattered most to Ambrose. The one thing he strived to protect.

"Yes, sir, and I find it despicable." Her hand fluttered to her chest, and she grew breathless. "Forgive me," she said in a mild panic. "I meant only that I find my sister's behaviour despicable and do not believe her lies for a second."

Intrigued by the comment, Devlin turned to face her fully. "You are aware of Miss Bromfield's devious traits?"

The words left his lips, but his mind became engaged in counting the tiny freckles on Miss Duval's nose. Her lips were rosebud pink, her eyes a penetrating jade green. There was something otherworldly about her, something bewitching.

"I believe my sister inherited her cold heart and callous manner from my father," she said, oblivious to his musings.

"Then I must assume you inherited your pleasant manner from your mother." He was not a man to partake in even the

34

mildest flirtation, yet there was a smooth tone to his voice that sounded foreign to his ears.

"I like to think so, and I thank you for noticing, sir."

Devlin considered her appealing countenance, her kind face and warm eyes. Perhaps this lady had value after all. Perhaps he, too, should attack the baron from the flank rather than plot a frontal assault. Miss Duval had an intimate knowledge of her father's household, knew Miss Bromfield's habits. Devlin had no hope of trapping Miss Bromfield into marriage now, but he could find other ways to ruin her, to gain the information he required.

"So let us return to the predicament that plagues us both," Devlin said in a logical tone far removed from any notions of fancy. "Are we to wed or not?"

Miss Duval jerked her head back, somewhat surprised. "You are considering an alliance?"

"Why not?" Devlin shrugged.

She seemed confused, bewildered.

"But you cannot accept." She shook her head numerous times. "They despise me. There is villainy afoot, and it suits their purpose to trap us both in a sham of a marriage. No. You won your bet, Mr Drake. If you know what is good for you, sir, you will not force your claim."

Devlin took a moment to absorb her impassioned speech. "Do you speak out of concern for my welfare or your own?"

"Why yours, of course." She blinked rapidly in surprise. "I'm simply a servant in my father's household. Abused. Tormented daily. One cannot help but dream of escape."

Hatred for the baron filled Devlin's chest. He despised those who preyed on the innocent. His pulse rose more than a notch, and he resisted the urge to storm into the study and take a letter opener to the lord's throat.

"But it would be unwise to shackle yourself to me," Miss Duval continued. "I have nothing to offer a gentleman of your elevated status, nothing to bring to the marriage."

The lady might not have money, but she had something far more valuable—integrity. To Devlin, that was worth a king's ransom.

Miss Duval glanced nervously back over her shoulder as if expecting the evil baron to jump out of the shrubbery. "I have seen the wicked glint in my father's eyes when he mentions your family name and must advise caution."

It wasn't the lady's concern for his welfare that stunned him. It was that she thought her father had the power and the means to intimidate him. Yes, Devlin might not look so threatening when seated on the stone bench, but could she not see the brawn and muscle that made him a man to fear? Could she not see the darkness in his eyes, the ugly bitterness radiating from his soul?

"Perhaps I do have a reason to shackle myself to you," he said.

Now was the moment to explain that he planned to ruin her sister's reputation. Now was the moment to tell Miss Duval that she would prove useful to him in this game of vengeance. A lady possessed of such rectitude deserved honesty.

And yet he could not bring himself to utter the words.

Miss Duval studied him. Suspicion flashed in her eyes. "And what possible reason might you have, Mr Drake?"

Devlin searched his mind for some semblance of the truth. "I think we will suit."

She had the courage to look him in the eye. That was a good start. Once away from her family, all signs of timidity had dissipated. She spoke with heart and feeling, with a depth of passion he'd never seen. An excitement for life radiated from every fibre of her being, and he wanted to feel it flowing through his veins, too.

"I admire your strength, Miss Duval," he continued. "I admire the fact that you seem not the least bit intimidated by what some would regard as my beastly countenance."

"Oh, I am not intimidated, sir, though I will admit to being unnerved."

"Your honesty is perhaps your greatest asset, Miss Duval." Along with her vibrant red hair, sweet lips and green eyes that had somehow managed to shine a little light into his tainted soul.

"The fact that you see it as such tells me all I need to know of your character, sir."

Devlin inclined his head. "Then shall we marry? Can you bear to leave your family behind and take your place as mistress of Blackwater?"

"Blackwater?" Her bottom lip trembled. She remained silent for a brief time. "Yes, Mr Drake. I believe I might bear it very well."

CHAPTER FOUR

BLACKWATER, HAMPSHIRE

T he travelling chariot rattled along the narrow country lane, heading to Blackwater.

Since leaving London a little after dawn, the tension inside the confined space proved suffocating. For the entire three-hour journey, the baron had watched Juliet intently from the seat opposite, one long-fingered hand resting on his knee, the other gripping the silver top of his cane for balance. Hannah occupied three-quarters of the seat next to Juliet, her pelisse spread wide to prevent creasing.

Though it had been hard to say goodbye to Mrs Wendell, Nora and all the other servants who'd made life bearable these last six years, Juliet couldn't help but feel a rush of excitement at her new prospects.

"Remember what you must do." Her father's cold voice sliced through the silence. How could she forget when he'd made the original demand with such vehemence? "You have three days, and then I expect to receive word of your progress."

Juliet nodded. The baron wasn't the only one capable of deception. While she had agreed to do her father's bidding—be his spy, his thief—she had no intention of delivering on her promise. Besides, once a lady married was her loyalty not to her husband?

The imposing figure of Devlin Drake entered her mind.

Never had she met a man whose countenance conveyed such strength and power. And yet Juliet found nothing sinister behind those obsidian eyes. Oh, they were dark—so dark. So dark it was as if a thick shroud covered the windows to his soul to prevent anyone who dared to peer inside.

"Three days," her father repeated. "I think I deserve some reward for permitting you to marry the blackguard."

"Must you be so vague?" Juliet asked, intrigued to know the reason behind his odd request. "If I'm to find a letter, am I not permitted to know of its contents?"

The baron banged the floor with the bottom of his cane. The dull thud made Juliet jump.

"God damn, girl, can you not simply do as I ask without all the unnecessary questions?" The baron's eyes brimmed with frustration rather than anger. He inhaled deeply and added in a calmer tone, "I shall be the one to determine its value."

The whole situation was odd, highly suspicious.

Had Hannah documented her vile diatribe in a letter to Ambrose? Did the baron fear it might serve as evidence in a case of libel? So why insist Juliet search the house for all letters written in a feminine hand?

"Must I remind you where your loyalties lie?" the baron continued in a glacial tone.

Hannah snorted. "This conversation is pointless." She cast Juliet a disdainful glare. "Do you honestly think a man like Devlin Drake would marry someone like you? This is all a ploy to prove a point, to claim some sort of victory. I guarantee we will not make it over the threshold."

Juliet had to agree that theirs was an unlikely pairing. And yet when sitting with Mr Drake in the garden, she had felt a tingle of awareness. A connection existed between them though it was as fine and fragile as a spider's web.

"It would have served our purpose if Drake had remained abroad indefinitely. Somewhere too far away to pry," the baron moaned. "For your sake, Hannah, you must hope he welcomes your sister with open arms."

So this *was* about Hannah's recklessness.

Juliet hoped she did find the letter. Nothing would please her more than to wipe the arrogant smirk off her sister's face.

As the chariot suddenly slowed and turned in through a set of majestic iron gates, Juliet lowered the window and leant out, eager to glimpse her new home.

The sight stole her breath.

They passed through an impressive tree tunnel of the most vibrant array of autumnal colours she had ever seen. Slivers of sunlight cut through the canopy to cast the long drive in a warm amber glow. At the end stood a square portico wide enough to serve as a shelter for a carriage on a rainy day.

"Close the window," Hannah complained. "I'm liable to catch a chill, and I have the Loxton ball on Thursday."

Juliet ignored her. Hopefully, in a little more than an hour, she would never have to answer to Hannah again.

As they neared the house, Juliet's thoughts turned to her wedding. Hope burst to life in her chest pushing away all her doubts and fears. At heart, she was a loving, loyal person. Surely she could make the marriage work. Despite being a stranger, Devlin Drake must have seen something good in her to encourage him to make the offer.

When the chariot rumbled to a stop beneath the portico, the butler appeared at the large oak door, one sturdy enough to keep an army at bay. Silas, the baron's groom, climbed down from his perch, opened the door and lowered the steps.

The baron climbed out.

Hannah pushed forward and exited next.

"Good morning, my lord. I'm Withers. Welcome to Blackwater." The butler—a plump man of average height and with a dour-looking face—inclined his head. "I trust you had a pleasant journey."

The baron whipped his watch from his pocket and examined the face before thrusting it back into his coat and releasing a huff of frustration. "We did not come all this way to stand on the doorstep making idle conversation. Where's Drake?"

The butler's expression remained impassive. "At the chapel, my lord. He asked that someone escort you there upon your arrival."

"Then make haste, man. Let us get the matter over with." The baron attempted to shoo Withers into the house.

"You can access the chapel via the path, my lord." Withers gestured to the left of the house. "A footman will escort you there at once."

"Only a heathen like Mr Drake would expect you to walk a mile to your own wedding," Hannah complained as they sauntered behind the footman.

They followed the gravel path down past the lush green lawns and crossed a small stone bridge over a babbling brook. Her father pressed the footman to hurry, chiding the servant for his slow, doddery pace. While Hannah chased their father's heels—for she despised being the last to arrive—Juliet ambled behind.

Nerves pushed to the fore.

Many women married for status, for convenience, to keep them from the workhouse. Most had no choice. Most were miserable and indulged in hobbies to replace the lack of love. The Blackwater Estate was vast. Running such a property would easily fill Juliet's days.

But what about the long, lonely nights?

Would Devlin Drake come to her bed? Would he be as forceful as the rogues her mother warned her about? Or would he be kind and understanding of her situation?

They arrived at the chapel, a quaint building set amongst the trees that looked hundreds of years older than the house. Being late October, there was a bitter nip in the air, but there wasn't a cloud in the sky. The tiny panes in the stained-glass windows shone and sparkled as the sun's rays bounced off the surface.

If Juliet searched the length and breadth of the country, she doubted she would find a prettier place.

The footman came to a halt at the church entrance. "Mr Drake awaits you inside, my lord." He raised the latch, pushed open the arched wooden door and gestured for them to enter.

Neither her father nor Hannah thought to ensure Juliet looked presentable. Neither had bothered to provide her with a dried posy or some other frippery to indicate she was the bride. Neither offered words of encouragement or comfort or hope.

Loneliness breezed through the cracks in Juliet's armour. Her chest constricted, squeezing her heart. Many times she had longed to feel her mother's warm embrace, but no more so than today. Juliet closed her eyes and conjured an image of the sweet lady who always cupped her cheeks and kissed her with genuine affection.

"Stop dawdling." Hannah's less than polite nudge in the back dragged Juliet from her reverie. "Your ogre awaits."

Years spent biting her tongue culminated in the sudden urge to speak the truth. "As I no longer need to appease you, Hannah, let me give you a word of warning. Lay a hand on me again, and I shall make it my life's mission to inform every lady I meet what a spiteful hag you are."

Hannah gave a wry smirk. "You're not married to Mr Drake yet. Until he says 'I will' you're still my servant."

"Does the fact that I'm your sister mean nothing to you?" Once, Juliet hoped they might be the best of friends.

"You're my father's by-blow," Hannah said, thrusting her button nose in the air. "You're a mistake. A stain on our family's reputation. And I for one will be glad to see the back of you."

Juliet was about to say the feeling was mutual, but they were suddenly cast in shadow. She turned to the door to find Devlin Drake's large frame filling the narrow space.

He cast Hannah a menacing glare. "Opinions are subjective, Miss Bromfield." Mr Drake's words hit like an arctic chill. Ice cold. Cold enough to freeze the flaming fires in hell. "Perhaps it is you, with your vile tongue, who is the blight of the Bromfields."

Hannah shivered, but it took more than a frosty tone to unsettle the ice queen. "Well, Mr Drake," she began, thrusting her fingers more firmly into her gloves, "after the disreputable way your brother behaved, you are hardly one to cast aspersions."

A volatile energy clawed at the surrounding air. Mr Drake ground his teeth and looked like a jaguar ready to pounce.

Juliet cleared her throat. She looked up into Mr Drake's onyx eyes, knowing it would take more than a few chosen words to break through the hard layers. "Pay her no heed, sir. These last six years, she has used every means possible to ruin my day. But I refuse to let her ruin this one."

Mr Drake met her gaze, those dark eyes softening just a fraction. A shiver of awareness shot through Juliet's body. Her stomach flipped more than once, and she felt suddenly breathless.

Mr Drake inclined his head. "Then let us proceed, Miss Duval. Your father has taken a seat in the pew and seems determined to remain there." His gaze drifted over her face, settled on her lips for longer than was deemed appropriate. "But you do not need his arm to lean on."

The hint of admiration in his tone gave her a rush of confidence. "No, Mr Drake. I am more than capable of walking down the aisle on my own."

"Why walk alone when you can walk with me?"

Juliet's stomach performed another feat of acrobatics. "But that is not the done thing, sir."

"Perhaps not, but neither of us cares much for propriety."

Hannah muttered something derogatory, but Mr Drake's penetrating gaze never faltered.

He reached for Juliet's hand and placed it in the crook of his arm. "From this moment forward, you need never walk alone again. From this moment forward, anyone who attempts to hurt you must answer to me."

Oh, every word that left his mouth eased the crippling loneliness within. She clutched the hard muscle above his elbow, looked up at him and smiled. "Then lead the way, sir."

The private chapel comprised of six box pews, a carved oak pulpit and a small altar situated at the foot of a less than majestic stained-glass window.

The reverend, dressed in his white surplice, raised a ginger brow as they approached.

"You may begin the service, Reverend Fisher," Mr Drake said as they came to a halt before the altar. "I wish this matter concluded with haste."

While Mr Drake's tone held a hint of frustration, nerves left Juliet desiring a swift conclusion, too.

After a moment's pause, the Reverend Fisher cleared his throat and bestowed a serene smile on the two undeserving people seated in the pew. "Dearly beloved …"

Hannah sniggered. "Oh, please."

Even the Lord was not worthy of her respect. She gave another snort of contempt when the reverend sought confirmation that there were no impediments to the marriage.

The Reverend Fisher ignored the rude interruptions and continued to speak in the loud and lofty tone often used to address a packed congregation. He addressed the groom, spoke of comfort and love and honour.

Mr Drake's black eyes turned a deep chocolate brown when he said, "I will." Not once did he stutter or flounder.

And then the reverend turned to Juliet and asked if she would obey this man, this tall, dark stranger. Would she serve him, love him, give herself unto him? Juliet's pulse raced. How could she lie before God? How could she promise to care for a man she hardly knew?

Silence ensued.

Her heartbeat pounded in her ears.

Heat rose to her cheeks.

The baron glared at her and mouthed a demand for her cooperation.

Mr Drake bent his head. "Trust in fate," he whispered before straightening again.

Fate?

Fate had hardly been kind to her thus far.

This day would prove to be either the best or worst of her life. He was asking her to jump into a fast-flowing river without knowing its depth, without knowledge of the dangerous undercurrents lurking beneath.

Juliet glanced at the only two people in the world she could call family. Compared to living with Hannah and the baron, the prospect of sharing her life with Devlin Drake did not seem so daunting.

"I will," she blurted before logic intervened.

Mr Drake's broad shoulders relaxed.

"And who giveth this woman to be married to this man?" The reverend's serene gaze drifted to the baron.

The muscle in her father's cheek twitched. Standing abruptly, he marched over to them and snatched Juliet's hand with such force it would undoubtedly leave a bruise. "I do," he snapped.

Mr Drake pinned her father with a hard stare. "That's the last time you'll manhandle her," he whispered through gritted teeth as he captured Juliet's hand and cocooned it between his large, hot palms.

Juliet's throat grew tight. Not because of nerves this time, but because she suddenly felt safe. Whatever happened between her and Mr Drake, she believed he would protect her until his dying breath. And that brought a brief smile of satisfaction to her face.

Hope fluttered to life in her breast as she examined the mysterious man standing before her. In a moment of fancy, she imagined he loved her. That she, a woman so small and insignificant, could tame this wild, fascinating creature. Was it possible for such a powerful man to feel something other than anger? Was it possible that an oddly matched couple might make a meaningful connection?

Feeding her fantasy, Mr Drake took her right hand and promised to love and cherish her.

When it was Juliet's turn to do the same, she couldn't help but smile again for her hand seemed so tiny and fragile against his. As she told him she would love and cherish him, too, she spoke with conviction—she had to believe it was possible. And although her body paled in comparison to Mr Drake's hulking form, her heart was large enough for both of them.

Somehow, she would come to care for him.

Somehow, she would find a way to make her marriage work.

The Reverend Fisher plucked an odd-looking ring from the open Book of Common Prayer. He handed it Mr Drake, whose eyes held a brief look of wonder as he took the black ring with gold engraving. A smile touched his lips as he slipped it onto the end of Juliet's finger.

The striking design distracted her temporarily. Gold leaves and flowers covered the black enamel. Tiny crystal teardrops made up the petals. It sparkled when the light caught the stones. It was a ring like none she'd seen before—exotic, breathtaking, far too unusual for a wedding band.

But were they not an unusual pairing?

"Do you like it?" Mr Drake said softly.

"It's beautiful."

"I wish I could say I chose it myself, but my friend Mr Dariell deserves the credit."

Prompted by the reverend, Mr Drake pushed the ring slowly down past her knuckle. The sensation caused heat to flare in her stomach. There was something sensual about the way he claimed her finger, made all the more seductive by his pledge to worship her body.

Judging by the look in his eyes, they were both surprised by the snug fit. Perhaps Mr Dariell had the gift of second sight. Perhaps he could predict the future, knew Mr Drake would marry a woman half his size.

Mr Drake kept hold of her hand when they knelt to pray. Tingling started in Juliet's fingers, journeyed up her arm to her heart. Twice, she felt Devlin Drake's searing gaze. Did he feel these odd sensations, too?

"… and may ever remain in perfect love and peace together …" The reverend's words struck Juliet like a bolt from the heavens.

What hope had they of finding a perfect love when everything about the match screamed of imperfection?

He was dark and dangerous. She was loyal and loving but had been forced to suppress it. They were marrying for all the wrong reasons—spite, revenge, to prove a point, to settle a wicked wager.

But it was too late for regrets.

The mistake was made.

The reverend bid them to rise, placed his hand over theirs and pronounced them man and wife.

For a moment, Juliet forgot how to breathe.

Thankfully, matters proceeded to the signing of the parish register. Despite having such thick fingers, Mr Drake possessed an aristocratic flare when it came to skill with a quill pen. Hannah scratched her name reluctantly, moaned and groaned that they had forced her to witness such a sham.

When all was done, Devlin Drake captured Juliet's hand and placed it in the crook of his arm. They left the church in silence. There were no cheers from a waiting crowd, no rose petals thrown to wish them good luck. No chariot to whisk them away to begin an exciting new adventure.

Mr Drake drew Juliet aside, away from the door. "While it is customary for guests to share a meal with the bride and groom, would you rather we were alone?" He towered above her, yet his voice held a hint of warmth that made him appear less threatening.

"I would hardly call our witnesses guests. They are here purely out of necessity."

"Then you have no objection if I send them home?"

Juliet glanced at the door as her father and Hannah exited the church. Never had she seen such stern faces. Six years was more than enough time to spend with people who despised the ground you walked upon.

"You may do as you see fit, Mr Drake."

"Devlin," he corrected. "I want no formality between us, Juliet. As my wife, I seek your counsel on this matter. Do you have any objection if I am rude to your family?"

How was she supposed to answer when her heart jumped about like a spring hare? Hearing her given name spoken in such a rich, deep voice was enough to raise her pulse a notch. Being referred to as his wife roused some rather odd sensations in an intimate place.

Gathering her wits, Juliet raised her chin. "I have no desire to listen to their constant criticism or ugly threats."

"Threats?" Her husband straightened to his full height.

"It's nothing." She had no intention of rummaging through his private correspondence. What could the baron do? Surely he wouldn't see any harm come to her over one of Hannah's foolish letters? "My family often uses intimidation to manipulate situations to their advantage."

"Not anymore."

Devlin captured her hand and held it in a firm grip. He led her over to her father, who was engaged in a heated discussion with Hannah.

"You'll do as I say and that's—" The baron stopped abruptly upon noting their approach. His gaze settled on their clasped hands and he snorted. "Now you're wed, I suppose you intend to force us to sit through a nauseating wedding breakfast."

"On the contrary." Devlin squeezed Juliet's hand in gentle reassurance. "I expect you to leave Blackwater immediately and never return."

Hannah stared down her nose. "Thank the Lord. I have no intention of staying a moment longer."

Deep furrows formed between her father's brows. "You intend to prevent me from visiting my own daughter?" He pursed his lips. "I know you married the girl out of spite, but to punish her on her wedding day. It's outrageous."

"As outrageous as spreading vile gossip about my brother?"

"The truth is often vile," Hannah blurted.

"Be quiet, girl," the baron snapped. He focused his beady stare on Devlin. "If revenge is your game, you have married the wrong daughter."

"Or so you think."

Juliet listened to the exchange, her head swirling in a cloud of confusion. Both men spoke as if she were insignificant, worthless. A pawn in their petty squabbles. Yet Devlin continued to stroke his thumb back and forth over her fingers. The act suggested he was her protector, supported the fact he'd told her no one would ever hurt her again.

"Leave!" Devlin glared at the baron. "Get the hell out now else I shall grab you by the collar and drag you to the gate." He stepped forward, taking Juliet with him.

Hannah and her father had no option but to retreat along the path. They ambled at first, the pair snapping and sniping at each other as they went. Juliet and Devlin walked behind though she had to jog to keep up with his long strides. Still, Devlin pressed on, forcing the baron to quicken his pace.

"Slow down," Juliet whispered, tugging on his hand. "I cannot keep up with you. And if you continue to hold my hand so tightly, I'll lose the use of my fingers."

"I'll not rest until I've seen them off my property."

"Then go ahead without me."

"You want to abandon your husband when we've only been wed for five minutes?" He cast her a sidelong glance, scanned her from head to toe. The corners of his mouth curled up into a faint smile. "Forgive me, but there is only one way to solve this problem, and I'll be damned before I permit your family to wander unsupervised around the grounds."

Without warning, Devlin Drake scooped her up as if she were as light as a child. The bulging muscles in his arms almost split the seams of his coat.

"Mr Drake, put me down. You cannot carry me in public." Her complaint fell on deaf ears, though she had to admit she felt a flutter of excitement at being held in such a strong embrace. Satisfaction settled in her chest, too, at the look of shock on Hannah's face. "You're giving them every reason to call you a heathen."

"Mrs Drake, accept that I'm a man who cares nothing for propriety. The sooner you understand that I do as I please, the easier life will be."

Juliet twined her arms around his neck though she was in no danger of falling. "But you have a wife to think of now."

"Did you not swear to obey my every command?"

"I also swore to love you and so I hardly think we can lend weight to either statement."

"Granted," he said as they crossed the stone bridge. "Both of us are wise enough to know we had no hope of marrying for love."

"No, but we must make the best of the situation."

"Agreed."

As they followed the baron to his carriage parked in the courtyard, Juliet considered the way Mr Drake's dark eyes masked all emotion. She considered the stubborn set of his jaw, the errant lock of black hair falling across his brow and realised he *did* terrify her.

It had nothing to do with his powerful build or commanding countenance, and everything to do with the way he held her close. What terrified her most was that she could easily grow to care for him. She could easily grow to love him.

CHAPTER FIVE

S till cradling Juliet in his arms, Devlin stood beneath the
portico and watched the baron's chariot rumble away down
the drive. He stared at the vibrant yellow conveyance—silently
cursing the occupants to hell—even after it trundled through the
iron gates and turned into the lane.

The next time he saw Miss Bromfield, she would not be
wearing the same smug expression. The next time he saw the
baron, he wondered if he'd thank him for tricking him into taking
a different bride. Despite the fact Bromfield cared little for his
illegitimate daughter, something about the ease in which he
accepted the situation bothered Devlin.

The baron's parting words to Juliet echoed again in Devlin's
mind.

Remember what I said.

Something told him not to ask his new wife what the devious
lord meant. They were practically strangers, had been married for
less than an hour, and it would serve neither of them if she felt
forced to lie. No. Devlin would bide his time, encourage her to
confide in him, divulge any secrets.

God, he was the worst sort of hypocrite for he had chosen not to reveal the reason he'd slipped the ring onto her finger and made her his bride.

"Well, do you intend to put me down or will you carry me around as some matrons do their pugs?"

Devlin couldn't help but smile at her comment. "That all depends. Will you bite me if I tickle your chin?"

"Most definitely. And I shall yap relentlessly if I grow tired and bored."

A chuckle burst from his lips. He could not recall the last time he'd found a woman so amusing. One thing was certain, his wife piqued his interest.

"You're not yapping now," Devlin said, looking into eyes that reminded him of the rare jade stones he'd seen on his travels. "Does that mean you like being held in my arms?"

Dariell once told him that jade brought good luck. That it symbolised a unity of mind and soul. His insightful friend was always right, and the thought brought a sliver of optimism.

Her cheeks flushed a pretty shade of pink. "It means I'm still unsure how best to deal with my master."

Devlin felt his smile slip. "I'm not your master, Juliet. You have free rein over this house, these lands. Make your demands, and you will discover I am not so disagreeable."

"Why would I think you disagreeable when you have been nothing but obliging?"

He lowered her gently to the ground, missed the warmth of her body instantly. In his arms, they seemed equal. Now, as he towered above her, she looked so delicate, so fragile. Fragile enough that the urge to protect her held him in a vice-like grip. They had been married for less than an hour, and already chivalrous thoughts entered his head.

The irony was that he would be the one to hurt her.

When a man lived for vengeance, he lacked the capacity to

love. Had a heart filled with nothing but bitterness and hatred. Like her father, he intended to use this innocent lady for his own gain.

And how the hell could he consummate this union when he was liable to bruise her, to crush her beneath his weight? For a man who applied logic to every situation, somehow he had failed to follow the same principles when it came to choosing a bride.

"Come," he eventually said. "Let me introduce you to the staff. Mrs Barbary will escort you to your apartments where no doubt your maid is unpacking." As the words left his lips, he realised his error.

Juliet smiled, and it suddenly felt like a promising spring day, not a chilly one in late autumn. "I am my own maid, sir," she said with a chuckle, "and it will take me five minutes to unpack the two dresses in my small valise."

"Two dresses? No one saw fit to provide you with a trousseau?"

What was he thinking?

A lady's family spent weeks preparing her new wardrobe. The baron wouldn't care if his daughter married him wearing nothing but a coal sack.

"No, Mr Drake." She tugged at the pale blue dress and pelisse she'd chosen for her wedding ensemble. "These are the best clothes I have and once belonged to my sister. But they're terribly out of fashion I'm told."

"Devlin," he corrected, eager to hear how his name sounded when spoken so sweetly. "Then we must send for a modiste."

"Oh, no." She waved her hands at him. "Please do not go to any trouble on my account."

"Then allow me to go to the trouble for my own sake." He'd not have his wife walking about looking like the hired help. "You'll need various dresses, gowns, nightclothes—"

"Nightclothes? But I never wear—" She stopped abruptly, and her cheeks flushed berry-red.

"Never wear what?" Devlin asked despite knowing exactly what she was about to say. "Nightclothes?" His pulse raced at the thought. "Not even in the dead of winter?"

"I hate to feel encumbered," she said though could not look him in the eye. "And I should tell you now that I do not ride or dance, so there is no need to go to extra expense."

An image of her assisting the maids in the scullery flashed into his mind. While Juliet lived in the shadows, her sister rode in the park during the fashionable hour, danced in silk gowns, wore diamonds at her throat.

"Then I shall teach you to do both." He had always been one to root for the less fortunate. "There is nothing like riding to get the blood pumping." How easy it would be for this conversation to turn salacious.

"Oh, no." Juliet swallowed. "I fail to see how someone so small might command such a large beast."

"Are you referring to your husband or the horse?" he said, unable to resist teasing her.

Juliet's eyes widened. "You are not a beast. You're just … just a rather large man."

They stared at each other for a moment until a deep, powerful bark and the sound of crunching gravel drew a muttered curse from his lips.

"Damnation," Devlin said, glancing over her shoulder. "Do not be afraid."

Juliet jerked her head back. "I'm not afraid of you, Mr Drake. I find your size a tad unnerving but—"

"I'm not talking about me. I'm talking about my dog." Devlin caught sight of the monstrous animal bounding towards them. "I suggest you turn around. Do it slowly else you might end up in a heap on the floor."

Juliet turned to witness the hound's approach. Her eyes grew wide, and her chin hit her chest. "Good Lord!" She stumbled back, her outstretched arms grasping for something stable to help keep her upright. "That's not a dog. That's a ... that's a ..."

"Beast?" Devlin wrapped his arm around her shoulder and drew her close to his side. "He's harmless. I can assure you."

"To you perhaps. Forgive me for being somewhat apprehensive when a dog is tall enough to look me in the eye."

"Rufus, stay." Devlin raised his hand in command, but the black hound galloped towards them, ears flapping, eager to meet his new friend. "Rufus!"

In a panic, Juliet shuffled behind Devlin. She clutched the back of his coat as the dog charged at them. The athletic animal jumped up and almost took Devlin clean off his feet.

"There's a boy." Devlin stroked the dog's ears and then tried to force the muscular creature back onto all fours. "Now sit so you may meet your new mistress. Rufus, sit."

Rufus climbed down but was more interested in what his master was hiding behind his back. He bounded behind Devlin, leapt and bounced on his hind legs in a bid to get closer to Juliet.

"Arghh, get down, Rufus." Juliet gasped as she released Devlin's coat. "Rufus. Good heavens. No. Stop it. That's enough."

Devlin swung around to offer his assistance and had to purse his lips at the comical sight.

Rufus stood on his back legs, his front paws draped over Juliet's shoulders as she struggled under the strain. She winced as he licked her face, and then pulled her head back to prevent him from repeating the friendly gesture.

"Rufus!" Devlin shouted in the harsh voice that made men quiver. But the dog had been without his master for five years and struggled to follow commands. "Let me help you."

"No, wait." Juliet wrapped her arms around the dog's chest, stroked and tickled his back affectionately. "If he thinks I need you to fight my battles, he'll jump at me every time he wants your attention."

The lady might be slight of frame, but she had a backbone of steel.

He liked that.

The dog slobbered over her, left mud stains on her blue pelisse. She looked up at Rufus—whose head was twice the size of hers—stared him in the eye and said in a firm but kind voice, "Get down, you daft dog, so I may stroke you some more."

Surprisingly, the hound obeyed.

Juliet continued to pet the dog and mutter words of endearment. She turned to Devlin. "Now, this is a beast."

"A beast you have managed to tame within minutes." Devlin wasn't surprised. There was a sweetness to her character, a quality that spoke of love and loyalty—the only things that mattered. "No doubt you'll be riding my Arabian stallion before the week is out."

The thought that this lady might possess the ability to command and conquer him, too, sent the hairs at his nape prickling to attention. His pulse soared, so much so that he became aware of his heartbeat thumping hard in his chest.

His wife of almost an hour had already touched him in ways no other woman ever had, or could. She had made him laugh twice—a rare feat in itself—had surprised him with her courage. The desire to hold her in his arms grew. The need to protect her, to make her smile, to be the best version of himself pushed to the fore.

Bloody hell!

Something told him theirs would not be a simple marriage of convenience.

"We should retire for a few hours," he said, but then realised he sounded like an eager husband desperate to bed his wife. "No doubt you would care to spend time in your chamber, familiarise yourself with the staff and the house. And I have a few business matters that need my attention."

Business matters? On his damn wedding day?

Juliet's hand came to rest on Rufus' head. Disappointment flashed briefly across her face. "Oh, you want to be alone."

No, for once in his life he didn't. Juliet was easy to talk to, pleasant to be around, entertaining company. But he could not lose sight of why he'd married her, and it would take time to grow accustomed to having a woman about the place. "We will dine together this evening."

"Of course. Your time is precious. I understand." His stomach tightened when her green eyes dulled. "And you're right. I have work to do and must learn all I can about running a house of this magnitude."

Guilt flared.

It didn't help that Rufus whined and stared at him with the same sad eyes and forlorn expression.

"Remember that you are mistress of the house, not a servant." Having spent years in servitude to her father, it would take some time for her to grow accustomed to her new position.

Juliet forced a smile. "Should I feel the need to make any changes, would you like me to seek your approval?"

Devlin shook his head. "As long as loin of peacock remains off the menu, I shall have no complaints."

She fell silent and the knot in his stomach wrung tight again.

The crunching of gravel underfoot drew their attention to the brick archway to their left. A stable hand appeared. The boy, Jack, clung on to his hat and broke into a jog when he spotted Rufus sitting beneath the portico. "Beg yer pardon, Mr Drake sir," he said in a state of mild agitation. "Rufus was sittin' inside the stables one minute an' gone the next."

"Rufus was eager to meet his new mistress."

The boy inclined his head to Juliet. "I'll take him, ma'am, though that's the first time he's sat still all day."

Juliet patted Rufus' head. "And does Rufus live in the stables permanently?" she said, locking eyes with the hound.

Devlin considered the look of affection in Juliet's eyes and couldn't help but feel a tinge of jealousy. Never had he felt threatened by a rival, let alone a damn dog. "He is not coming into the house if that is what you're about to suggest."

"I wouldn't dream of bringing him inside."

"I'm glad to hear it."

"Not until he is fully trained."

"Trained? You think you can tame that wild beast?" Devlin had to admire her enthusiasm.

Not wanting his staff to be party to their private conversation, Devlin dismissed Jack. The only way the boy could get the dog to follow him was to tap him on the nose and then run away. Rufus bolted, caught up with the boy on the lawn and brought him to the ground.

"You see," Devlin said, finding the whole scene amusing. "Rufus only sat still because you showered him with affection." Hell, Devlin would lie on the chaise all day if she stroked his hair with the same devotion.

"Perhaps," she said, raising a coy brow. "But I won't know if he can behave unless I try to teach him to be submissive."

"It will be a waste of time and effort. He's been alone for too long and cannot obey the simplest commands."

Juliet pursed her lips. "So he is the only dog of that size you own?"

"Indeed."

"I see." The corners of her mouth curled up into a sweet, innocent smile, yet those hypnotic green eyes sparkled with mischief. He liked that, too. It seemed there were many things he liked about his wife. "Well, you're a man who likes to gamble. Would you care to make a wager?"

Devlin folded his arms across his chest. "A wager? That depends on the stakes."

Her gaze lingered on the expanse of muscle in his upper arms.

"Should I fail to train Rufus sufficiently enough that he may spend a considerable amount of time indoors, you may ask anything of me and I shall grant your request."

A host of possibilities raced through Devlin's mind. Sabotaging her efforts in order to ask questions about Ambrose was not his first thought. Neither was asking her about her father's cryptic message.

No.

He wanted to teach her to ride, to dance, wanted to lounge on the bed and watch her bathe. He wanted a kiss, a caress, to bed her in the hope the goodness filling her heart might cure him of the bitterness plaguing his own beating organ.

"You won't win," he said, feeling another frisson of guilt that this charming lady had curtailed the need to avenge his brother. "I tend to succeed in most things I put my mind to."

"And yet while you won your last bet, did you not come away with the second prize?"

Devlin wasn't entirely sure what to say to that. "Not when I judge integrity to be a most valuable asset. In that regard, every lady in London trails miserably behind you."

Damn. He despised men who spouted sentiment to win favour, but it was the truth.

Her porcelain cheeks flushed pink again. "What better compliment could a lady have on her wedding day?"

Her words carried no hint of sarcasm. Still, it occurred to him that he'd not told her she looked beautiful. To do so would sound insincere when they both knew that was not the reason he'd married her. "You should know that I rarely express my good opinion."

"Then you do me a great honour."

Their eyes locked and the air between them crackled to life.

Had he married Miss Bromfield, he would have deposited her in her chamber within minutes of returning to the house. The next few hours would be spent plotting all the ways he might make her rue the day she spoke so cruelly of Ambrose.

But he had married this petite creature with her broad smile and beguiling eyes. For some obscure reason, the thought of hurting her made his stomach coil in revulsion. For his sanity, he should put some distance between them, make it clear theirs was a marriage of convenience. He should focus on discovering what the hell had happened to Ambrose.

Which was why he surprised himself when he said, "Then I agree to your wager and shall think long and hard about how you might reward me when I win."

She must have noted the salacious tone in his voice—one he failed to suppress—for her gaze fell to his lips. And then he saw the one thing in her eyes he dreaded most—the flicker of fear that told him he was wrong to assume his size didn't matter. Wrong to assume her courage knew no bounds. They were mismatched, unsuited, odd.

Juliet swallowed deeply. She opened her mouth, but he did not give her a chance to speak.

"Well, we cannot stand conversing under the portico all day." His voice carried his frustration. "I have matters to attend to and shall see you this evening at dinner."

"Of course," she said but did not present him with one of her wide, beaming smiles. "Will you at least introduce me to your housekeeper before you retire to the study?"

Devlin inclined his head. No doubt his staff were lined in the hall waiting to greet their new mistress. "Mrs Barbary is eager to meet you."

He chose not to tell Juliet that she should expect some hostility as he did not want to worry her unduly. But Mrs Barbary had served his family for fifty years, had come to the house as a girl of twelve, had cared for Ambrose like a son and blamed the Bromfields for his demise.

"Should you encounter any problems with the staff then you

may seek me out." Devlin continued, hoping she would learn to embrace her new role.

"There will be no problems," she said, and though she straightened her back and lifted her chin, he could hear the nervous edge in her voice. "If there's one thing I do know, it's how to deal with unreasonable people."

CHAPTER SIX

"And the household linens? Have you inspected them this month?" Juliet said in a firm but friendly tone as Mrs Barbary gave her a tour of the house.

Within minutes of meeting the staff, it soon became apparent that the housekeeper was not a woman who welcomed interference from the mistress. Aware of the lengthy time Mr Drake had spent abroad, Juliet decided that Mrs Barbary had been left to her own devices for far too long, and that was perhaps the reason for her reluctance to disclose any information relating to the running of the house.

"When the master is in residence, I inspect the linens on Fridays," Mrs Barbary said, her pinched face and thin lips suggesting suppressed annoyance.

The housekeeper stood a foot taller than Juliet—as most people did. Clearly the woman knew of Juliet's inferior birth else she would not speak with such veiled disdain.

"And when he is not in residence?"

Mrs Barbary looked down her pointed nose. "I inspect them once a quarter."

"Then I ask that you take a full inventory and we will discuss the matter tomorrow." The last thing Juliet wanted was to cause animosity, but she had to make a stand. She had to show she was capable of holding her position.

"Yes, Mrs Drake."

Juliet's stomach performed a flip at the sound of her married name. A dark, brooding image of her husband invaded her mind. For some inexplicable reason she felt drawn to him, craved spending time in his company, even though there were plenty of reasons she should be frightened.

Devlin Drake was too tall, too broad, too strong. His countenance screamed of virile masculinity. And those eyes—heavens above—they were like dangerous pools with fathomless depths. When the sun's rays caught the black irises, they turned an inviting chocolate brown. When he smiled and laughed, they grew warmer still.

"And these are your apartments." Mrs Barbary's words drew Juliet from her musings. The servant stood in the gloomy corridor and gestured to the chamber door. "All the rooms are exactly as they were when the mistress was alive." The housekeeper's mouth twitched in a half-smile of admiration. "Now, there was a lady of high standards and unshakable integrity."

The indirect insult did not go amiss.

Nor had the earlier comment about there being no need to unlock the music room door.

"Then I hope to prove myself a worthy replacement as mistress of Blackwater."

Mrs Barbary pursed her lips and gave a curt nod. She opened the chamber door and stood back for Juliet to enter.

Like all the rooms in Blackwater, the bedchamber was a gloomy, oppressive place. The panelled walls, the faded tapestries, the green velvet bed hangings made the space feel sombre and morbid.

Juliet's heart sank.

It was as if a solemn presence lingered within the walls, one eager to invade her spirits, to suck every drop of hope and happiness she possessed, leaving a shrivelled wreck. A sense of melancholy gripped her, ready to drag her down into the depths of despair.

She had married a man who'd left her alone on her wedding day, in a strange house with servants who obviously disapproved of the match. Never had she felt so lonely, not even in her father's home. Now she knew why a lady took her own maid when she married. A familiar face would be a welcome distraction.

"What with the sudden news of your wedding, there's been no time to air the place properly." Mrs Barbary moved to the window and pulled back the curtains. "There's a dressing room through there," she continued, pointing to another door. "And a sitting room where the mistress used to take her breakfast and write her letters."

No doubt the rooms were just as dismal. But how was she to broach the subject of new furnishings when the chamber was like a shrine to Mr Drake's beloved mother?

While Juliet had a multitude of questions regarding the running of the house, including a curiosity to examine the last three months' accounts, she needed time alone to gather her thoughts.

"Thank you, Mrs Barbary. That will be all for now." At all costs, she must shake this morose mood. "We will meet tomorrow and go over the menus for the next two weeks."

"Yes, ma'am." The housekeeper hovered for a moment. Perhaps she sensed Juliet's unease, for she said in a more personable tone, "There's a pleasant view of the gardens and the fountain from the window. The path leads down to the brook if you're in the mind for a stroll. The mistress used to sit on the bench and read her correspondence."

She didn't want to hear any more talk of reading letters.

"Thank you." Juliet forced a smile. "Perhaps I might go out

tomorrow." A walk would distract her mind and give her an opportunity to build a relationship with Rufus.

"I shall send Tilly up to you." Mrs Barbary's critical eye focused on the mud stains on Juliet's pelisse. "She'll attend to all your needs until you're ready to take a maid of your own choosing."

Juliet nodded. Only when the rattle of Mrs Barbary's chatelaine faded into the distance did she breathe a relieved sigh. Her stomach twisted in painful knots, much like the first day she'd spent under her father's roof, feeling overwhelmed and out of her depth. The desire to run had been stronger then. The desperate longing to feel her mother's loving arms wrapped around her proved equally intense.

Wallowing in pity was a fool's pastime, and so Juliet unbuttoned her pelisse, shrugged out of the garment and threw it onto the chair. Then she braced her hands on her hips and surveyed the room. A brighter colour was needed, pale yellow or gold, something to bring life to the mausoleum. A vase of dried flowers on the side table and a few lively paintings on the wall would improve the room immensely.

Feeling more optimistic, she wandered over to the washstand and poured water into the porcelain bowl. As she immersed her hands, her gaze fell to the black and gold wedding band. The choice of ring was as intriguing as the man who'd slipped it onto her finger and made a host of promises he couldn't possibly keep.

Devlin Drake.

The words drifted through her mind like a haunting melody, and she found she rather liked the air of mystery contained within each note.

If a few furnishings could brighten her bedchamber, what would it take to light the fire in her husband's obsidian eyes?

Nothing superficial or conventional or predictable.

A smile touched her lips.

She would just have to be herself.

Dinner was a formal affair. Footmen busied about bringing in platter after platter. Lamb in a piquant sauce. Wild duck. Ham and veal patties. Pigeon. Enough French beans to feed a battalion. Clearly, Mr Drake's appetite was as large as his frame. Not that Juliet could enquire as to the reason for such excessiveness. They sat at opposite ends of a long table, too far away for her to read any emotion in his eyes, too far away to partake in idle conversation.

"Must we sit so far apart?" she asked, craning her neck to peer over a gilt centrepiece of a Grecian temple with winged maidens draped around the pillars.

The contrived scene was incongruous to what she already knew of her husband's character.

Mr Drake dabbed his mouth with his napkin and said, "Forgive me, did you say something?"

"Can we not sit together?"

He brushed a lock of sable hair from his brow and looked at her blankly.

Juliet turned to the footman who stood in the background as if made of stone. "Would you ask my husband if I might move closer?"

The footman inclined his head, walked sombrely to the other end of the table and conveyed the message.

Mr Drake looked at her. She thought she saw his mouth twitch in amusement, but it was impossible to tell. But then he pushed out of his chair and strode towards her, power emanating from the thick thighs bulging in his breeches.

Towering above her, he offered his hand. "You do not need to ask permission to move."

Juliet stared at his face, then at the width of his palm, the length of his fingers. "The aristocracy can be rigid when it comes to etiquette."

"Do I look like a man who abides by the rules?"

Her heartbeat pulsed hard in her throat. "I do not know you well enough to answer." Lord, he looked like a man capable of crossing swords with the devil.

"Then let us rectify the situation." He extended his hand further, and Juliet slipped her small hand into his without hesitation.

The reaction was instant.

A jolt of awareness shot up her arm to play untold havoc with her nerves. Heat spread from her neck to her cheeks. She couldn't look him in the eye but simply allowed him to assist her from the seat.

A curt nod to the footman and the servant seemed to understand his master's request. By the time Juliet sat comfortably in the chair to her husband's right, her place setting had been moved.

"Forgive me," she said, hoping conversation would banish these strange sensations. "I'm used to dining in the kitchen and find I'm not comfortable following convention."

Mr Drake sipped his wine. "I can see that." Hungry eyes devoured her over the rim of his glass. They drifted over her loosely tied hair, considered the unruly red curls that always escaped any attempt to keep them at bay.

Juliet tucked a stray curl behind her ear. "Are you disappointed I did not make more effort for dinner?"

Well, he did say he admired honesty.

"Not at all." His rich, velvet voice stirred the hairs at her nape. "I despise the contrived, and it's important you feel comfortable here at home." He paused and then said, "You have beautiful hair. Why hide it with fancy combs and ridiculous feathers?"

The compliment sent her pulse racing. Never before had a man expressed his admiration and she couldn't help but smile.

"May I ask you something?" She swallowed a spoonful of veal broth while waiting for his answer.

"You do not have to tread lightly around me, Juliet." He

glanced up and dismissed the footmen. "Say what you will and accept that I will do the same. That way, there can be no misunderstanding between us."

Guilt flared. Honesty had its limits. How could she tell him she was sent to spy?

"Then I must ask you two questions." She would ask the easiest question first. "Is it not a waste for the kitchen to prepare so much food when an army of men would struggle to eat such a quantity?"

He scanned the table and shrugged. "The staff know little of my current tastes and needs. And for a reason I am yet to fathom, they are too nervous to broach the subject. But I agree it is excessive."

"Then I shall speak to Cook and Mrs Barbary in the morning and make alterations to the menu."

His lips curled into a sinful smile as he raised his glass in salute before downing the contents. "And your second question?"

Juliet glanced at the wedding band gracing her finger. "Tell me about the ring. How is it you bought my exact size when I have unusually small fingers? When I was not your chosen bride?"

Mr Drake swallowed deeply. She saw the same look of surprise in his eyes as she did when he realised he'd bought a perfect fit.

"There is only one possible explanation, only one answer to your question, Juliet."

"And what is that?"

"I was meant to marry you."

Their gazes locked. The power of his words struck her heart. If he truly believed what he said, then there was hope for them yet.

"But I did not choose the ring," he reminded her.

"No, your friend Mr Dariell did."

"Indeed. Dariell has the gift of insight, the gift of intuition.

The man has a way of seeing the truth while those around him are oblivious. Don't ask me how he knew of this odd turn of events. He simply insisted I make the purchase, despite the fact it is a rather unconventional design."

Juliet held up her hand and admired the pretty pattern. "I think it's the most enchanting thing I've ever seen. It conveys a certain mystique. It draws the eye and holds one captive, although I think that has something to do with how the glass petals sparkle in the light."

Mr Drake cleared his throat. "They're not glass. They're diamonds."

"Diamonds!" She could not contain her surprise. "Diamonds? All of them?"

"All of them."

"Oh!"

Good Lord. It must have cost a king's ransom.

"I would never permit my wife to wear cheap imitations."

The sudden rush of excitement coursing through Juliet's veins was tempered by the fact he would have given the ring to Hannah had their father not played his ace card.

"You would have had to tell my sister about the diamonds before you attempted to force the ring on her finger else she would never have agreed."

Mr Drake opened his mouth to speak, paused for a second and then said, "I had no intention of giving Miss Bromfield that ring."

"You didn't?" Confused, Juliet shook her head and frowned. "But you purchased it for your wife."

"And my wife is wearing it."

Perhaps she had drunk too much wine. Perhaps the trials of the day made it impossible to form rational thoughts. "You are not making any sense," she found the courage to say.

"The thought of giving your sister that ring filled me with loathing." He shifted uncomfortably in the chair, hesitated before speaking again. "I purchased a plain band to use in its place."

So why had he given it to her?

Why give the inferior choice such an expensive, such a breathtaking piece of jewellery? Regardless of his reason, she couldn't help but feel flattered. But his answer raised another important question. Why make a wager in the first place when one was repelled by the prize?

"Dariell taught me to listen to my intuition," her husband continued. "It felt right to give you the ring. The fact it fits confirms it was a wise decision."

If the ring was meant for her, then there must be some higher force at play. The knowledge that fate would guide their way was like a reassuring arm around her shoulder.

"You mentioned meeting my brother," Mr Drake said as he stood and performed the duties of the footman: moving the china bowls and serving a selection of food from the silver platters.

"Yes, I met him many times."

"So you bore witness to his relationship with Miss Bromfield?"

"Indeed." Whatever it was he wanted to know, these evasive tactics would not work. "What are you asking? If they loved one another? Because I can tell you the answer is no."

Mr Drake took his seat at the head of the table. She was rather glad as it eased the pressure on her neck.

"You seem confident in your answer."

"Hannah couldn't possibly love anyone as much as she loves herself." Loving someone meant making sacrifices, meant a willingness to compromise. "Had she loved your brother she would never have slandered his character, even if he did break her heart."

His expression darkened. "And you know of the vile things she said, about his fondness for—" He stopped abruptly, a frown marring his brow. "Did you just say Ambrose broke her heart?"

Juliet nodded. "Hannah was most upset when your brother ended their betrothal." She remembered the night clearly. The argument started in the garden, went on for an hour or more. It was the only time Hannah had ever cried herself to sleep. "Though I am the only person who knows the truth."

Mr Drake sat forward, intrigue playing in his eyes. "But everyone believes Miss Bromfield was the one who decided they would not suit."

"As a gentleman, perhaps your brother did not wish to cause her any embarrassment. Perhaps my father threatened him, insisted Ambrose do something to save her reputation. I don't know." A rumble in her stomach drew her gaze to the sumptuous meal before her. "Do you mind if we eat now?"

"Not at all." Mr Drake glanced at her plate. "You will need your strength if you plan to train the hound."

While Juliet slipped a piece of cold lamb into her mouth, Mr Drake sat in an odd meditative silence, the tips of his steepled fingers touching his lips.

"Were you party to their private conversations when Ambrose came to call?" he suddenly said in the suspicious tone one might expect from a barrister attending in the Old Bailey. "Do you know why my brother decided against marrying Miss Bromfield?"

Something about his brother's death troubled him deeply. It went beyond grief. Was it that he had been absent in his brother's time of need? Was it the vile things people said? Did Mr Drake feel it necessary to try to salvage his brother's ruined reputation?

For now, she would answer his questions. But she needed to conduct a more in-depth enquiry.

"No, I'm afraid I don't. I remember hearing various snippets of their conversation but you can hardly expect me to recall them three years later." Juliet drew on the few mental pictures stored in her mind. "But theirs was a volatile relationship."

"Volatile? How so?"

Juliet's cheeks grew hot. She could hardly tell him that she spied on them, that at times she was a little envious of the romantic connection they shared. She could hardly tell him

Hannah had slapped Ambrose's face so hard it had left an angry red welt.

"Oh, they would kiss with a passion that would affect anyone who saw them. It is why I find it difficult to believe your brother had a distaste for women."

"Trust me. Ambrose was not interested in men."

"No. I am inclined to agree."

A relieved sigh breezed from his lips. "Passion can be all-consuming." His obsidian eyes roamed over her face. "It can rob a man of all logical thought."

"Only a man?" The odd stirring in her breast when he slipped the ring on her finger suggested otherwise.

"I am sure women possess the same propensity for lust." He watched her as he brought the glass of claret to his mouth, sipped the wine and licked the burgundy residue from his lips.

The air thrummed with an intensity that made it hard to breathe. She imagined him kissing her, touching her, believed she might actually come to enjoy the experience.

"I'm quite sure they can." The tremble in her voice revealed her apprehension. In a matter of hours he would expect her to consummate their union. But whenever she showed any signs of fear or anxiety, she felt Mr Drake retreat into the depths of his dark, dank lair.

"Yet while you spoke of their passion," Mr Drake said in a more detached tone, "the word *volatile* suggests a violent, rather explosive relationship."

Explosive was indeed the right word to describe her sister's sudden outbursts. "Hannah finds it hard to control her emotions when things do not go her way."

"She is unpredictable, then." It was not a question. He fell silent again, a silence that stretched on and on until they had finished their meal.

A yawn escaped Juliet's lips, and then another.

"Do you find my company tiring?"

"Not at all," she said, feeling quite the opposite. She found him fascinating. "Conversation seems to flow naturally between us, but it has been a long day." And might well be an equally long night.

"Then allow me to escort you to your bedchamber."

Juliet sucked in a breath as he pushed out of the chair. She considered the broad expanse of his chest, considered how suffocating it must feel to have such a weight squashing her into the mattress. "Of course."

As they ascended the grand staircase, the tension grew palpable.

Every painting they passed conveyed yet another solemn face. Fear took hold. Each step, each breath drained her energy, seemed to suck the life from her limbs. By the time they reached the bedchamber door her hands were shaking, her knees barely able to support her weight.

"This is where I shall leave you and bid you goodnight," Mr Drake said stiffly.

"Goodnight? Oh. I see. Are … are you not coming in?" Despite these crippling emotions, a part of her wanted to further their connection, longed for fate to draw her down this unfathomable path.

"No." He captured her chin between his fingers, lowered his head and pressed his lips to hers. They were warm, tasted rich and exotic like wine and spice. She suddenly realised it was what she needed, realised how much she craved his touch, but he pulled away. "I shall visit you later once you have rested."

Juliet looked up into eyes so shockingly black. Black as the night. "You must forgive me. I lack the experience necessary to quash any awkwardness." And she didn't have the first clue how to seduce her husband.

Mr Drake inclined his head. "No doubt we will muddle through." His low voice carried a hint of dejection. "Goodnight, Juliet."

"Goodnight."

Juliet watched him walk away, shoulders slumped. He looked weary, his spirits deflated.

Oh, how she wished this was a love match, wished they could have come together in a night of blinding passion. She wanted to bring him comfort, hoped he could soothe away her fears, ease the years of loneliness.

Juliet thought about her husband's perplexing personality while she stripped and washed. She thought about his sensual lips as she slipped in between the cool sheets and lay quiet and still.

For four hours she waited patiently for his return.

But Devlin Drake did not come back.

CHAPTER SEVEN

Alone in his bedchamber, Devlin sat in front of the fire, a glass of brandy cradled between his palms as he watched the dancing flames. Hours had passed since he'd left Juliet with a promise to return, an unspoken promise to consummate their union.

Never had he taken a woman who didn't want him, and he had no intention of doing so now. So why did every fibre of his being implore him to navigate the dark corridors to her chamber? Why did the need to prove he had made the right decision to wed burn so fiercely in his veins?

Vengeance was proving to be more trouble than it was worth. Ambrose was dead. What did his brother care if Miss Bromfield paid the price for spouting lies? He had cared about furthering their family's bloodline, about building a prosperous estate for future generations. Ambrose cared about honour and principles and duty. All the things that made a man forget what really mattered—things like honesty and friendship and love.

Perhaps that was what ailed Devlin. In seeking retribution, he had lost something of himself. Now he was married to a woman who trembled whenever he stood, a woman who affected him more than he cared to admit.

Damn, were he not so attracted to her it would be simple. But he'd wanted to kiss her from the moment he pushed the ring onto her finger. At dinner, he had watched her intently while she ate tiny morsels of food. He imagined the taste of her rosebud lips, imagined those vibrant red curls sprawled over his pillow, those delicate hands caressing the muscles in his chest—until his pleasurable thoughts were replaced by a nightmare vision of her crying out in pain as he thrust inside her.

Half a decanter of brandy hadn't helped to rid him of these conflicting emotions.

Part of him wanted to capture her in his arms and make her his own—a woman with such a huge heart would easily learn to love. Part of him wanted to distance himself. The thought of hurting her, of hearing the cruel taunts he'd endured as a younger man proved too much to bear. And so he stayed away.

Three days passed, three long, restless nights.

Valentine's arrival distracted Devlin from his troubles.

"Forgive me for mentioning the obvious," Valentine said as he lounged in a chair in the drawing room. "But there appears to be a major flaw in your plan."

Devlin settled his long frame into the adjacent seat. He glanced out of the window at the delightful figure of Juliet racing about the manicured lawn. "And what flaw would that be?" he said, teasing his friend.

"That the lady dancing with your dog is not the dreaded Miss Bromfield." Valentine pushed his hand through his mop of golden hair. It was a gesture that often left the ladies breathless. "In your haste to settle the wager you've married the wrong woman."

"Juliet is not dancing with Rufus. She's training him."

Devlin couldn't help but smile at the comical sight. Every day beginning at noon, Juliet took the dog through a specific set of tasks, rewarding him for his obedience, returning him to the stables when he failed to obey her commands. Still, even though she wore her cloak, it was too cold to stay outdoors for long periods, and he made a mental note to caution her on the effects of the inclement weather.

"It may have been some time since I graced a ballroom," Valentine said in his usual suave, sophisticated voice, "but the dog has his paws on her shoulders while she twirls him about the garden. Is that not dancing?"

"It's a sign of affection. Rufus likes her. What can I say?"

Valentine chuckled. "Rufus isn't the only one salivating. It seems his master is also quite taken with the petite beauty. You've barely dragged your gaze from the window since we sat down."

To say Devlin's wife fascinated him was an understatement. She might be small in stature, but her presence dominated the corridors of the dusty old house. He'd lost count of the times he'd hidden in the study only to hear the sweet melodic tones of a country tune echoing through the halls. Her animated conversation at dinner each evening held him fixated. And when she smiled, his stomach shot to his mouth.

"So," Valentine continued, "are you going to tell me what the hell happened after we parted company at Brooks'?"

"Must I?"

"Yes, if you have any hope of getting rid of me."

No man wanted to admit to being duped, but Devlin explained how the baron had tricked him, how he'd married the illegitimate daughter in the hope of still ruining the legitimate one. And yet that wasn't the whole truth. The more time he spent with Juliet, the more he believed he'd been snared by an enchantress.

Valentine narrowed his gaze. "And it did not occur to you that there are other ways of seeking vengeance on Miss Bromfield without marrying the poor relative?"

"Not at the time, no."

"And do you regret your hasty and somewhat reckless decision?" With sharp eyes, Valentine studied Devlin intently.

"No, I cannot say that I do." He never lied to his close friends.

The corners of Valentine's mouth curled into a wicked grin. "Then she must be remarkable in the bedchamber for it is rare to see you so enamoured with a woman."

Devlin glanced out of the window for the umpteenth time. Juliet had managed to get the dog to lie down. Her beaming smile broke through his hard demeanour to touch his heart.

"I wouldn't know as I've not had the pleasure," Devlin said, relishing the sudden look of shock on Valentine's face.

Valentine's jaw dropped. "You've been married for four days, and you have not bedded your wife? Do you have a problem in that regard? For if you do, there is a shop on Jermyn Street—"

"God's teeth, Valentine, everything works exactly as it ought."

"Then why the hell have you waited?"

It was difficult to explain without sounding like a smitten fool.

"Because when I do enjoy her company, it will be because she desires me. Once we consummate the marriage, she is tied to me indefinitely, and I would rather know she wants to stay with me of her own volition." Despite all protestations to the contrary, was he still hoping to find love?

Valentine chuckled when he stared out of the window to see Juliet kiss Rufus on the nose. "I cannot see her leaving here. Not when she is hopelessly in love with your dog."

"It seems she has skill for controlling beasts." Devlin suspected he, too, might do her bidding for such a handsome reward.

Valentine, being a highly intelligent man, one proficient in hearing the unspoken, gave a curious hum. "And yet I cannot help but sense fear plays a part in your problem."

Damnation.

As one of Devlin's closest friends, Valentine knew his hopes and dreams, knew of his minor insecurities, his weaknesses and doubts.

"I'll not bed a woman who shows the slightest sign of fear," Devlin reiterated. "You know that." He hauled himself from the chair over to the row of decanters on the side table. "Brandy?"

"Need you ask? But you are attempting to steer me off topic." Valentine raised a brow. "I am not speaking about your wife's fear. I am speaking about yours. What could a man with your strength and power possibly be scared of, Drake?"

After filling two crystal tumblers, Devlin returned to thrust one at Valentine. His friend accepted the drink, but his mocking smile only made Devlin restless. He couldn't sit still in the chair for it offered a perfect view of his delectable wife playing games with Rufus. Juliet looked so happy, so carefree, not as nervous as she was in his company.

"Well?" Valentine continued. "Are you going to ignore my comment?"

Valentine possessed a persuasive charm one could not ignore.

"What is it you want me to say? That I'm scared of hurting her? You know damn well that's the case. You can see how small and fragile she is."

"Good God, you speak as if your wife were a child." For a man who displayed cool indifference for most things, Valentine surprised him by raising his voice. "She's a grown woman. Anyone can see that."

Jealousy stabbed Devlin's heart. Valentine only had to look at a woman and she was panting. "You've had the gall to peruse my wife's assets?"

"What virile man does not admire the female form?" Valentine was taunting him, seeking a reaction, out to prove a point.

"Then you would have had to look hard to notice anything in that unflattering dress."

A wicked glint flashed in Valentine's bright blue eyes. "I'm a master at most things, Drake, you know that. I have an immense ability to use my imagination, though I do believe that in paying your wife a compliment I have struck a nerve."

"Perhaps you should worry about your own affairs. Did you not come home to convince Lady Durrant that you're a man capable of commitment?"

A look of uncertainty passed across Valentine's face, but he soon replaced his mask of indifference. "I gave her a reason to doubt me once before, and she married someone else. Now the lady is widowed, I have no intention of making the same mistake."

"And you believe her lack of loyalty provides a solid foundation to forge a relationship?"

Sometimes, when it came to women, intelligent men failed to see the flaw in their logic. Yes, Valentine needed a strong woman who refused to pander to his whims. Someone his equal in intelligence and mental agility. The last thing he needed was a woman who manipulated men and played the coquette.

Valentine needed someone unlike any other woman he had ever met—a bluestocking with the seductive wiles of a courtesan. If such a lady did indeed exist.

Just thinking about unique women drew Devlin's gaze back to the window. His heart sank when he found no sign of Juliet or Rufus on the lawn. The urge to hunt them down, to join them in mindless frivolity took hold. He wanted to smile, to laugh, to love, to feel something other than bitterness.

"Five years ago, I left Lady Durrant no choice but to seek a husband elsewhere." Valentine swallowed the remains of his brandy and snorted. "But it seems I am not alone in seeking the lady's affection. A Mr Kendall is eager to pursue her hand, and the lady is taking full advantage of the situation." Valentine shook his head, the indolent wave that followed suggesting an end to that particular conversation. "It is of no consequence. I came to see how you were faring with the vicious harlot. I came to offer my support, only to find you married a kind-hearted beauty instead."

Devlin contemplated the bizarre turn of events. "Perhaps we all thought we knew what we wanted when we decided to come home. But perhaps we're not being true to ourselves and fate has intervened."

"It is not like you to offer such a philosophical appraisal," Valentine said with a chuckle. He proffered his empty glass to prompt Devlin for a refill.

"No. I find I am not myself of late." Devlin's gaze flitted back to the window. It was not like him to lose focus when he'd set his mind on a task. It was not like him to pine after a woman, either.

CHAPTER EIGHT

"Don't you ever grow tired?" Juliet patted Rufus' head as they stopped to rest on the stone bridge. Rufus sat obediently at her side, his long tongue lolling as he panted for breath, and she couldn't help but feel a sense of satisfaction at her accomplishment.

And yet part of her wished she would fail in her mission to tame the hound. The desire to learn what Devlin Drake would ask for should he win the wager burned in her chest.

Was it wrong to hope he might dare ask to spend the night in her bed?

For three nights she had sat with him at dinner. They'd spoken about the theatre, about his lengthy travels abroad, and she had barely been able to contain her excitement when he described the exotic food, the strange languages, the stifling heat. Whenever it was her turn to speak, his obsidian eyes devoured every inch of her face and body until she was so hot she almost believed she might be thousands of miles away in India.

During the hours spent in conversation, she felt his equal in every regard. She forgot about the difference in size, forgot about her inferior bloodline, forgot that they had somehow felt obliged to marry.

He had been watching her today as she played on the lawn with Rufus. Her awareness of him grew more acute by the day. Her need to bring comfort, to ease the tiredness that lingered in his eyes grew with each new day, too.

Rufus' whine brought Juliet's thoughts back to the present.

"What is it now? Have I not given you enough attention?" Juliet tickled the spot beneath the hound's ear, and his eyes flickered closed in response. "If only your master reacted to me so easily."

If only she had the skill to tame the mysterious man who proved elusive after dark.

Rufus stood and nudged her leg with his head whenever her attention waned.

Two earth-trembling barks and she knew the dog needed to spend his insatiable energy.

"Come on. We could run from Land's End to John o' Groats, and still, you'd want more." Juliet wrapped her cloak more firmly around her shoulders and broke into a jog while Rufus galloped on ahead. "I shall certainly sleep well tonight." At least then she wouldn't feel quite so inadequate when her husband failed to come to her bed.

As they crossed the field that ran parallel to the boundary wall, Juliet wondered if Mr Drake regretted his decision to marry. Perhaps the thought of siring an heir with a woman who society deemed inferior was part of the problem.

But he *had* been tempted to knock on her door.

Only last night, she heard his heavy footsteps pace the landing before coming to a sudden stop outside her bedchamber. For one long, drawn-out minute Juliet had waited for the turn of the doorknob. But her wait was in vain.

Clearly he was determined to probe her mind about his brother's relationship with Hannah, but the conversation always left him in a sullen mood, and she had started to avoid mentioning her devious sister.

The clip of horse's hooves on the lane beyond the low stone wall captured her attention. Juliet stopped to catch her breath. At first, she wondered if it might be Lord Valentine returning to London. Mr Drake's friend was an incredibly handsome man, although not to her tastes. He was more angel than devil, and she had developed a sudden fondness for the dark, brooding type.

The horse trotted past, though the rider did not raise his hat, did not even glance in her direction. Miserable blighter. And she'd heard country folk were far friendlier than those in town. Then again, with Mr Drake's commanding countenance there was no telling who he'd upset.

Pushing the thought from her mind, Juliet found a stick, called Rufus to her side and then threw it as far as she could manage. The hound bounded off to retrieve it, but rather than return with his prize, he charged into the distance.

"Rufus! Come back here." Juliet braced her hands on her hips as the animal bolted towards a small cluster of trees. "Damn that daft dog. Rufus!"

She was so preoccupied calling Rufus, that she failed to hear the pad of footsteps behind her until it was too late. Juliet swung around, shocked to come face-to-face with the gentleman who had passed by on the horse.

"Heavens, you scared me out of my wits." The tremble in her voice supported her claim, as did her racing heart. Anyone capable of trespass was someone to be feared.

"I was told you'd be expecting me." The man looked not the slightest bit familiar. His accent bore the coarse tones of someone who hailed south of the Thames. Beneath his greatcoat, his clothes looked to be of reasonable quality, though not the expert tailoring that might mark him a gentleman. "Why else would you be alone and so far from the house?"

Juliet's throat grew tight. "Who are you, and what do you

want?" She managed to keep her voice even while silently wishing Rufus was at her side.

"I come at Lord Bromfield's behest. On account that I work for Mr Middle, his man of business."

"Oh, I see." Juliet felt a little more at ease knowing who had sent him, although when her father said he expected to see results in three days, she didn't think he meant it. "I imagine he wishes to learn of my progress concerning the matter of spying."

"I've been sent to retrieve the letters. To take back any you've found."

"Then you have had a wasted journey, Mr …"

"Biggs."

While Mr Biggs was nowhere near as tall as Devlin Drake, he looked down on her with the same air of condescension as her father.

"I have searched the house numerous times," she lied, "and have found nothing of interest."

For a second, Mr Biggs looked appeased, but then the menacing glint in his eyes suggested otherwise. He gritted his teeth and scowled, grabbed her by the elbow so tightly a stabbing pain shot up her arm.

"You'll find those damn letters no matter what the cost." Mr Biggs shook her roughly. Letters? So she was looking for more than one. "And I'm here to make sure you do."

"Ow! You're hurting me." Juliet tried to tug her arm free, but Mr Biggs held her in a vice-like grip. "I shall be certain to tell my father of your violent treatment."

Mr Biggs sneered. "It was your father who instructed me to beat you. I'm to make sure you understand your responsibilities to your family."

"Beat me?" The pain in her elbow shot to her heart. Why was she so surprised? Hannah's reputation came before anything. "What? And rouse my husband's suspicion? I think not."

The comment did not deter the villain. With his free hand, he pinched her chin and pulled her face so close to his she caught a whiff of his rancid breath.

"You don't want me to mar that pretty face of yours. Else you'd have to tell your husband about your plan to steal private letters from his household."

Your honesty is perhaps your greatest asset.

Devlin Drake's words invaded her mind.

Despite their utter unsuitability, he valued her integrity. Perhaps it was time to tell him the truth, explain her father was equally obsessed about Hannah's involvement with Ambrose. Oh, all this angst, all these lies, and all because Hannah had written something slanderous in her missives.

"Perhaps I will tell my husband," Juliet countered. It was the only thing her conscience would allow. "I can assure you he will seek revenge should anything untoward happen to me."

Anyone who attempts to hurt you must answer to me.

Mr Biggs' grubby nails dug into her cheeks as he squeezed hard. "You'll bring the letters to me tomorrow night. I'll wait by the fountain at midnight. If you don't, then Mr Drake might find himself involved in a nasty accident." Biggs grinned, revealing the brown rot covering the top of his teeth. "He wouldn't be the first gentleman to fall off his horse and break his neck."

Panic choked her throat.

A man of Mr Drake's size would hit the ground hard.

"He wouldn't be the first gentleman to slip from a faulty saddle, neither," Biggs added, taking pleasure from these vile threats.

"My father would condone murder just to save his daughter's shame?" Did anyone really care about the silly things Hannah had written? Those who'd spent time in her company knew she was a heartless witch.

"I'm paid to get the letters regardless of the cost. If you know what's good for you, you'll do as the baron asks."

Knots formed in her stomach.

What had she ever done to warrant such cruel treatment?

Tears threatened to fall, but she kept them at bay.

"Happen you need a taste of what to expect should you fail to obey." Biggs released her, and she stumbled back. He drew closer and raised his hand ready to wallop her hard across the cheek.

Juliet winced. She screwed her eyes shut as she waited for the sharp sting. But then a monstrous growl filled the air, followed by the blood-chilling bark of a killer.

Rufus! Thank God!

"What the hell—"

Juliet opened her eyes just as Mr Biggs took flight. He sprinted towards the stone wall as Rufus came bounding past, almost knocking her clean off her feet. Biggs tried to clamber over the wall, lost his footing twice, and for a moment Juliet wondered if the hound would leap after him.

"Rufus!" Juliet called out to the dog as he lunged at Mr Biggs. "Come back here."

"Get off me!" Biggs tumbled over the wall. He scrambled to his feet, whipped a blade from out of his boot and jabbed it at the animal. "Perhaps I'll cut out that blasted tongue."

"No! Rufus." Juliet whistled. "Come here, boy."

With his paws resting on the top of the wall, the hound bared its teeth at Biggs.

Juliet wasn't sure what to do—drop to the ground in the hope of rousing the inquisitive animal's attention or run. She chose the latter.

"Rufus!" Juliet turned on her heels, picked up her skirts and ran as fast as her legs could carry her. She glanced back over her shoulder to find the energetic animal bounding behind. Lord, she was liable to break a bone if he brought her to the ground.

With the stone bridge in sight, she did the only sensible thing. She stopped, collapsed in a heap on the grass and covered her face with her hands as the dog slobbered her with affection.

But the urge to see Devlin Drake forced her quickly to her feet.

What if Mr Biggs had an accomplice working in the stables?

What if Devlin went riding with his friend Lord Valentine and she was too late to warn him?

"Come, Rufus." She slapped her thigh and broke into a jog.

Juliet ran until the burning in her chest reached her throat, until she could no longer feel her legs. Rufus ran beside her, his ears flapping, his eyes wide with excitement. She knew she should stop to catch her breath but the desire to ensure everything was as it ought to be at home outweighed anything else.

Home.

The word echoed in her mind.

Despite the housekeeper's austere demeanour, Juliet had grown attached to Blackwater during her short stay. If only she could forget about her sister's troubles and focus on building a relationship with her husband. But the baron seemed set on spoiling all hopes of happiness.

Just when Juliet had convinced herself all would be well, she charged into the cobbled courtyard to find Lord Valentine sitting astride his horse. Devlin stood beside him, no doubt waiting for his mount, too.

"No!" The word reached the ears of her husband before she had the chance to reclaim it.

Devlin's head shot in her direction, as did Lord Valentine's.

Rufus reached them first, forcing Devlin to pet the animal to prevent him from pawing his immaculate blue coat.

Breathless and exhausted, Juliet came to an abrupt halt. "You're not going riding?"

Devlin raised a brow. "Is that a question or a command?"

"A question, of course." She glanced up at the handsome figure of Lord Valentine. "Good day to you, my lord." She slapped her hand to her chest and gasped. "Forgive me, we were running and—"

"One requires a lot of energy when trying to tame a beast," Lord Valentine said, offering an amused smile. "I imagine they can be quite demanding."

Juliet struggled to form a response. Her only thought was that she couldn't let Devlin leave, had to warn him of the threat. "Most demanding indeed." She turned to her husband. "Must you go out?"

"Valentine is leaving," he said, a concerned frown marring his brow. "It was not my intention to provide an escort."

"And I had best be on my way if I'm to make London before dark." Lord Valentine touched the brim of his hat and inclined his head. "Good day, Mrs Drake. May I wish you every success with your protégé?"

"I hope you're referring to the hound," Devlin teased.

"Who else?"

Lord Valentine rode out of the stables. The clatter of horse's hooves on the cobblestones sent Rufus racing to the gate, eager to give their guest a proper farewell.

"Is everything all right?" Devlin drew Juliet around to face him. "You seem agitated."

The feel of his large, powerful hands on her shoulders was her undoing. She flew at him, wrapped her arms around his waist and rested her head on his chest. "I thought you were going riding with Lord Valentine."

She could feel the uneasiness in his hard body, could hear the rapid beat of his heart.

"And why should the prospect cause you distress?" he asked with some confusion.

"You know how terrified I am of horses." That was not the whole truth, and she knew she had to find a way to tell him of Mr Biggs' vile threats, of her father's unreasonable demand.

His body relaxed. He wrapped his arms tightly around her and held her in a protective cocoon. "I am an accomplished rider, Juliet, although I am touched you feel some concern for my safety. It is promising, considering the fact we married as strangers."

But they were not strangers anymore.

From that first meeting, that first conversation in the garden, she had felt the need to put his welfare before her own. One did not do that for a stranger.

"But now we are better acquainted," she said, trying to keep the panic from her voice. "Now, we are friends and confidantes." At dinner they spoke with ease, discussed matters close to their hearts—when he was not questioning her about Ambrose and Hannah. "Which is why there is something I must tell you."

He pulled away. The sudden uncertainty in his eyes gave her a rare glimpse of his vulnerability. "From your tone, I suspect it is something unpleasant."

She nodded. "I didn't mention it before because I believed they were idle threats."

"Threats!" He straightened as a dark expression replaced one of uncertainty. "Damnation. Does this have something to do with your father?"

Juliet swallowed deeply. "He wants me to act as his spy, wants me to find the letters Hannah wrote to your brother." Oh, her shoulders felt lighter having relieved herself of the heavy burden.

"His spy?" After a second's pause, Devlin gritted his teeth and muttered a curse. "Whatever she wrote must be damning."

"We both know she can be cruel and vindictive."

"*Evil* is a more accurate word."

Juliet touched his sleeve. "I had no intention of carrying out his request. You must believe me."

He glanced at her hand, met her gaze. "I do."

"But it seems my father's need to protect Hannah has affected all sense and logic. While out with Rufus I was accosted by a thug, by the man hired—"

"Accosted?" He did not sound at all pleased. "A man attacked you?" Wild, obsidian eyes scanned every inch of her face and body.

"Mr Biggs threatened to beat me unless I find the letters my father seeks." Juliet rubbed the spot on her cheek where she could still feel the imprint of the rogue's grimy fingers.

A growl resonated in the back of Devlin's throat. It was as if the devil had burst up from his fiery grave ready to torch those who dared defy him. "Why the hell didn't you tell me right away? Where is he? When I find him, I'll bloody well kill him."

"Rufus chased him off."

"Did he hurt you?"

"A little."

"More than you want to admit?"

"Yes."

He dragged his hand down his face and sighed. "You're not to wander the grounds alone, not until I've dealt with this matter. First thing in the morning we must search the house for the damn letters, learn what the hell your sister wrote." He placed a comforting hand on her upper arm. "Good God, he must have scared you out of your wits, else you would not be trembling."

"It is for you I fear."

"Me?" he said incredulously. "Do I look like a man incapable of warding off an attack?"

Panic took hold again. "Mr Biggs said that if I fail to cooperate he will make sure you have an accident, cut the straps on your saddle, frighten your horse."

Devlin's eyes turned inquisitive rather than angry. "And I ask you again. Your fear is for me and not yourself?"

"Of course it's for you. One hears of such accidents all the time. Strong, virile men thrown from their horses for no apparent reason."

For a moment he simply stared at her, those penetrating eyes warm and caressing as they moved over her face. Without warning, he pulled her into an embrace and wrapped his strong arms around her.

"Then allow me to put your mind at rest. It would take more than vicious threats to bring me down." The heat from his body penetrated her clothes. "And men who threaten women are not really men to fear at all."

"You're not worried?"

"Not in the least."

A comfortable silence ensued.

His chin came to rest on her head, and he inhaled deeply.

Never had she felt so safe.

A rush of warmth filled her chest, and she looked up at him. His black eyes softened and the need to prolong the intimacy of the moment took hold. If she let this opportunity pass, there might not be another. She reached up with trembling fingers, stood on tiptoes and cupped his neck.

"Will you not ease my fears, Mr Drake?" The tremor in her voice was unmistakable. "Will you not touch your lips to mine and assure me all is well?"

The sudden flash of heat in his gaze stole her breath, and yet he hesitated.

Unable to fathom the reason for his lack of eagerness when he held her so intimately, she pulled his head down to hers and pressed her lips to his.

The kiss was soft, chaste, left her lips tingling, desperate for more. The brief touch told her all she needed to know—that she felt connected to him in a way she could not explain.

"Is this marriage not worth more to you than two names listed in the parish register?" she said, pulling away for he seemed unresponsive, lacked the drive to give more of himself. The pain of rejection made it hard to breathe. "When you said we would suit, tell me you meant as more than friends."

Devlin closed his eyes briefly. "I don't want to hurt you," he whispered.

"Hurt me? You're hurting me with these conflicting moods. You stare at me when you think I'm not watching. Push me away when we have an opportunity to grow closer."

He shook his head. "I mean I don't want to hurt you physically." Perhaps her sudden shock at his comment was evident in her eyes for he added, "I often don't realise my own strength, and you're much smaller than I."

Juliet took a moment to consider his words. "You do want to kiss me, then? You do want me as your wife for all the reasons marriage was intended?" The three nights spent alone in bed had convinced her otherwise. And yet the mystical ring on her finger gave her hope.

"I don't want you to fear me."

Why could he not simply answer the questions she posed?

"I don't fear you." Would she wrap her arms around him if she did? "But I fear if you do not kiss me there shall forever be a barrier between us." She moved to pull away, but he held her in an embrace. "I cannot promise it will be a pleasurable experience. How can it be when I lack the skill—"

Devlin Drake's mouth came crushing down on hers without warning. Strong, muscular arms held her captive while he assaulted her senses with a kiss so hot, so wild it robbed her of all rational thought.

His exotic cologne—some unusual spice from a faraway land—filled her head. It was so strong, so potent, so utterly masculine. She would remember it long after they parted.

A fire in her stomach ignited. Touching his chest, running her tiny hands over the solid planes stoked the flames. And when his tongue traced the seam of her lips, when he entered her mouth, heavens, she thought she might melt beneath the heat.

For a few seconds, she was out of her depth. He dominated the kiss, controlled it, manipulated her mouth to do his bidding. Large hands cupped her cheeks as he deepened his hold on her.

Oh, she had every right to fear him. This man loved with a savagery she found intoxicating.

But the need to conquer the master, to prove that being small did not mean she was subservient took hold. After all, did a roaring fire not stem from a tiny spark?

Daring to be bold, Juliet grabbed the lapels of his coat in her fists and stroked her tongue against his. The sensation sent her head spinning. The drum of a pulse between her legs left her aching for something though she knew not what. But it gave her the strength to take control of this mating of mouths, and before she knew what she was about, she controlled the speed, the tempo.

A growl resonated in the back of Devlin's throat.

Soon they were moaning into each other's mouths, clawing at each other's clothes.

The internal inferno grew, leading her to a reckless place that promised a wealth of pleasure. She had forgotten they were standing in the courtyard in full view of the grooms and stable hands.

Rufus was the one who brought them both crashing back to reality.

The excitable beast jumped up, the sheer power of the lunge forcing them apart.

Devlin's dark gaze never left hers as he fought to catch his breath.

Juliet's chest rose and fell so rapidly her pants filled the air between them. She touched her fingers to her swollen lips as her body begged for a deeper satisfaction.

Rufus barged in between them, only ceased whining when Juliet laid her hand on the hound's head.

"Well," she began in the hope conversation might calm her racing heart, "I think we have broken down at least one barrier today."

"Indeed." Hungry eyes moved over her face. "That was … unexpected."

"Delightfully so."

A faint smile touched his lips. "Perhaps I underestimated you."

"How so?"

"Despite my size, one touch of your tongue brought me to my knees."

Juliet was not used to speaking so intimately, though she liked that her husband was in a playful mood. And knowing she had pleased him boosted her confidence.

"Perhaps I have uncovered a weakness in your strategy." He could no longer play the fear card in this game of wits. Not when she had devoured his mouth like a reckless wanton.

Devlin shrugged. "A man must lose sometimes. Defeat is necessary when one has their eye on a greater prize. And it seems I am on my way to winning the wager when it comes to taming that dog."

Juliet glanced at Rufus who kept forcing his giant head under her hand so she would stroke him. "A few more days and I shall have him mastered."

"A few more days and I imagine Rufus won't be the only beast crouched at your feet."

CHAPTER NINE

The wild, erotic kiss Devlin shared with Juliet had roused more than a burning desire to claim his wife's body. A man could only lie to himself for so long. And clearly, Juliet found nothing overtly terrifying about his countenance. Else she would not have ravaged his mouth as if desperate to sate a clawing hunger.

By God, one taste of her sweet lips and he'd been lost in a haze of lust and longing. Her passion, coupled with her unquestionable honesty, had done more than break down the barrier of fear. Other buried desires pushed to the fore, too. Music had been his first love—his only love thus far—but men of his size did not play the piano. Men with clumsy hands did not master the keys. Men so broad looked awkward seated on the bench.

And yet music touched him in a way his family never understood.

Hearing Juliet's melodic tones drifting through the dark corridors had reawakened something inside him. Her voice brought life to the house where previously there had been death and decay. Her captivating presence, her laughter and gaiety, brought hope for something infinitely more rewarding.

And now, as he sat once again in the fireside chair in his bedchamber, his body eagerly awaiting the moment he stalked to Juliet's apartments to claim the passionate woman as his own, what he had seen at dinner held him rigid in his seat.

The blue bruises tainting the porcelain skin at her elbow confirmed what he suspected. All his protestations of providing protection, and he'd failed her at the first hurdle. All the time she spoke about Rufus, asked questions about Valentine, all the time he should have prompted her memory to reveal new information about Ambrose, all he could do was stare at the rogue's imprint as shame and loathing filled his chest like a bitter poison.

No doubt her delicate skin bore Devlin's searing mark, too, on her waist and her hips, the places he'd grabbed and held as the depth of his passion had left him unsteady on his feet.

God, how he hated the voice in his head. It fed on every negative thought and feeling, gobbled up his misery as a starving man would a hearty meal.

You must shift your thoughts to your heart.

Dariell's wise words penetrated his mind.

Devlin glanced back over his shoulder expecting to see the Frenchman, for that was how distinctly he heard them. His friend had the gift of oratory, a skill, an eloquence, a way of getting under a man's skin, of making him see clearly after a lifetime of wandering blindly.

And so Devlin sat there, listening to the crackling fire, staring at the flickering flames. He had never attempted to shift his thoughts. How could he when his head was so full of plots for vengeance? Did the heart not lack the capacity to think?

He focused on the organ beating in his chest and felt instantly calmer. The longer he sat there, the more peaceful he felt. What surprised him most was that bitterness did not live in the heart. It lived in the mind. In a moment of clarity, the desire to make love to his wife pushed to the fore, as did the desire to tinkle the ivory keys.

Devlin shot to his feet.

Not once, as he descended the stairs as if late for an appointment, did he give the voice in his head permission to speak. Not once, when he charged into the study and ransacked the drawer, did he stop to question his motives.

The brass key tingled in his palm as he turned left along the corridor leading from the hall. The metal object grew hot, encouraging him to hurry. Musical notes—remnants of his favourite tune —echoed as he approached.

He unlocked the door and stepped inside.

The sight of the grand piano sitting alone in the corner of the large, empty room sent his pulse racing. The wing-shaped case and the warmth of the walnut wood drew him closer. What he called the music room was in truth a ballroom with polished oak floors and a set of double doors leading out into the garden. It was a room meant for pleasure. A room meant for music.

During the years spent abroad, he had enjoyed listening to the strange tunes that rang through the bustling bazaars. The drums, sitars, the sarangi, odd-shaped pipes that produced unique sounds unlike anything he'd heard before.

Devlin moved closer and ran his hands over the smooth wood covering the keys. Then he rolled up his shirtsleeves, took his seat on the bench and flexed his fingers.

He played the compositions he remembered, let the music flow through his body. He played the pieces he'd composed as a younger man when he'd dreamed of entertaining excited throngs. The more he played, the more the notes breathed life into every fibre of his being.

But something drew his attention away from his music. Something infinitely more powerful drew his attention towards the door.

He saw her then—Juliet—gripping the jamb with her slender fingers, her wide eyes watching him, mesmerised, enthralled.

Their gazes locked.

She gasped, shrank back into the shadows.

Devlin jumped up from the padded bench. "Wait. Don't go. Please, come and join me."

Juliet hesitated, but then slowly pushed open the door and stepped inside. "I did not mean to spy. I did not mean to invade your privacy, but I heard the music and simply had to come." She smiled. "You play beautifully."

No one had ever bestowed such praise. Men lacked the heart for music. Large men were cumbersome and clunky on the keys.

Knowing that the voice in his head sought to ruin the moment, he shifted his awareness back to his heart.

"My fingers are not as nimble as they used to be."

"Who taught you to play like that?"

Juliet closed the door and moved farther into the room. She wore the same ugly brown dress she'd worn to dinner. It was dull, poorly fitted, yet her radiance shone through. No wonder Miss Bromfield banished her sister to the servants' quarters. The woman despised competition.

"I taught myself one year while my parents were travelling abroad." He closed the gap between them, his slow movements like the first steps of a seductive dance. "One can master most things if one is willing to practise."

"I would say you have a natural gift, a talent, an ear for music."

She was alone in her judgement, but he was not about to wallow in self-pity. "It has been many years since I last played."

"Because you were abroad?"

"Partly."

With wide eyes, she twirled around and surveyed the room. The moonlight streaming in through the terrace doors illuminated the renaissance paintings on the ceiling and the detailed architrave that gave the place an ethereal air.

"Mrs Barbary misled me when she said this was the music room."

"My parents rarely used it for its intended purpose. They were rather pious people, interested in assisting those in need not pandering to those who live life to excess." Consequently, they were harsh to their privileged children, judgemental.

"Heavens. I imagine they would turn in their graves to learn you married a woman born out of wedlock."

Devlin raised a brow. "It would be nothing compared to what they would do if they knew of the unholy things said about my brother."

Juliet's gaze fell. "I'm sorry Hannah feels it necessary to be so spiteful. I doubt anyone believes her."

The same morbid questions entered Devlin's head.

But now was not the time to dwell on the past. He would search for the letters in the morning, discover what he needed to know, rip out the snake's fangs so she could not infect others with her venomous diatribe.

"We can discuss the matter tomorrow." He gestured to the empty space. "It seems a pity to waste the time we have here on something that causes us both such anguish."

A smile touched her lips. "What would you have us do?"

She could sing her sweet songs while he accompanied her on the piano. He could kiss her again, try not to hurt her this time. But they were in a ballroom, and she could not dance, and he needed to do something to distract him from thoughts of ravishing her body.

"I shall teach you to waltz."

She shook her head. "But I don't want to learn. I lack coordination and the elegance required to master the dance."

"Say what you mean. You're scared I will step on your feet and break your tiny toes."

Juliet arched a censorious brow. "If I meant that I would have said so. I'm scared I shall embarrass myself when I have an overwhelming desire to impress my husband."

The surrounding air was suddenly charged with a vibrant energy.

No woman had ever cared for his good opinion. And yet here stood a lady willing to trust him, willing to bare her heart despite the possibility of rejection. She could not possibly impress him more than she had already.

Devlin could not help but cup her cheek. Her skin was as soft as silk, warm to the touch. "You impress me every day just by being yourself. I know no one with a sweeter voice, no one who can command a beast with the mere click of her fingers."

Water welled in her eyes though she was smiling. "I fear I must correct you. That dog doesn't listen to a word I say."

"I wasn't speaking of Rufus." His rich tone carried the essence of his desire for her. "Is it that you believe we will look clumsy together?"

She gave a coy shrug. "It's not that we might look odd, but more that it might be difficult for me to look into your eyes as we move about the floor."

"Because I am too tall?"

"Because I am too short."

His hand slipped from her cheek. He glanced over her shoulder to the full-length looking glass on the far wall. He had to admit, that even with a foot and a half difference, they did not look as odd as one might think.

"I have a perfect solution for our first dance," Devlin said with affection, losing all trace of his gruff countenance when in the company of his wife.

Juliet's eyes widened. "You do?"

"Before one can master the steps, it helps if one gets a sense of the rhythm."

"Are you going to play?"

"No. For it will be impossible to stare into each other's eyes when we're so far apart." Devlin slid his arm around her back and without warning lifted her until they were eye level. "There. You may be more than a foot off the floor, but at least you won't have a crick in your neck."

A chuckle escaped her lips. It was the most enchanting sound he'd ever heard. But then she did something that stole his breath, something that robbed him of all rational thought.

Juliet placed her hand on his cheek, pressed her lips to his in a chaste kiss and said, "You are very kind to me, and for that, I will always be grateful."

God damn, he'd never been called kind in his life. "You make being kind easy."

Her eyes sparkled, and she looked … she looked happy. "Then dance with me, Mr Drake. Let us pretend I am not as hopeless at dancing as I am at training dogs."

"It would be my pleasure, Mrs Drake, though I do wish you would call me Devlin."

Devlin instructed her how to hold his hand, to place her other hand lightly on his shoulder. Once he was certain he wasn't squeezing all the air from her lungs, he set about the floor, twirling and gliding to a hummed melody.

Not once did she tear her gaze from his. The feel of her breath breezing across his cheek sent the blood racing in a southerly direction to pool in his cock. He throbbed and ached with the need to claim this bewitching enchantress. Everything about her enticed him, her carefree manner, her lighthearted laughter.

Feeling the urge to excite her further, Devlin swung her around so quickly her head lolled back. Springy red ringlets flew free from their pins. She gripped his hand, burst into fits of laughter.

"I'm slipping," she said with a beaming grin.

"I'll not let you go."

"Not ever," she joked.

"Not ever." The sudden realisation that he meant it, that he spoke of something infinitely more profound than this playful dance, forced him to come to an abrupt halt.

Juliet's eyes dazzled in the muted light. Their breathless pants filled the air.

"Oh, I think … I think I might like waltzing, Devlin."

It was the first time he'd heard her say his name. How strange that one simple word could shake him to his core. "Then we must practise daily."

"And I shall wear heeled shoes when we work on the steps."

He didn't want to teach her the steps. He wanted to hold her like this, wanted her to look at him with pleasure in her eyes, not fear.

"There are other things I might teach you, too." Lust raged hot and needy through his veins when he imagined cementing their alliance.

Fear did flash briefly in her eyes, and he was relieved when she said, "You'll not get me riding one of those muscled beasts."

Erotic images danced in his mind when he pictured her straddling his large thighs.

Devlin kissed her once, a soft, open-mouthed kiss that promised so much more. "I was thinking of a different dance, a different form of riding. I was thinking that if you can't tame the dog, you might like to focus your efforts on taming your husband."

CHAPTER TEN

Alady did not need to be skilled in seduction to recognise the look of desire in a man's eyes. Juliet could hear the husky sound of lust in Devlin's voice, had felt something licentious in his kiss.

All the air in her lungs dissipated when she thought of running her hands over his bare skin. "What are you suggesting?" She did not want to be presumptuous. "Are you referring to your conjugal rights?"

"Conjugal rights?" he said incredulously as he lowered her slowly down the hard length of his body until her feet came to rest firmly on the floor. "You make relations sound one-sided."

"But is that not the correct term?"

"Well, yes, if you're talking to the vicar."

"And if you're talking to your wife?"

Devlin thrust his hand through his black hair. "I want to make love to you, Juliet. Show you the pleasure a couple might find in the marriage bed. But the more we discuss the matter, the more my mind screams of caution."

Make love? That was not how her mother described the act.

Nerves almost rendered Juliet speechless, but Devlin's last

comment caused her to frown. "Why caution?" Was it that he was mindful of her innocence?

"I'm told it will be far from pleasant the first time, but things should improve dramatically after that."

Juliet took a moment to gather her wits. After three nights spent alone in her bed, she'd wondered if there was something wrong with her. Clearly, her heathen husband was possessed of romantic notions.

"Then you know to be patient?" she asked even though she knew the answer. "You know I don't have a clue what to do?"

A sinful smile illuminated his features. "And I shall be more than happy to be your guide, your tutor." He reached for her hand. "Let us retire to your chamber and take matters from there."

That sombre place?

"No." A mild sense of panic ensued. She could not be intimate in a room that was like a shrine to his mother. When Devlin's smile faded, she quickly added, "The room is dreary, so morbid. I couldn't possibly relax in there."

"If it's simply a matter of decoration, then you're welcome to make changes."

"Yes, but that does not help the situation now."

Oh, things were easier, more natural, when they were gliding around the floor. Juliet glanced around the ballroom. Moonlight streamed in through the terrace doors, catching the crystal teardrops on the chandeliers so that they sparkled like diamonds. The ceiling was a colourful canvas of cherubs playing harps, of Greek gods swathed in red robes, of naked nymphs luring their lovers.

"We can stay here," Juliet said, without giving a thought to their comfort.

Devlin's curious gaze dropped to the hard floor. "I don't think you appreciate—"

"Please, Devlin. Let us remain in here." She didn't mean to sound like a coquette, like a woman skilled in the art of manipulating men. "Let us stop talking. I hear the waltz is a prelude to seduction." Or so Hannah said. "Dance with me again."

Without further discussion, Devlin inclined his head and then lifted her into his arms.

This time, he did not hum a tune as he held her close. They did not twirl about or break into fits of laughter. This time, they stared into each other's eyes, moved in a slow, seductive rhythm that made all the blood in her body pool at the apex of her thighs.

She wanted this man.

She wanted her husband.

Was that not the greatest achievement of their union so far?

"You look devilishly handsome tonight," she found herself saying.

The heat in his gaze sent a shiver rippling to her toes. "And you are by far the most beautiful woman I have ever laid eyes on."

Oh, she knew he was exaggerating, but she drank in the compliment regardless.

"Then perhaps you should kiss me, Mr Drake."

"Perhaps I should."

When he stopped moving, she knew she was about to feel those hot lips on hers. Excitement fluttered wildly in her chest like a flock of finches eager to escape an aviary.

The first touch of his mouth was electric. The sudden rush of energy lighting her from within. It lacked the urgency of their first kiss, though that was not a complaint. On the contrary, the way his mouth moved languidly over hers proved far more enticing. With every teasing movement, he gave her a little more, until the need to thrust her tongue into his mouth became overwhelming.

Impatience, coupled with a raging hunger, forced her to penetrate the seam of his lips.

She sensed the shift in him immediately. Needy and desperate, Devlin moaned into her mouth as their tongues tangled.

"Damn, Juliet," he muttered, dragging his mouth away.

"You're determined to rouse the ravenous beast when I am trying to be a gentleman."

She was about to chastise him for mentioning the word *beast* again, but they had come this far, and any conversation would only dampen the mood. So instead she pressed herself against his solid chest, rained kisses along his jaw, pressed her mouth to the sensitive spot just below his ear.

His groan of pleasure echoed through the vast room. "By God, for an innocent you have the skill of a temptress. Hold on to my neck and don't let go."

She did as he asked. She would do anything he asked.

Devlin released his grip. He caught hold of the hem of her dress and shoved her skirts up to her thighs. Large hands slid up over her stockings, up over her bare skin. He cupped her buttocks and urged her to wrap her legs around him. The sensation of having her legs wide and gripping his waist only heightened the pulsing in her sex.

"Your skin is like the softest silk," he said as he kissed her neck, as he moved slowly around the room in this dance of seduction.

Juliet's head fell back as his hot mouth trailed towards the neckline of her dress. Oh, how she wished she wore the scandalous dress of a courtesan. How she wished the curve of her breasts bulged so he might lavish them with attention, too.

"I need more than this," she said brazenly. Desire affected her like a drug, sent her head spinning, her body tingling. "I need to see you, Devlin. I need to touch you. Lock the door."

With his hot palms gripping her buttocks, they glided over to the door. He pressed her back against the wooden panel as he reached down and turned the key. And then he kissed her again, in the wild, untamed way that told her he wanted this, too.

"You affect me as no woman has before," he said as he broke to catch his breath.

The compliment meant more to her than he could know. It

went some way to filling the cavernous hole in her chest, the one left by grief, by her dreadful mistreatment at the hands of those who might have loved her.

"Then make love to me as you want to." It took a tremendous effort to keep her nerves from her voice. She would not give him a reason to retreat. Not now. Not when she longed for the closeness of his body.

They stared into each other's eyes, and the warmth she saw stole her breath.

"I cannot promise it will be comfortable, not here, not without the luxury of a bed."

"It will be perfect." She trusted that fate would make it so.

Holding her securely, Devlin swung her around, and after a moment's pause carried her to the piano. "Lift the prop stick and lower the lid."

"Is it heavy?"

"On second thought, hold on to my neck and I shall do it."

It was heavy. The dull thud reverberated through the instrument. But Juliet had no time to consider the matter further. Devlin lifted her up on top of the piano.

He kept his heated gaze fixed on hers as he stepped back, tugged on the knot in his ivory cravat, unravelled the material and threw it to the floor. His burgundy waistcoat followed. And then he gathered the hem of his shirt and dragged the garment up over his head.

Juliet watched, awestruck. All the air left her lungs.

She tried to take in the full magnificence of the man she'd married. A dry mouth left her licking her lips. Lord, no doubt she held the same ravenous look that lingered in his eyes. Her gaze flicked frantically back and forth, drinking in the glorious sight. Devlin Drake was like a living monument to the gods of Olympus. Every muscle, every sculpted contour screamed of power, of strength, of an ability to command anyone, anything. And yet there was something graceful, something sleek about the way the muscles worked together, about the way his bronzed skin contained such raw masculinity.

Her fingers thrummed with the need to touch him, to push through the dark hair on his chest, to follow the teasing trail that led down beyond the waistband of his breeches.

"Judging by your wide eyes and open mouth, am I to assume this is the first time you have laid eyes on a man's bare chest?"

"I have only ever seen a man in his shirtsleeves, though nothing could have prepared me for the sight of you, Devlin."

"Is that a compliment?" He sounded unsure.

"Of course it's a compliment. Look at you. I have never seen a more breathtaking sight in my life."

The corners of his mouth curled up into a sinful grin. "Does that mean you'd like to see the rest of me?"

"The rest of— Oh, you're referring to …" She couldn't say the words and so pointed to his breeches. "Do you think an innocent might handle the shock?"

"Juliet, innocent or not, I think you can handle anything."

Yet more praise. The comment forced her to straighten her back, gave her the confidence to say, "Then, by all means, let me see you in all your naked glory."

The bulge in his breeches told her he was aroused, and she wondered if her mother had made another mistake when she described a gentleman's manhood as the rod of Satan.

The thought was fleeting. Devlin unbuttoned his breeches and pushed the garment down past his hips and over his thick thighs. Oh, heavens. He was aroused, highly so, and though she wondered how on earth she could join with a man so large, it wasn't at all as grotesque as her mother had made out.

It took three attempts before her eyes accepted that she could look at his manhood for longer than a second. He stood proudly, no longer bore the countenance of a man who thought himself large and beastly. Did that have something to do with her hum of approval?

To tease her, Devlin ran his hand down the solid length. "Now you have seen everything I have to offer it is only fair you reciprocate."

"But I am seated on top of a piano." It was more than a plausible excuse.

He closed the gap between them. Stepped so close she could feel the heat radiating from his skin. "I'm a man who knows how to turn a situation to my advantage." Taking hold of her foot, he removed her shoe and threw it onto the pile of clothes on the floor.

"Do you mean to undress me, Mr Drake?" she said with a giggle.

"I mean to undress you, pleasure you, thrust inside you until you're panting my name." He moistened his lips. "Do you think you might bear that, Mrs Drake?"

Juliet swallowed down the hard lump in her throat. "Yes, I think I might bear it very well."

"Then let us begin. You'll need to lie down."

A host of questions flitted through her mind, but she placed her trust in him and did as he asked. Her other shoe joined the pile, but he did not roll down her stockings. Instead, he pushed her skirts up to her waist and bent her knees.

"Don't be afraid," he whispered as he lowered his head.

Hot lips seared her thigh, leaving a blazing trail as he moved higher. Juliet batted at her skirts for the position left her exposed. "Devlin, wait."

The first flick of his tongue sent her heart shooting up to her throat. Her mother mentioned nothing about a man performing— Oh, Lord! The erotic rhythm sent waves of pleasure rippling through her body. Devlin licked her, sucked and teased. She couldn't help but thrust her hips to meet his greedy mouth. The smooth surface of the piano lid gave her nothing to grab. But then Devlin wrapped his arms under her knees and drew her to the edge. She could touch him then, could feel the scorching heat of his skin, the bulging muscles in his arms.

Juliet held on to her husband as the coil of pleasure inside wound so tight she feared she might explode. And explode she did. Her body spasmed and shuddered and shook.

"Devlin, oh …"

The slick sound of Devlin's fingers entering her slowly was enough to start the pulsing all over again. The muscles in her core clamped around him. But she needed something more. Her breasts were heavy, aching for his attention. And oh, how she wanted to press herself against his muscled chest.

"As much as I have a newfound fondness for the piano, making love to you like this will not be without problems." He captured her hand and brought her to a sitting position. "Let's move to the floor."

Juliet's cheeks burned from embarrassment, but the sight of Devlin's jutting manhood distracted her mind from all thoughts of awkwardness.

With his strong hands on her waist, he lifted her down to the floor.

"Should I lie down?" Her heartbeat still pounded in her throat.

"Let's divest you of this ugly dress first. The modiste assures me she shall have your wardrobe completed by the end of the week."

Juliet didn't want to think of anything other than this magical moment. Many times, she had watched her mother rehearse for various roles. A good actress had a way of appearing confident, could tease and torment the audience. But Devlin wanted honesty, and that is what she would give him.

"I don't know how to do this in such a way as you might take pleasure from it." Juliet bit down on her bottom lip as she stood before the majestic figure that would put Hercules to shame.

Devlin's gaze softened. "Tell me how I can make this easier for you."

Her heart melted a little at those words. "Don't give me time to think, time to panic."

A sensual smile crept up his face as his eyes journeyed over her. "Then come here."

He took her hand and drew her to his chest. His wicked mouth came crashing down on hers, so hot and wet. The thick evidence of his arousal pressed against her. Tongues tangled. The mood grew urgent. She ran her hands over his back, dared to grip his firm buttocks. The feel of his skin ignited a fire deep in her core.

And then he whipped her around, fiddled with buttons and stripped her of her dress. Her petticoat, stays and chemise soon followed. He reached up, his fingers delving into her hair, pulling out the pins until red ringlets came cascading over her shoulders and down her back.

"Good God," he said as he stepped back to survey the sight. "I knew you were beautiful, but you take my breath away. I shall make my apologies now. Visiting your bed will be a regular occurrence."

The thought of being like this with him every night flooded her body with a rush of euphoria. "Make love to me, Devlin." She loved the way he had described the prospect of their union. "Make me your wife."

He took her hand and brought her down to the hard floor. "Sit astride me."

Astride him? Her mother had only mentioned the crushing sensation when a man—spent and exhausted—collapsed on top.

Sensing her hesitation, Devlin smiled. "Your fear of horses has no place here."

Juliet peeked at his jutting erection. "It is not horses I fear." But then she saw the brightness in his eyes fade, saw the dark veil fall. She had said the wrong thing, the only thing that caused him to withdraw into himself.

Without further thought she straddled his hips, lay on top of him, her breasts crushed against his chest, and kissed him with every fibre of her being. She wanted the amusing and carefree Devlin, not the brooding man who called himself a beast.

Juliet tore her lips from his, placed a hand on his cheek and whispered, "I'm just a little nervous, that is all. But I want you, and so I ask that you excuse my trembling fingers."

"Then let me touch you in the hope of banishing any anxiety."

Hot hands settled on her waist, explored the soft lines of her hips, moved up to cup her breasts. Despite her short stature, she had been fortunate enough to be endowed with breasts ample enough to hold this man's attention. Indeed, Devlin held her in place as he sat up to suck her nipples to peak.

The jolt of pleasure was wild, explosive. All thoughts abandoned her as she writhed in his lap, as she curled her fingers around his neck and urged him to continue. The hard evidence of his arousal pulsed beneath her sex and the desperate urge to mate with him made it impossible to keep still.

"Take me now, Devlin. Don't wait."

She did not need to say it twice.

His fingers slicked over her sex. She came up on her knees as he took himself in hand, watched him intently as the head of his manhood eased inside her. For a few seconds, her body resisted the intrusion, but he was patient, surprisingly gentle for a man so large.

"God, Juliet, you're so wet, so tight."

Juliet swallowed. "Is that a good thing?"

A chuckle escaped his lips, and the solid length inside her pulsed with amusement, too. "It means I'm struggling to keep control of my desire."

"Oh." He pushed a little deeper. "Oh." The word meant something entirely different this time.

"Hold on to me. I need to thrust harder."

She clung to the rippling muscles in his arms as she welcomed the whole length of him into her eager body. The sudden stab of discomfort tore a gasp from her lips while *he* moaned with pleasure.

Devlin stilled and held her close. "You must be the one to move. You must be the one to gauge how best to proceed."

After taking a moment to catch her breath, she nodded. "Then you must guide me."

He clasped her buttocks, lifted her slightly and lowered her down. "Move like this."

The more times she rose and fell to sheath his manhood, the easier it became. With her discomfort soon forgotten she found a rhythm that left them both groaning and panting.

Their damp bodies moved together in exquisite harmony. There was no pain, no anguish, no wishing she might be somewhere else instead. For all her mother's experience, it seemed she knew nothing about relations between a husband and wife.

But it was not the shudders of ecstasy that stole Juliet's breath when she came apart in Devlin's arms. It was not the rush of possessiveness when he cried her name and spilt his seed inside her. It was the sudden realisation that she had not lied before God. She had given herself to her husband, cherished every moment they spent together. And her heart swelled in the knowledge that she fancied herself a little in love with Devlin Drake.

CHAPTER ELEVEN

"I think we should begin our search for the letters in your bedchamber." Juliet offered Devlin a beaming smile before biting into her toast. Fixated by the way her mouth moved, he watched and waited for her to swallow. "How fortunate that you did not think to remove your brother's belongings when you claimed the master room."

Devlin stared at her, wondering why the hell desire thrummed through his veins during something as simple as a conversation at breakfast. His rampant imagination saw him swiping the crockery to the floor, lifting his wife onto the table, gripping her thighs and driving home, driving into the only place he'd ever felt a profound and lasting satiation.

"Mrs Barbary would not dispose of Ambrose's belongings without permission," he said, shifting in his seat to ease the throbbing erection pressing against his breeches. Damn. This would not do. He could not look at Juliet without recalling her passionate reaction to him the previous night. "And since my return, I've been too preoccupied with my wife to undertake the task."

Juliet must have noted the sensual undertone in his voice for her porcelain cheeks flushed a pretty shade of pink. After a failed attempt, she looked him in the eye. "Is that a complaint?"

"Most definitely not."

Guilt stabbed his chest. The many letters he'd received over the last three years informing him of Miss Bromfield's predilection for gossiping had fuelled the fire of vengeance. Now, the bubbling inferno was reduced to a simmer. Knowing that a woman was his weakness did not sit well with him.

Ambrose deserved better.

Ambrose deserved justice.

But that was not the only reason for his sudden pang of shame. His hypocrisy was laughable. Juliet's honesty and loyalty to her husband—a man she had known for a week—roused a deep level of affection within. While he, on the other hand, had not been truthful about his reasons for marrying her and needed to address his failing as a matter of urgency.

"Besides, I doubt we'll find the letters from your sister to Ambrose in my chamber," Devlin said, pushing all thoughts of bedding his wife from his mind.

"And why is that?"

He told her about the baron's unexpected visit to Blackwater, his demand to have the letters returned, Mrs Barbary's refusal to grant him entrance and the consequent theft. "I suspect the baron hired a man to break into the house. The thug ransacked the room. Had he found the letters, your father would have had no need to hire a man to threaten his own daughter so violently."

Juliet fell silent.

Devlin noted her distress: her eyes moist with unshed tears, the lines on her brow furrowed. The urge to make her smile took hold. But he could not bring her mother back from the grave, could not make her father love her as he ought.

"While my mother never gave me cause to question her judgement," she said with an air of melancholy as she gazed out of the window, "I cannot see what possessed her to give herself to such a cruel and wicked man."

"She was younger then, perhaps not as wise as she would have had you believe. Parents strive to ensure their children do not make the same mistakes." Devlin caught himself. Dariell would be proud to hear such a thoughtful response.

Juliet turned to him, her eyes brighter than he expected. "It seems she was wrong about a few things when it came to intimate relations." Those green gems flashed hot as they scanned the breadth of his chest and finally settled on his mouth.

Damnation.

Lust surged through his veins.

But he refused to behave like a wild beast.

Devlin shot out of the chair, threw his napkin onto the table and straightened his coat. "Let us search the room just to be certain." He was about to offer his hand, but the bulge in his breeches forced him to skirt behind the chair and play footman. After helping to ease Juliet's seat from the table, he gestured for her to walk ahead.

"Afterwards, we should move to the study and then the library," she said, glancing back over her shoulder. "I can think of nowhere else one would attempt to keep private correspondence."

"We don't know if Ambrose kept the letters. But he was a stickler for propriety. If Miss Bromfield slandered him, I imagine he would seek to contest her opinion out of moral principle."

"Perhaps he hired someone to deal with the matter," Juliet said, sounding slightly breathless as they reached the top stair.

Talk of his brother dampened Devlin's ardour. Which was just as well considering they were heading for his bedchamber. He placed his hand at the small of Juliet's back and guided her along the corridor to the west wing.

"Is it not customary for a husband and wife to have adjoining apartments?" she asked as he opened the door to his room and motioned for her to enter. "How is it I am in the east wing while you sleep on the opposite side of the house?"

Devlin thought to lie, to make an excuse as to why he felt the need to maintain some distance but found he could not.

"There is a suite of rooms adjoining yours. I could have moved in there. But Ambrose preferred the west wing, and I thought by moving into his chambers it would afford you time to grow accustomed to your surroundings."

Juliet raised her chin in acknowledgement as she came to a halt in the middle of the room. Hands braced on her hips, she studied the gold bed hangings, the chinoiserie furniture and the Chinese silk wallpaper depicting village scenes from a distant land.

"What a beautiful room. It's so light and airy, not at all a place where I would expect you to feel comfortable sleeping."

As always Juliet was right. He found the decor too feminine for his tastes, although that was not the reason he'd lain awake most nights since his wedding day—except for last night of course. Last night, he'd drifted into a peaceful slumber, the smell of lavender that clung to his wife's skin still swirling about in his head.

"Is that because you assume beasts prefer caves?" Devlin teased.

She arched her brow by way of a reprimand. "I meant it isn't nearly masculine enough."

The veiled compliment only reignited his lust for his wife. "Ambrose found dark colours depressing." Devlin felt the need to defend Ambrose's tastes for his choices in no way defined his sexuality. "Dreams of the Orient inspired him, but commitments at home prevented him from venturing farther than town."

Juliet turned to face him, her honest eyes alight with enquiry. "And you slept in here because you believed I would feel safer knowing you have to navigate two long corridors to reach my chamber?"

"I slept in here because it is important that you feel comfortable." It was not a lie, just not the whole truth.

"Comfortable at night?" she asked as she closed the gap between them and placed her dainty palm on his chest. Just like the rest of him, his heart kicked against his ribcage as he relished even the smallest contact. "Comfortable enough that I don't fear you charging into my apartments to claim your husbandly rights?"

"Indeed."

Juliet held his gaze. The air crackled and sparked to life. Her hand snaked up over his chest, up to tangle in the hair brushing his nape.

"And now," she whispered, her voice more a seductive lilt, "does it not occur to you that I might feel safer knowing you're close?"

God, he'd never wanted a woman as much as he wanted her. Was it because she belonged to him that he had the overwhelming need to join with her? Was it because she smiled at him when his mood turned morose, chuckled when he was overly stubborn? Was it because she made him feel strong, her protector, not clumsy and awkward?

"What are you saying?" Devlin cupped her cheek. "That you want me to move into the adjoining suite of rooms?"

She turned her head and kissed his palm, kissed his large, ugly hand, a hand made for fighting, for maiming. "I don't want to traipse along dark corridors to find you."

Devlin studied her face as a warm sensation flooded his chest. She was like a flower in the height of summer, open, stretching for the sun. There was no artifice, nothing hidden, nothing deceitful or devious. Never had he admired a woman more.

"If it pleases you, I shall have my things moved this afternoon." His voice sounded somewhat fractured, uncharacteristically high.

"Only if it pleases you."

Lord, surely after all that occurred last night, she knew how much he wanted her.

"It would please me immensely."

A wide, beaming smile illuminated her face. "Then it's settled." She stepped away. "It's good that we can be honest with each other."

Guilt surfaced.

It was a perfect opportunity to broach the subject of his original motive for marrying her.

"Juliet."

"Yes?" She moved to the window, excitement radiating from her like a bright beacon as she considered the lush landscape beyond.

Devlin tried to form the words but all the air in his lungs dissipated. He cleared his throat. "In the years since my brother's death, I have grown somewhat obsessive, somewhat desperate to clear his name. It formed the basis of my decision to return. It formed the basis of my decision to … to marry."

Juliet's gaze drifted from the window, and he became the subject of curious examination. "You wish to disprove Hannah's account of your brother's character?"

Hell, she was as sharp as a hunter's blade. Perhaps she already understood the reasons why he'd felt compelled to marry her.

"It was my intention to ruin her name enough to discredit her opinion."

Juliet's face revealed nothing of her thoughts, yet she remained fixed at the window. "How did you propose to do that?"

"As her husband, I would have had ample opportunity to make her rue the day she spouted her vicious lies. I would have controlled every aspect of her life with an iron hand." Bitterness dripped from every word. For the first time in days, he felt like the savage beast men feared.

"And because Hannah despised your family, the only way to achieve your goal was to make the wager with my father."

"Indeed."

A frown creased her brow, and he silently begged her to ask the only question that mattered. "I cannot blame you for despising her, and revenge had to be your motive. While many men will forgo character if a woman is beautiful, you are not one of them."

He did not deserve the compliment woven within her statement.

"What I fail to understand," she continued, "is why you were willing to sacrifice your own happiness in the process. Is your need for satisfaction so great? Do you think Hannah's ruination would have eased the pain of your brother's death?"

God, it was like listening to Dariell. The probing questions forced him to bolster his defences. "One must seek justice for those deprived of a voice."

"How noble. Would parliament not be a better place to serve your needs, acting on behalf of those who truly suffer?"

Anger stirred from its slumber. "Every man's life has value. Just because Ambrose lived a life of privilege does not mean he suffered less. Besides, one must have one's own house in order before tackling the problems of the world."

A weary sigh left her lips. She offered a curt nod. "You're right. Forgive me. If Hannah orchestrated your brother's downfall out of spite, then she deserves to pay. But since you were denied the opportunity to make her your wife, I suspect finding any answers to account for the odd turn of events will prove difficult."

Ask me the damn question.

Did you plan to use me to achieve your goal?

Why was she stalling?

"If I'm to discover the truth I need your help." Devlin studied the language of her body. Her stance was stiff, the vivacious energy that captivated him had dissipated. "You are the only one who bore witness to the conversations they shared. You're the only one who can offer any insight."

She remained silent for a time, her gaze fixed on the hem of her plain brown dress. He could feel her withdrawing, shrinking into the shadows, far away from him. The muscles in his stomach twisted into painful knots, and in his head, he cried, *Don't go.*

"Juliet."

"Yes?" She looked up, but her eyes lacked vitality.

"Is there anything you wish to ask me?"

"No. Your motives are clear."

The tension in the air was stifling. "I meant everything I said the day I offered marriage in the garden. We suit better than I could ever have hoped."

She nodded. "Your offer was generous for a woman like me, and I am truly grateful."

Devlin did not want her gratitude. He wanted things infinitely more precious. He wanted her trust, her respect. He wanted her love. The thought shocked him.

"And in recompense for offering me a glimmer of happiness," she said though she sounded far from content, "I shall do everything in my means to help you." She straightened and cast him a weak smile. "Finding the letters must be a priority, and at dinner tonight you must—" She broke on a gasp, her head shooting back to the window.

Panic flashed in her eyes. She wore her sudden terror like a masquerade mask, hiding all innocence and beauty. All thoughts of how he might salvage something after this awkward conversation abandoned him.

"What is it?" Devlin wanted to reach for her, to take her in his arms and soothe away her fears, but a wall existed between them now, and he wasn't sure how to break it down.

"Tonight!" She clasped her hand to her chest. "How did I forget?"

"Forget what? You are not making any sense."

"The fountain." She touched the sleeve of her dress, the place that hid the evidence of her bruises. "I'm to meet Mr Biggs at the fountain at midnight."

Panic gripped Devlin by the throat. "Like hell you will."

"If I fail to bring the letters as requested, he promised to punish you." A tear trickled down her cheek, and Devlin couldn't help but think that their early conversation was the cause.

"You'll not leave this house," he said, the command carrying the full weight of his authority. "Is that clear?"

In a voice barely louder than a whisper, she muttered to herself, *accident* the only coherent word.

"Juliet." When she failed to meet his gaze, he repeated, "Juliet. I shall meet Mr Biggs at the fountain." Blood rushed to his hands until his fingers throbbed with the need for satisfaction. "And when I do, you may trust that he shall not darken our door again."

CHAPTER TWELVE

"Are you certain you're feeling well?" Devlin put down his cutlery and dabbed his mouth with his napkin. "You've hardly eaten anything this evening. Are you worried about my impending confrontation with Biggs?"

"Partly." A myriad of thoughts flitted about in Juliet's head. Their lack of success in finding any letters from Hannah proved frustrating. And while she had every confidence her husband possessed the strength and ability to tackle a rogue like Mr Biggs, it took one mistake, one random shot with a pistol to end a man's life.

The tension in the air was palpable.

She was at fault.

Disappointment hung like a lead weight in her chest, dragging her down. She was not naive enough to think Devlin Drake had married her for her wit or beauty. He had married her to prove a point to her father, and because she had the integrity Hannah lacked. Oh, one could not deny desire had sprung to life from practically nowhere, but it hurt to hear that his only motive was to use her as a source of information.

But when one married for the wrong reasons what else could one expect?

Another man might have punished her, abused her to get what he wanted. For all his faults, Devlin acted like a caring husband which only confused matters all the more.

"How many times must I tell you?" Devlin reached across the table and touched her arm. "Four men would struggle to take me down. One flick to the throat is all it takes to render Biggs helpless."

For a man of Devlin Drake's size, it was easy to imagine him in the midst of a violent brawl. Only last night, she had run her hands over hard, bulging muscle, excited by the raw power contained beneath his bronzed skin. She had witnessed the darkness in his eyes, felt the angry undercurrent that invaded his aura, which made him a man to fear.

"I know how conniving my father can be when he wants something," she said, staring at the asparagus spears on her plate. "Based on his actions so far, I cannot help but think this amounts to more than a few malicious comments written in a note."

Devlin fell silent for a moment. He sipped his wine though his dark eyes remained trained on her over the rim of his glass.

"And correct me if I'm wrong," he began, "but I suspect your solemn mood stems from more than our failure to find the letters."

Juliet daren't look at him. She was not one who sought pity and had tried to pretend that learning of his motive for marriage hadn't changed things somehow.

"Juliet." Devlin's rich voice caressed her.

"Yes?"

"Look at me."

"Must I?"

"Unless you want me to straddle your lap at the dining table."

She glanced at the footmen who held their stone-like expressions.

"I would consider that unwise unless you want to break the chair legs. I doubt either of us wishes to end up in a heap on the floor."

"It did not seem to bother you last night."

The comment brought the memories of their passionate encounter flooding back. Her body reacted instantly, sending pulses to the intimate place that craved his touch. When she found the courage to look at him, her stomach flipped.

"Nothing would have bothered me last night," she said.

"Then perhaps we should retire to the music room and converse in there." Devlin swallowed another mouthful of wine, and his lips curled into a sinful grin. "I will have the truth from you even if I have to tease it from your mouth."

Juliet's heart fluttered up to her throat. While her body relished the prospect, her mind focused on the two words that rendered her helpless—*the truth*.

"I'm not a naive chit at her come-out ball, but, foolishly, I imagined you'd experienced the same sense of connection when you suggested marriage. I am simply trying to come to terms with the fact that I appear to be somewhat gullible."

Devlin leant back in the chair, a smile touching his lips. One jerk of the head and both footmen left the room.

"Would you have had me lie to you this morning?"

"Of course not."

"Did you not marry me because I offered a means of escape?"

Juliet blinked. "Well, yes. But that was not the only reason."

Devlin raised a curious brow. "And what other reason possessed you to shackle yourself to a stranger?"

The stark reality of the situation hit her. Since the day he'd pushed the magical band onto her finger, nothing but romantic notions filled her head. He was her protector, her saviour, the only one ever to unlock these sweet sensations that plagued her mind and body. She trusted him, cared for him.

"You made me feel safe, comfortable. I liked that we were

different in so many ways. It sounds silly and perhaps a little conceited, but I had the overwhelming sense that you needed me, that we needed each other." She stopped to take a breath. "And that is why I married you, Mr Drake."

The smile slipped from his face only to be replaced with the same heated look she'd witnessed when in the throes of passion. Fire flashed in those dark eyes. "Besides needing to address the situation with Ambrose, I married you for exactly the same reasons."

Her heart swelled in her chest. "I was hurt earlier, that is all."

"I know. And I will make sure I never hurt you again."

"Then there are no more secrets between us?"

"None."

The tension in the air lifted. Any awkwardness melted away, replaced by the thrum of suppressed desire. She felt the brush of his leg against hers beneath the table. But as much as she burned for his touch, all thoughts turned to Mr Biggs. Until her father had the letters, he would hound them to the ends of the earth. There was no telling what he would do if she defied him.

The chime of the long-case clock in the hall only heightened her anxiety. Juliet counted each sombre strike.

Six.

Seven.

Eight.

Another four hours until Devlin confronted the rogue.

Another four hours of uncertainty.

"Stop thinking about my midnight appointment," Devlin said as he sank his knife into a piece of venison pie. "You should eat something. You'll need your strength as there might well be more dancing once I've disposed of Biggs."

Devlin Drake defied all logic. Did he not fear the outcome? Was he not the least bit concerned that they might have underestimated the threat?

"How can you think of dancing when we have grave dealings ahead?"

A devilish smile graced his lips, one that spoke of hot lust and sin. His molten gaze slid down her body. "I have spent every minute of the day dreaming of *dancing* with you tonight."

Oh, Lord!

"Is … is that what you plan to tell Mr Biggs when he demands to see the letters?"

Devlin swallowed his food and straightened. "After Biggs has had a painful conversation with my fist, I doubt there will be anything left to say." A dark, sinister grin obliterated all traces of his amorous mood.

"What good will that do? Is it not better to press him for information?" It would help if they knew what they were looking for. Was it a matter of libel? Was it something more vindictive? "What if Hannah blackmailed Ambrose over his fondness for men?"

"Ambrose did not pursue relations with men. I would have no objection if that were the case. Everyone deserves happiness, but it goes against everything I know of his character."

From the little she knew of Ambrose, Juliet had to agree. "Knowing Hannah as I do, blackmail is within the realms of her capabilities. And her arguments are rarely based on fact."

Oh, she could picture Hannah's ugly sneer upon delivering her vile threats, contempt written over her—

A sudden thought hit Juliet like a sharp gust of wind, forcing her to draw her head back.

Hannah's words bombarded her mind.

Only wallflowers have time to write letters. Society ladies prefer less mundane pursuits.

During the six years she'd lived with Hannah, not once had Juliet seen her sister sitting at the escritoire. Her mornings involved studying the latest fashion plates from Paris or gossiping about another lady's lack of womanly wiles. Expressing her thoughts in ink was out of character. But had Ambrose refused all requests to meet and given her no other option?

If you hope to play a role in this family, you will find the letters.

I want all letters written in a feminine hand.

Juliet had believed that her father's odd request stemmed from the need for caution, the need to protect Hannah at all costs. But now she wasn't so sure. Perhaps Mr Biggs might provide a clue to help solve the mystery.

"I have an idea," she said, her voice laced with a smooth, sensual undertone for she expected her husband's fierce objection. She reached out and touched his arm, stroked back and forth with obvious affection. "I have a plan that might improve our hand in this game."

Devlin's coal-black eyes fixed her to the chair. "And you think you might seduce me into submission?"

"Perhaps."

"Then I must assume your idea is foolish, and that you hope my passion for you will overrule my sense of logic."

Rather than feel frustrated by his sharp intellect, a warm glow of pride filled her chest. "You are extremely alert and quick-witted."

"As my friends will tell you, my skills in negotiation are legendary. Coupled with my intimidating manner, I always walk away from deals with more than I want."

A tickle of excitement sparked to life in Juliet's belly. It gave her an opportunity to forget about the threat from Mr Biggs, if only for a short while. She rose slowly from the chair, moved to stand behind Devlin and placed her hands on his broad shoulders. Even through his coat, the muscles flexed beneath her palms.

"I do not profess to have your skill for negotiation," she said in a husky voice she could not recall ever using before. "But perhaps I might at least tempt you to consider my proposal."

"No doubt you could tempt the devil to take confession."

"I could but try." Throbbing fingers forced her to touch his skin, to massage the spot just above the collar of his coat, up into his hair.

A pleasurable hum resonated in his chest as he relaxed his head into her hands. "What is it you want me to do, Juliet? For I doubt our thoughts are aligned."

He was wrong. The spicy scent of his cologne teased her nostrils. Touching him stoked the fire within. But while her body craved this man, her mind was determined to ensure he did not meet Biggs alone.

"A comment my father made leads me to wonder if he wants something else besides Hannah's letters." Juliet rubbed his temples in a circular motion. "And so I think we should test the theory out on Mr Biggs."

One coherent word cut through Devlin's relaxed breathing. "We?"

Juliet bent her head and whispered in his ear, "I shall forge a letter from Hannah and hand it to Mr Biggs. It will give us an opportunity—"

"Like hell you will." In three swift moves her husband shot out of the chair, gripped both her hands and swung her around until her bottom perched on the edge of the table.

"At least give me a chance to explain."

He towered above her, so dark, so menacing, and yet she was more aroused than frightened. "I'll not let that rogue lay a hand on you again." His mouth came crushing down on hers, so urgent, so possessive. Blazing lips locked her in a scorching embrace.

Juliet relished the taste. Perhaps it was the potent essence of the wine that made her dizzy. Delirious. Perhaps it was the sizzling energy in the air that robbed her of all rational thought. She clutched his shoulders as their tongues fought a wild and intense battle for control.

Pure, unadulterated lust rendered them both incapable of forming a word.

He delved deeper into her mouth as he pushed her farther back onto the table. Cutlery clattered on the china plate. A crystal goblet toppled over, splashing wine on her dress. A cool breeze drifted over her legs as Devlin bunched her skirts up past her thighs.

"Do you want me to stop?" he said, tearing his mouth from hers. "Tell me now while I still have a grip on the last thread of control."

Gasping for breath, Juliet placed her hand on his heart. The organ thudded against her palm. Taking him into her body brought comfort as well as immense pleasure.

"My mother told me relations always took place in bed. I cannot recall her ever mentioning a piano, a ballroom floor or a dining table."

Guilt flashed in his eyes. "Forgive me. Sometimes the savage part of my character overrules all else."

She could sense his retreat. Oh, she had said the wrong thing. "No, you misunderstand." Juliet reached for the buttons securing the fall of his breeches. "It excites me that you lack the control to wait. It makes me feel that you desire me."

A sinful smile replaced the brief look of shame. Hot hands slid up under her skirts to cup her buttocks. "Oh, I desire you more than you know. Say you want to redefine what it means to take dessert."

Despite trembling fingers, she undid a button. "When I think of tasting anything rich and moorish, I shall think of your mouth. But promise me, when we settle down for a glass of port, that you will listen to my proposal."

Devlin bent his head and traced her lips with the tip of his tongue before thrusting inside. The kiss lasted seconds though it tugged at the muscles deep in her core.

"I promise to give your plan my full consideration," he said in a rich, husky voice that never failed to heat her blood. "I promise that once we have dealt with Biggs, I shall do whatever is necessary to ease your fears."

His words were like an aphrodisiac. One minute they were kissing, the next he was filling her full, sliding in and out of her hungry body in a slow, seductive rhythm. The maddening ache for him grew in intensity. Wrapping her legs more firmly about his waist, she urged him to hurry. It was not her pleasure she sought. But she would see the look of satisfaction banish the darkness from his eyes. She would see every flicker of emotion on his face, feel the power in every sleek stroke.

The clatter of crockery behind only inflamed her desire. They were wild, reckless, bound together by the hand of fate. Never had she felt so ravenous. Never had she experienced emotions so profound.

"God, Juliet," he panted. "You drive me insane."

He pounded harder, faster, again and again and again. His hand edged under her skirt, the soft pad of his thumb circling the one place desperate for his touch.

She came apart in seconds. "Devlin … yes …" Violent tremors shook her body, the shudders reaching her toes. "Devlin. I …" The word *love* clung to the tip of her tongue, but she chose to hold on to it for a while longer.

Three slow, measured strokes and her husband's head fell back. His guttural growl filled the room. He thrust inside her one last time, clutched her hip and held her there while he gasped for breath.

"This is the only place I belong." Devlin's muttered words were barely coherent.

His muscular arm snaked around her back, held her firmly in position as he collapsed back into the chair, taking her with him. Their bodies remained joined even when he softened inside her.

Juliet placed her head on his shoulder while still straddling his body. "I keep expecting to wake from this dream and find myself staggering down Bond Street overladen with Hannah's parcels."

"I share your sense of relief that we've both been spared such a cruel fate."

"Yet I cannot help but think the worst." An uncomfortable sense of foreboding refused to be tempered. "My father will stop at nothing to get what he wants."

Devlin sighed. "Then our next move must be strategic."

"Strategy involves having some knowledge of the game. In this instance, it would help if we understood my father's motive for making such demands."

Devlin fell silent for a moment before offering a curious hum. "Then tell me again of your plan for Mr Biggs."

CHAPTER THIRTEEN

Black clouds crept across the night sky to obscure the waning moon. With the absence of any natural light to illuminate her way, Juliet relied only on the small lantern to guide her through the garden. Gusts of wind attacked the flickering flame, making it impossible to hold the lamp aloft. The sound of trickling water drew her down the three stone steps leading to the lower tier and the ornate fountain—the place of her midnight assignation.

A frisson of fear rippled across her shoulders. She glanced back at the sprawling mansion, thought she saw someone watching from her bedchamber window, but Devlin had left the house thirty minutes earlier on a quest to find the perfect place to hide.

Juliet shook her head in a bid to focus on the task at hand and continued her journey towards the strange shadows she knew to be the trimmed topiary. Like soldiers on sentry duty, the cone-shaped trees flanked all sides of the magnificent water feature, and yet she knew her husband would not hide in such an obvious place.

But Devlin was out there somewhere, lurking in the depths of the darkness. She could feel the intense heat of his gaze following her every movement.

Mr Biggs was not waiting at the fountain.

Minutes passed.

The hoot of an owl and an odd scurrying sound forced her to squint at the eerie silhouettes in the distance. The sharp autumnal wind whipped her cheeks. Dead leaves blustered about her feet. The snap of a twig drew her frantic gaze to the path leading down to the brook.

A figure appeared—an ominous black shape that swayed in time with the trees.

The mass moved ever closer.

Oh, she should have brought Rufus, but she couldn't trust the dog to obey her commands, hadn't the strength to hold him on a leash. And the last thing they needed was to send Biggs fleeing in fright.

"The baron will be pleased to hear you've finally proved your worth," Biggs' gritty voice cut through the crisp night air. He came to a halt a few feet away.

"Family loyalty is everything, is it not?" Juliet kept the sarcasm from her tone. It would not do to aggravate a man who thought nothing of beating a woman. If Biggs put a grubby hand on her, it would be the end of all conversation. Devlin had made that clear.

"You have the letters then?"

"I have one letter. Despite an endless search that is all I could find."

Biggs bared his gritted teeth. "One? One! Wait till the baron hears about this." He closed the gap between them, looming large. "Happen I'll need to give you a reminder of what's expected."

Juliet flinched. Her pulse thumped hard in her throat. "Don't you want to see the letter first?" she said, trying to buy more time before Devlin charged out from his hideaway and beat Biggs to a pulp. "It might prove to be exactly what my father seeks."

"Let me see it." The rogue beckoned her to hand over the letter. "For your sake, you better hope you're right."

Juliet placed the lantern on the ground, reached into her pelisse and withdrew the missive she had written an hour earlier. The ink was too dark, the paper not nearly creased enough. It lacked the potent smell of neroli that clung to everything Hannah touched, a scent that lingered for months if not years.

Biggs snatched the letter but did not peel back the folds to scan the contents. He turned it over in his hand, examined the name on the front and the broken wax seal, then brought the paper to his nose.

"This isn't it." Strong fingers scrunched the letter until it was a ball in his fist. He threw it to the ground, rubbed his hand over his bristled chin and cursed.

"How do you know when you haven't read it?" Juliet clenched her hands at her sides, her nails digging into her palms as she waited for his violent outburst. She had to press him for more information. "That was a letter written by Miss Bromfield and sent to Ambrose Drake. It details her ugly threats, her attempt at blackmail. Is that not exactly the thing my father seeks? Or is there something else he considers more valuable?"

Tell me, tell me something.

"You ask too many questions." Biggs snarled and stabbed his finger at the mansion behind. "Are you tellin' me that's the only letter you could find in a house that size?"

So this had nothing to do with the disparaging gossip hurled at Ambrose Drake.

Did it have something to do with him breaking the betrothal?

"You're welcome to search the house yourself once you've explained the nature of your enquiry to my husband. Though I doubt he will permit you to set foot over the threshold."

Biggs seemed undeterred by the warning. "And while I'm there, happen I'll tell him his wife is a spy."

"I wouldn't if I were you. Mr Drake has quite a temper." Or so he had led her to believe. "He can kill a man with a simple flick of the wrist."

"Not with a broken neck he can't. Now get back to the house and bring me what I need else you'll feel the flick of my wrist across that pretty face of yours." Biggs offered a menacing grin as he raised his hand in warning.

The moment you feel threatened call out.

Devlin's instructions flitted through her mind, but she needed more information from Biggs.

"Dare lay a hand on me, and it will be the last thing you do." How she found the confidence to challenge him, she would never know.

"We'll see about that." Biggs curled his fingers into a fist just as a loud, ear-piercing howl rent the air. The thug froze as his frantic gaze scoured the gardens. "Wh-where's that blasted dog?"

"Rufus? He's about somewhere. But he is trained to wait for my signal." If only that were true, but the hound lacked discipline and refused to bow to authority.

Biggs shook his head and trained his beady eyes on her. "You've until tomorrow to bring me what I ask. I suggest you search amongst her ladyship's trinkets."

Her ladyship?

"And let this be a warnin' to you."

The backhanded slap took her by surprise. The power of it caused her to stumble back.

A thunderous roar echoed all around them. Bloodthirsty. Savage.

In a sudden panic, Biggs swung around and around, searching for the source of the brutal battle cry.

Juliet could see nothing but a host of shadows. And then, like a devil in the darkness, she saw her husband's hulking form appear behind Mr Biggs. A brief sliver of moonlight illuminated a section of Devlin's face to reveal a menacing mask of rage. His large, muscular arm slipped around the scoundrel's throat. "One wrong move and I shall snap your bloody neck."

∞

Anger burst through Devlin's veins—hot and molten. Fury almost blinded him. The need to extinguish all sign of life from the bastard who had the audacity to strike his wife vibrated through every taut, tense muscle.

He couldn't look at Juliet. To do so would render him helpless, would serve to bury the blade deeper into his heart. He should never have agreed to her plan, but the woman held him captive with her honest eyes and beguiling smile.

Biggs' strangled croak encouraged Devlin to tighten his hold. The man would know how close he'd come to losing his life. Devlin squeezed until Biggs punched and slapped his arm, begged for mercy, until he choked and spluttered.

"You have five seconds to tell me what the hell the baron wants from my house." Devlin relaxed his grip but kept hold of his prisoner.

Biggs coughed, the wracking sound like music to Devlin's ears. "Go ... go to hell."

"Very well." Devlin tightened his grip, this time lifting the blackguard clean off the ground. Biggs kicked and thrashed for freedom but to no avail. "I shall ask you again. If you're not looking for the letters from Miss Bromfield, what are you looking for?"

He gave Biggs another opportunity to speak.

"I don't know what the baron ... what the baron wants."

Frustration only enraged Devlin further.

"Then let me see if I can be a little more persuasive."

Juliet stepped forward, drawing his attention. "What do you intend to do with him?" The sight of the red mark on her face brought bile bubbling to his throat.

"I intend to throttle the bloody life out of him until he spills his guts." And then he would partake in a form of self-flagellation, penance for permitting his wife to meet with the blackguard.

Juliet blinked rapidly. "Oh, and if he refuses?"

"He won't."

Desperate to try a different tactic, Devlin grabbed Biggs by the back of his collar and dragged him backwards across the lawn. Arms flailing, the fiend staggered. He slipped on the dew-soaked grass and hit the ground hard, but Devlin continued to haul him to the brook.

"Get the hell off me," Biggs complained. "Let me stand, and I'll walk."

"Did you show my wife the same courtesy when you struck her so viciously?" The memory of the incident flamed the fires of vengeance.

"I'm only following the baron's orders."

Devlin cursed. "And in a moment you'll be following mine."

Having played in the brook many times as a boy, Devlin was well aware of its depth. He pulled Biggs down the bank and into the water. The man splashed and spluttered when his head went under.

Juliet stopped on the grass verge, watching him intently. "You mean to drown him?"

"I do." The water lapped around Devlin's thighs as he wrestled Biggs onto his front. He grabbed the scoundrel by the hair and forced his head beneath the murky depths.

Biggs thrashed.

Devlin gritted his teeth, the muscles in his arm bulging as he used his strength to keep Biggs down.

"Release him!" Juliet cried. "He's been under for far too long."

Not wanting to cause his wife any more distress, Devlin hauled the sopping wet figure up. "Tell me what the baron really wants."

Rivulets of water ran down Biggs' face. Droplets clung to his lashes. "The letters," he said, gasping for breath. "The baron wants the letters. That's all I know."

"The letters written to Ambrose Drake?"

"No ... not those."

"What other letters would be of interest to him?" Had it something to do with business dealings? Had Ambrose taken the baron's investment and died before legal proof could be established?

"I can't say."

"Can't or won't?" Devlin thrust Biggs' head under the water once again and held him until the air in his lungs had surely diminished, until the burning pain in his chest proved excruciating.

"Devlin," Juliet called. "Enough of this. He doesn't know."

"He knows something."

Juliet gasped suddenly. She hurried down the bank and rushed into the brook despite crying out in shock as she hit the cold water. "Let ... let me speak to him."

"Good God, woman. You'll catch your death."

Eager to get his wife out of the water, Devlin yanked Biggs to the surface. This time, the man retched and heaved.

Juliet grabbed Biggs by the arm. "You were looking for something when you examined the letter I gave you. What was it? Tell me, and I shall beg my husband to set you free."

Devlin was about to argue, there were two possible outcomes his conscience would allow, but he bit his tongue when Biggs nodded.

"The baron ... he's lookin' for old ... for old letters."

"Old letters?" Juliet glanced at Devlin and frowned. She turned back to Biggs. "How old?"

"F-fifty years." Biggs coughed and spewed a mouthful of dirty water.

Fifty years?

"What else can you tell me?" Juliet persisted. "You examined the wax seal, and the name scrawled on the front. To whom are these letters addressed?"

"I don't—"

Devlin gripped a clump of Biggs' hair, ready to force him under.

"Wait! The baron will kill me if he knows I've told you anything."

It was the time to give Mr Biggs a choice. Devlin could not allow the rogue to go free, to inform the baron of all they had learnt tonight. There was only one proposal he could make—one that left Biggs with no choice but to surrender.

"Let me speak plainly." Devlin hauled Biggs to his feet. Water cascaded from his sodden coat, a coat that whiffed of algae and rotten vegetation. "I cannot let you leave here."

A sound akin to a whimper vibrated in the man's throat.

"Not unless you agree to do my bidding," Devlin continued. "You can either languish in Blackwater's cellar until we have solved this mystery, or you can work for me. The baron need not know of your treachery and double dealings. I shall pay you for information."

Biggs remained silent for a brief time.

Perhaps he needed a little prompting in the right direction. "Know that should you betray me, or attempt to hurt my wife again, I will hunt you down, to the far reaches of the earth if necessary. When I find you, I'll kill you."

Biggs' shoulders slumped. "Looks like I've got no choice."

"Excellent." Devlin released his hold on the fellow and slapped him hard on the back. "Now tell my wife what she wants to know. You owe her that for the despicable way you've behaved."

"You must know to whom the letters are addressed," Juliet reiterated.

"I only that know that they're old," Biggs said with some

reluctance, "that they were addressed to the mistress of the house."

"To the mistress?" Fifty years ago, Devlin's grandmother was the mistress of Blackwater, but she would have been a young woman only recently married. "To Charlotte Drake?"

So what prompted the baron to show an interest in correspondence sent to a woman before Bromfield was born? And why was it considered pertinent now after all this time?

Then another thought struck him.

"Did the baron hire you to break into this house three years ago? To ransack my brother's room?" Devlin loomed over the scoundrel. "Did he pay you to kill my brother?"

Biggs raised his hands in surrender. "No, no. I swear, I had nothing to do with any of that, and have only worked for Mr Middle these last twelve months."

"Mr Middle?" Devlin asked.

"My ... my father's man of business," Juliet replied on the rogue's behalf.

A man of business that dealt with more than the overseeing of the accounts, Devlin thought. Mr Middle's involvement did suggest it might be a financial matter. Did Devlin's grandfather owe the baron's family a debt and the letters pleading for his grandmother's assistance were a means of proof?

God damn. There were so many conflicting thoughts racing about in Devlin's head.

"You will return to your master and inform him that my wife needs more time to find the letters." Devlin grabbed Biggs by the arm. "You will make no mention of speaking to me but confirm that you feel confident in Mrs Drake's cooperation."

Biggs nodded.

"Now, I shall escort you to the gate and see you on your way." Devlin could not let the scoundrel leave without giving him a parting token. Though he would take great pains not to mar the man's face. The last thing he wanted was to alert the baron.

Afterwards, he would see to it that Juliet soaked her cold bones in a warm bath. He may even join her. It would give him a chance to clear his mind for he needed full use of his faculties if he had any hope of solving this mystery.

During their game at Brooks', the baron had informed the crowd exactly what he deemed important—money and reputation. As his hunt for the letters clearly had nothing to do with salvaging Miss Bromfield's character, that left but one avenue of enquiry.

Had Ambrose ended the engagement because of the baron's financial failings? A man like Ambrose married to secure his estates. He did not marry for love. The lack of a dowry would certainly explain why the baron had offered Juliet as payment for the wager. Particularly when Miss Bromfield would not have hesitated to rip Blackwater apart in her hunt for the evidence.

"How do I know you won't kill me?" Biggs' croaky voice drew Devlin from his musings.

An opportunity suddenly presented itself. Devlin cast the thug a wicked grin. "Because I want to see the baron's account ledger, and you're going to steal it and bring it to me."

CHAPTER FOURTEEN

Water squelched in Juliet's boots and dripped from her sodden dress as she hurried up the stairs to her bedchamber. The cold water in the brook had held her in its frigid grip, leeched every ounce of heat from her bones. The spasms had started, the shaking, the chattering teeth, the inability to place her feet on the stairs without her knees buckling. But thoughts of a warm fire, of sinking her limbs into the steaming hot bathtub forced her to the bedchamber door.

Mrs Barbary's hollow cheeks and disdainful gaze had conveyed the extent of her disapproval. "The mistress must rise above these boisterous antics," the woman had said, believing the story that Juliet and Devlin had slipped down the bank and into the water during their midnight stroll. "The mistress of the house must be beyond reproach."

What gave the housekeeper the right to judge?

What gave her the right to express her opinion?

Perhaps she believed those born out of wedlock lacked morals, believed that Juliet would be the downfall of the Drake family. That her children would have tainted blood and run amok like wild rapscallions.

Shaking thoughts of Mrs Barbary from her mind, Juliet pushed open the chamber door. Upon first glance the room was unchanged. But the gap in the curtains told her she had not imagined seeing a figure at the window.

Juliet scanned the dimly lit room, found no sign of disturbed drawers. Yet she could not shake the feeling that someone had violated her private domain.

A knock at the door brought the maid Tilly, accompanied by two footmen laden with buckets of water.

Tilly bobbed a curtsy. "Oh, ma'am, let me move the tub and then I shall help you out of those wet clothes." She hurried to the far corner of the room, folded back the dressing screen and hauled the bath to a position closer to the fire.

While the footmen emptied the steaming buckets, Tilly rushed to Juliet's side. "It's too dark to go walking by the brook at night. Thank the Lord it's only knee deep."

"Knee deep for most people, waist deep for me." Juliet chuckled. The young maid reminded her of Nora, of one of the few things she missed about living in the baron's home. "That's how the water seeped into my stays."

"We will soon have you warm, ma'am, and tucked snug in your bed."

Sleep would elude her tonight.

How could she settle after what they had learnt from Mr Biggs? Where did one begin to look for letters that were fifty years old? And judging by the callous look in Devlin's eyes as he escorted Mr Biggs to the gate, the scoundrel might not survive to tell more tales.

"How long have you worked here at Blackwater?" Juliet asked the maid, though from the girl's youthful complexion it could only be a matter of years.

"Three years, ma'am." Tilly tugged Juliet's dress down to her ankles and helped her step out of the garment. "The previous master hired me just before he … before he died."

Juliet sighed. Death seemed especially cruel when it took those in the summer of their lives. "It must have been difficult here, what with my husband living abroad."

Upon hearing the trudge of footsteps on the stairs, Tilly drew Juliet into the dressing room. It would take the footmen two more journeys to complete the task.

"What with the mistress passing a month earlier," Tilly said, "it left the house in turmoil."

"The mistress?" From their conversations, Juliet presumed Devlin's mother died before he left for the Far East. She was certain that's what he had said. "Are you referring to Mr Drake's mother?"

Tilly shook her head as she untied the laces on Juliet's front-fastening stays. "No, ma'am, his grandmother."

The news came as a shock. "You speak of Charlotte Drake? Charlotte Drake died a month before her grandson?"

An abrupt cough drew Juliet's attention to the dressing room door. Mrs Barbary stood watching them with her hawk-like gaze.

"Take Mrs Drake's wet garments to the laundry, Tilly," the housekeeper snapped. "I shall assist her into the tub."

Tilly stood frigid for a few seconds, but then scooped up Juliet's clothes and hurried from the room. Juliet shivered, too. One glacial stare from Mrs Barbary and it was as if a winter chill breezed in through the window to freeze the blood in her veins.

Mrs Barbary took a silk robe from the armoire and draped it around Juliet's shoulders. "You should direct any personal questions about the family to me. The maids are prone to gossip and bouts of exaggeration. As mistress of Blackwater, you must not let them think you ignorant else they will ride roughshod over you every chance they get."

While she was in no doubt that Mrs Barbary meant well, her tone lacked the warmth needed to put Juliet at ease. And although she felt the urge to chastise the servant for forcing her opinion, the heat of shame flooded her cheeks. She was the daughter of an actress, not a lady of the ton. She knew how to work with servants not command them.

A hushed conversation from the bedchamber drew Mrs Barbary from the dressing room.

Tears prickled Juliet's eyes.

Oh, it was ridiculous that she should let the woman affect her mood.

Mrs Barbary barked instructions at the footmen, and their retreating steps preceded the click of the bedchamber door.

"Your bath is drawn, ma'am," Mrs Barbary called.

Juliet sucked in a breath, straightened her shoulders and exited the dressing room. "Thank you, Mrs Barbary, you may leave me. I wish to bathe alone."

The housekeeper's face remained expressionless. "Then I shall stoke the fire before I do."

Juliet slipped out of the robe, the silk garment pooling to the floor. Her numb fingers stung a little as she dipped them into the hot water. The same would be true for her limbs, and so she took her time, slowly immersing herself into the steamy depths.

Questions bombarded her mind—the persistent voice eager for answers.

"When you said the mistress read her letters on the bench by the brook, were you referring to Mr Drake's mother or his grand-mother?" Juliet spoke with an air of authority and would demand a reply if necessary.

As an unmarried man, Ambrose Drake would surely have sought his grandmother's assistance—a lady familiar with Black-water—in the running of such a large house.

Mrs Barbary straightened. She returned the poker to its fire-side stand and turned to face Juliet. "I spoke of his grandmother."

"Of Charlotte Drake?"

"Indeed."

"And these were her apartments?"

Mrs Barbary gave a curt nod. "The lady returned to live at Blackwater when her daughter-in-law died."

"And how did Charlotte Drake die?" From old age, no doubt, for the lady must have been in her dotage.

"Mrs Drake passed peacefully in her sleep." Mrs Barbary glanced at the large poster bed. A brief flash of pain marred her haggard features. She dabbed her finger to the corner of her eye, perhaps for effect. "I found her cold in her bed."

Another icy shiver ran the length of Juliet's spine. The warm water did little to keep the chill at bay. Was that why she had the sense someone lingered in the shadows? Watching. Waiting. For what she did not know.

Ambrose Drake had ended his betrothal less than a month before he died. Had grief over his grandmother's death persuaded him of the unsuitability of the match?

It could not be a coincidence.

"Had she been ill?" Juliet pressed the housekeeper for more information.

"Not ill. Just tired and weary the last few weeks and so kept to her bed. But that's to be expected for someone of her declining years."

"And the silver brush and mirror on the dressing table, the clothes in the armoire, they all belonged to Charlotte Drake?" Knowing the lady had died in the room did little to ease Juliet's anxiety.

"Everything is exactly as it was on the morning the mistress passed."

Conversation flowed a little easier now. Mrs Barbary's fondness for Charlotte Drake was evident in the tender tone of her voice. And so Juliet found the courage to ask the questions burning on her lips.

"And what of the lady's correspondence? Did she keep her private letters?"

"Her private letters?" Mrs Barbary cast a look of suspicion

before lifting her chin. "If they're not in the escritoire in the sitting room, then I don't know what she did with them." Her abrupt tone suggested she had better things to do than answer silly questions. "She may have used them for fire kindling."

They were not in the escritoire, nor any of the drawers, nor in a box under the bed. Juliet had spent the first few lonely nights at Blackwater growing accustomed to her new apartments.

She was still contemplating the housekeeper's reply when the bedchamber door burst open and Devlin marched into the room. Raw, masculine energy followed him, emanated from every fibre of his being. Water dripped from his clothes onto the wooden boards. His dark gaze skimmed past the housekeeper to settle on Juliet's bare shoulders. Purely to save Mrs Barbary any embarrassment, Juliet wrapped her arms across her chest.

"Let me call Mr Jasper, sir." Mrs Barbary moved to shield Juliet's naked form. "You must get out of those wet clothes before the cold seeps into your bones."

"I've spent five years dressing myself and have no need to wake the man at this late hour." Devlin shrugged out of his coat. The fine lawn of his shirt clung to the bulging muscles in his arms. The riveting sight banished all thoughts of the cold.

"You should take a hot bath," Juliet said, wishing there was room in the tub for two. "Mrs Barbary will alert Mr Jasper."

"I intend to take a hot bath." Devlin cast a sinful smirk. "Though I confess I lack the strength of will to remove myself from your bedchamber."

Mrs Barbary sucked in a breath. Juliet could feel her burning disapproval. The mistress of the house should not tempt the master. The mistress of the house should act with decency and decorum.

Devlin met the housekeeper's gaze and said, "Leave us. I shall attend to Mrs Drake."

"As you wish, sir." Head bowed, the woman left the room without a word or backwards glance.

Devlin locked the door.

"Please tell me you didn't murder Mr Biggs." Juliet scanned his face and hands looking for scratches or cuts or bruises, though in the firelight it was impossible to see in any detail.

"The man may have a cracked rib," he said as he stripped out of his clothing, "but he was breathing when we parted company at the gate."

"And you think you can trust Mr Biggs to keep his word and not mention our conversation to my father?" Juliet swished warm water over her shoulders to distract her wayward thoughts as her eyes feasted on Devlin's naked form.

"If Biggs has any sense, he'll be on the first coach to Edinburgh." He came and knelt down beside the tub and began tracing teasing circles on the surface of the water. "I doubt the man has a trustworthy bone in his body, and imagine he'll say whatever suits his purpose at the time. Pity though, I hoped your father's account ledger might provide us with a clue."

"Mr Biggs is in fear of his life. I doubt he will make a return visit."

"I agree."

Juliet remained silent while she watched her husband draw patterns in the water. Every muscle in her body wrung tight while she waited to discover where his fingers might venture next.

"What a shame the tub isn't big enough for two," Juliet said to tempt him to touch her.

"Most ladies would find the idea of sharing bathwater abhorrent."

"I am not most ladies," she said with a seductive grin. "And I could think of nothing more pleasing than settling between my husband's thighs as he massages my back with soap."

A hum left Devlin's lips. "Then first thing tomorrow I will send word to London and have Nash dispatch one of his architects to Blackwater. We'll have a Roman-inspired bathhouse built. One made just for two."

A sudden rush of love for her husband filled Juliet's heart.

Despite her wet hand, she cupped his cheek. "You would do that for me?"

Devlin gave an amused snort. "Well, as you require nothing but honesty from me, I admit that my own needs play some part in the decision, too."

"Can we have statues of Roman gods in the alcoves, and sconces on the walls with torches?"

"We can have whatever your heart desires."

Her heart desired but one thing—him. She would bathe in the icy brook if it meant being enveloped in his strong embrace.

Juliet drank in the sight of his broad shoulders, of the lock of ebony hair hanging over his brow. The orange glow from the fire's flames enhanced the brown flecks in his eyes, and his lips were a faint shade of … of blue!

"Heavens," she said, shooting up out of the water. "You must be frozen to your bones. Quickly, step into the tub."

Devlin stood, gripped her hand and assisted her out of the copper bath.

Before she knew what she was about, he dragged her into his arms and devoured her mouth. Desire pooled low and heavy in her loins, but concern for his welfare overruled all thoughts of seduction.

"Get into the bathtub, Devlin," she said, reluctantly tearing her mouth from his. "I shall kiss you once you're immersed in warm water."

He smiled. "And will you wash me as well?"

"You want me to massage soap over your back?"

"My back, my chest, a few other parts of my anatomy that need your caring touch."

Oh, he really was incorrigible.

But while she wanted nothing more than to lose herself in a moment of bliss, a nagging thought in her mind refused to be tempered.

"Climb into the water. When you're warm, I will assist you with your ablutions."

After kissing her once more on the lips, he obeyed her command. He was so tall he had to bend his knees to submerge his feet. Juliet grabbed her robe, slipped into the garment and then returned to kneel beside him.

"I spoke to Mrs Barbary a moment ago about your grandmother Charlotte," she said.

Devlin relaxed back as best as a man of his size could in such a confined space. "Did you ask her about the letters? I seem to recall that Mrs Barbary was once my grandmother's lady's maid. If anyone can shed any light on her private affairs, it is our housekeeper."

He said *our* as if they were equals in every regard.

Juliet had spent her whole life dealing with some form of inadequacy—she'd lacked a father growing up, lacked a mother much later, and consequently lacked love.

And yet the love she felt for this man was ready to burst from her in a tidal wave of emotion. She would tell him soon. Once she'd bolstered her courage.

"I asked, but Mrs Barbary knows nothing about your grandmother's correspondence." Previously, the housekeeper had mentioned that the mistress read her letters on the bench by the brook. Was that an important clue?

Oh, Juliet's mind was in a muddle.

"Despite the fact she had a close relationship with my grandmother," Devlin said, "Mrs Barbary is in her sixties. Too young to have born witness to the letters your father seeks."

"That doesn't mean she wasn't aware of their existence."

"Granted. Perhaps she thought you were prying. She was always quite protective of my grandmother." Devlin shivered visibly. "My shoulders are numb. Do you think you might warm them until the blood flows freely again?"

"Of course." Juliet scooped the warm water into her cupped

hands and poured it over his shoulders, repeating the action numerous times. "There is something that bothers me about your grandmother."

"And what is that?"

While Juliet's palms pulsed as she rubbed her hands over her husband's shoulders, the sudden pang in her chest stemmed from an apprehension to speak her mind.

"Do you not find it odd that your grandmother died around the time Ambrose broke his engagement to Hannah? Is it not odd that he died so shortly afterwards?"

A frown creased Devlin's brow. "She was old. Perhaps her passing forced Ambrose to reconsider all that is important in life. He wrote to inform me of her death, but by the time I received his letter he was dead, too."

"But knowing that my father seeks old letters changes things, do you not agree?"

Juliet's hand came to rest on his chest, covering his heart. The organ thumped hard against her palm. Evidently, he found the questions troubling. Had he heard the unspoken words? Was he open to the possibility that his grandmother died by a villain's cruel hand? Was he willing to accept that her father might be the one responsible?

"The word *coincidence* springs to mind, but Dariell would chastise me for my foolishness. He believes that one's destiny is not decided by a series of random events. There is no such thing as luck or chance."

Juliet wasn't sure she believed that. Had luck not played a part in Devlin winning the wager? Was she not lucky that Hannah refused to sacrifice her life to settle their father's debt?

"I should like to meet Mr Dariell. He sounds like an intriguing fellow."

"He is." After a moment's contemplation, Devlin said, "And you will meet him. Shall we invite him to dinner? Valentine will come, too, and Greystone and Lydia."

"Oh, I would love to meet your friends. And what of Lockhart?"

Devlin cleared his throat. "Lockhart is in hiding. No one must know he has returned home, for reasons I shall explain later."

Heavens, no wonder Devlin had spent so long abroad. When surrounded by such fascinating gentlemen, one would never suffer from boredom.

"Juliet," Devlin said in a tone that meant he was about to throw water over the fire of excitement burning in her chest. "My purpose for inviting them is not just so they may meet you, but I thought we could extend the invitation to family. I thought we could invite the baron and Miss Bromfield."

In an instant, her happiness sizzled and hissed as the fire inside died. "But why? They would shame me in front of your friends. Oh, Devlin, the thought of having them here makes me want to cast up my accounts."

"They will not dare insult you while I have breath in my body," Devlin said, his tone brimming with conviction. He took her hand in his although the water had wrinkled his skin. "And my friends will not permit their disrespect. You will like Greystone's wife. She is kind-hearted, and she loves him."

Juliet sighed. She could not hide from the baron forever. And at some point, hers and Hannah's paths were sure to cross.

"Then if I am to suffer the stress of dining with my family, at least tell me why it serves your purpose to have them here."

"It won't just be for dinner," Devlin said, wincing as he spoke. "I hoped they might stay the night."

"Stay the night? Oh, no, Devlin. I have spent six years sleeping under the same roof, don't ask me to do so again."

"Not even if it gives us an opportunity to trick your father into revealing more about the letters? We may learn something about what it is he truly wants. And as mistress of the house, your sister will have no option but to give you the respect you deserve."

While the thought of putting Hannah in her place proved

tempting, it was not in Juliet's nature to boast or flaunt her good fortune. "I doubt they will come."

"Your father paid a man to beat you, so you might provide the answers he seeks. Trust me. He will accept an invitation to spend the night in this house. The baron is desperate. Desperate men make mistakes."

A deep sense of foreboding shook her to her core. "Then I shall make sure I sleep with one eye open." And a blade hidden beneath her pillow.

"We won't be sleeping at all. We'll be spying on them, amongst other things." Devlin brought her hand to his mouth and pressed a tender kiss on her palm. "I shall not leave you alone for a second."

"Make sure you don't."

"Does that mean you agree?" He sounded hopeful.

Juliet nodded. "If you think it might help to solve the mystery of your grandmother's letters and put these troubles behind us for good, then yes."

He flashed a devilish grin. "You do know that I will do my utmost to embarrass your sister. It's the least I can do for Ambrose."

"She deserves nothing less." In all likelihood, Hannah would refuse the invitation. But then she doubted the baron would enter the lion's den alone. "Someone needs to knock her off that giant plinth. Hannah will never be happy if she continues to treat people with contempt."

"Is there any soap?" Devlin asked, changing the subject.

"Just a minute." Juliet hurried to the washstand and returned with the bar. She moved to hand it to Devlin, but he shook his head.

"You'll need to wash me." His seductive gaze swept over her. "I am too cold to see to the task myself."

"Too cold? Then I had better do something to heat your blood."

"My thoughts exactly." Devlin leant back against the copper rim. "But there's no need to hurry. You have all night to work on the task."

Juliet dipped her hands into the water and then worked the bar soap between her palms. A faint whiff of cloves and lemon wafted past her nostrils. She lathered Devlin's chest first, enthralled by the way her hands slipped over the hard contours, fascinated by the way his nipples peaked at the slightest touch. He was magnificent, all muscle and maleness.

"Does that feel better?" Juliet's voice dripped with lust and longing.

"Much better. But I'm a large man, Juliet." Those midnight eyes devoured her. "There are plenty of other areas vying for your attention."

"Any in particular?" she said, lathering the soap.

"Why not use your intuition?" His velvet voice slid over her skin to tease her senses.

Feeling far braver than she'd ever felt before, Juliet delved beneath the water. Her hand came to rest on the solid length of his manhood.

"I don't think you have to worry about the cold affecting you here," she teased as she wrapped her fingers around his shaft and massaged in slow strokes.

A pleasurable hum left her husband's lips. "When it comes to chills, it is wise to take precautions."

CHAPTER FIFTEEN

"Valentine, he has told me what happened at the gaming table." Dariell stood at the window in the drawing room, hands clasped behind his back as he stared out into the darkness. He wore his usual blue tunic and relaxed trousers—the dress worn by men in hotter climates—his hair tied back in a queue.

Devlin swallowed a mouthful of brandy and leant back in the chair. "And I'm sure he told you about the fateful event that followed."

"I didn't need to tell him," Valentine said from his fireside chair. "Apparently, you were never destined to marry Miss Bromfield."

Dariell turned and offered Devlin a knowing smile. "This is true."

"Then why the hell did you not say so before?" During the last three years, Dariell had listened patiently to Devlin's plans to ruin the harpy's good name.

Dariell shrugged. "I gave you enough clues as to your destiny."

He spoke of the mysterious ring, of his constant reminders

that vengeance tainted the soul, that love would find him if only he followed his heart.

Lydia, Lady Greystone, placed her sherry glass on the side table and settled back into the sofa so that Greystone—who draped his arm over the back in a languid fashion—could continue stroking her neck.

"Thank the Lord you're not married to that dreadful woman," Lydia said, and it was evident by her disgruntled tone that Greystone had told her of Miss Bromfield's slanderous lies.

"No one is more thankful than I." Devlin glanced at the ceiling and sighed. That dreadful woman was currently occupying one of the bedchambers. Perhaps it was a mistake to invite the Bromfields. "Juliet is rather anxious about having them to stay."

They had arrived late. Miss Bromfield complained about the road, the weather, the lack of notice. And then the snake's eyes slithered over Valentine and she hissed with pleasure. Try as she might, she failed to lure him into a hypnotic trance. It took a damn sight more than a pretty face and full breasts to tempt Valentine.

Still, Miss Bromfield would slink around him for the duration of her stay.

The baron appeared less hostile though reeked of insincerity. Being acquainted with Valentine's mother, Bromfield asked after the lady's health, spoke briefly to Greystone about his interests in shipping.

Dariell had hovered in the background, silently assessing the scene. The Frenchman knew a devil upon sight. A corrupt soul leeched into the air, looking to cling on to the weak, eager to suck the life out of its unsuspecting victims.

"As your friend, I will not tolerate their disrespect." Greystone's words dragged Devlin from his musings.

"You may have to tolerate it to a certain degree. As I said, I need the baron to remain here for the night." Be that as it may,

Devlin would throttle the lord if he dared to insult Juliet. "What Miss Bromfield does is of no consequence."

"You have willpower beyond that of any man I know," Greystone said with a hint of admiration. "You want to murder the baron for the way he has treated your wife, want to shame Miss Bromfield for what she did to Ambrose, and yet tonight you will break bread with them both."

"Juliet's safety is paramount." The thought of losing her chilled Devlin's blood. "That blackguard will stop at nothing to get what he wants, and if I continue stumbling about in the dark, how am I meant to protect her?"

"The enemy at the door is easier to defeat," Dariell said in the wise tone that made one stop and take note.

Valentine stood. He sauntered over to the row of decanters on the console table and refilled his glass. "We are at your command, Drake, and will do whatever we can to assist you."

Collectively his friends agreed.

"I look forward to making Juliet's acquaintance," Lydia said, no doubt eager for female companionship in a room full of men.

Devlin inclined his head. "She will be down shortly. The modiste arrived with her wardrobe and insisted on dressing her this evening."

Juliet's inner beauty shone through no matter what she wore. The old dresses were fit for the bonfire, and he hoped she incinerated them along with all terrible memories of the past.

A knock on the drawing room door brought Withers who introduced the baron and his insipid daughter. They all stood to greet the guests. Much to his chagrin, Devlin poured them both a drink though Miss Bromfield complained that the sherry was a little tart for her taste.

"And where is Juliet? Is she lost?" Miss Bromfield sniggered as she glanced around the room. "Has she forgotten she's to come to the drawing room and not the scullery?"

Spiteful witch!

"You surprise me, Miss Bromfield," Valentine said in a voice as smooth as the finest claret. "I thought a lady of your standing would know that the mistress of the house is always last to make an entrance."

"Of course I know. But what could be keeping her so long?"

"Most ladies of my acquaintance take an age to dress for dinner," Valentine replied.

Miss Bromfield tittered. "Well, perhaps she is mulling over which shade of brown suits her best."

"Having had the pleasure of meeting Mrs Drake," Valentine said, unruffled, "I can assure you she will look splendid in anything she wears."

"Then you must have been chirping merry when you met, my lord," Miss Bromfield countered.

Devlin remained rigid—his temper held in check by a flimsy thread. Once it snapped, he was liable to rip through the room in a whirlwind and destroy everything in his path.

"I can assure you, Miss Bromfield, that even in my cups, I am a man who recognises true beauty."

"Indeed," Dariell added. "Clothes, they do not make the man."

Miss Bromfield's eyes narrowed as she observed Dariell's unconventional attire. She screwed up her button nose. "And judging by your odd dress, I imagine you have spouted that nonsense many times before."

Dariell never lost his temper.

Nothing could rattle his composure.

"And I have another mantra you may find amusing." Dariell did not wait for a response. "How people treat others is often a true reflection of how they feel about themselves." Dariell inclined his head and smiled. "Is that more pleasing to your ears?"

"That is utter poppycock."

"If you say so, madame."

The baron cleared his throat. "And how is married life,

Drake?" His mocking tone grated. "Do you find the girl agreeable?"

The girl? Could the man not bring himself to call Juliet his daughter?

Devlin forced a reply. "I could not be happier and can only express my gratitude to you for presenting me with a much more appealing prize."

"You do strike me as a man who demands subservience," Miss Bromfield interrupted rudely. "It is why we would never have suited."

He would rather stab pins in his eyes than suffer her vile tongue each morning.

"You know nothing of my wants or needs, Miss Bromfield, though I happen to agree with your last comment. When it comes to you, incompatibility is in my blood. My brother found you disagreeable, too, I'm told."

Miss Bromfield's arrogant countenance faltered for a few seconds. "Your brother was less of a gentleman than your butler, Withers."

Devlin bit the inside of his cheek so hard he tasted blood. "He was gentleman enough to tell everyone you ended the betrothal when we all know the opposite is true."

Miss Bromfield's cheeks flared red. She swallowed numerous times but struggled to maintain her composure. It was ungentlemanly of Devlin to mention the affair openly, but he didn't care what they thought of him, and Miss Bromfield deserved her shame for the way she had spoken about Juliet.

Had they been anywhere else, the baron would have retaliated with a cutting quip, would have removed himself and his daughter from the house. Outraged. Insulted. The fact he said nothing only supported Devlin's theory that the lord was desperate to remain at Blackwater.

"Greystone," the baron said, clearly eager to change the

subject, "I hear it won't be long until you own your father's shipping company in its entirety."

Greystone stared down his nose. "Foolish men make it easy for others to succeed," he replied in a tone sharp enough to slice through the baron's facade.

The creak of the door drew everyone's attention.

Juliet entered the room.

For a moment Devlin struggled to catch his breath.

Dazzling them in emerald-green silk that enhanced the hue of her eyes to perfection, his wife stepped forward. She smiled though he could sense her nerves. The soft curve of her breasts swelled above the neckline of her gown. With her vibrant red curls styled in a fashionable coiffure, it drew his eye to the elegant column of her throat, to the porcelain skin he longed to kiss.

"You appear to have married an angel," Greystone whispered. "No wonder I've not heard from you this last week."

"I have been busy."

"Dariell is right. While her clothes enhance her beauty, it is her smile and honest eyes that are thoroughly captivating."

"Dariell is always right."

Greystone patted Devlin on the back. "You can close your mouth now."

His wife looked ravishing, enchanting, and a host of other words that bombarded his mind, that made lust throb in his loins, that made his heart sprout wings and take flight. She deserved the best life had to offer, and he wanted to be the one to satisfy every dream, every desire.

"Good evening," Juliet said in the kind voice that sent his head spinning. He wanted to reach out to her, take her in his arms and tell her not to worry. "I did not mean to keep you all waiting."

She offered their guests an exuberant smile, and Devlin knew then he was lost. Lost in a blissful euphoria. Lost in a whirl of powerful emotions. Lost in abiding feelings of love.

The neckline was too low, her stays too tight, the gown far too flimsy for an autumn night such as this. Juliet forced a smile as she greeted their guests though it took a tremendous effort to prevent her heart from bursting out of her chest. Seven pairs of eyes stared, scanned her from head to toe. While Devlin's friends looked upon her with an air of wonder, the same could not be said for her father or Hannah.

The baron held a detached gaze, the look he cast his servants to show they were in his house to provide a service—nothing more. Hannah had the look of a wildcat on the hunt—back arched, claws extended ready to attack. She glared at Juliet as if she might scratch out her eyes and use them to lure the crows.

Could Hannah not find it in her heart to be happy for the girl who had served her faithfully these last six years? Could she not find it in her heart to hide her true feelings, just for tonight?

Feeling a sudden flutter of nerves, Juliet looked at Devlin, and her anxiety drifted away like petals in the wind. While he, too, looked upon her in awe—and something vastly more licentious—his admiration stemmed from somewhere beyond his penetrating gaze, from somewhere deep inside. Indeed, it was as if his soul stretched across the space between them to touch and twine with hers.

The power of it invigorated her spirit. It gave her the confidence to straighten her shoulders, to look at Hannah directly and smile.

Devlin cleared his throat, but the other lady in the group rushed forward, hands outstretched.

"Forgive me, but I lack the patience to wait for introductions." The lady took Juliet's hands and clasped them tightly.

"You must be Lady Greystone. My husband speaks fondly of you."

"Does he?" she said with some surprise. "I must admit that I was rather rude to him when we first met. And please, you must call me Lydia." The lady held Juliet's arms wide, her bright blue eyes gleaming as she studied Juliet's dress. "Your modiste has outdone herself. You look captivating."

"Thank you." A blush crept up Juliet's cheeks for she was unused to accepting compliments.

"And your sister looks positively green with envy," Lydia whispered.

"Does she? Oh, I'm afraid she struggles to cope when the attention is not directed her way."

"My sister-in-law was the same."

Was?

Devlin had mentioned Lord and Lady Lovell. The lady had suffered a terrible accident, though he had said nothing about her dying from her injuries.

"Please accept my condolences," Juliet said, squeezing Lydia's hand as a sign of sincerity. "While I knew of the accident, I did not realise she had passed."

"Oh, Arabella isn't dead. My brother sent her to an asylum, so he could move his mistress into the house. It's a terrible scandal, of course, but when one's relation is a fool it cannot be helped."

With honesty being a trait Juliet most admired, she warmed to Lady Greystone instantly. "Well, I have spent my whole life living under a cloud of disgrace. It will be good to have company."

Devlin appeared at Lady Greystone's shoulder. "Forgive the interruption. But I must introduce you to my friends."

"Of course."

"Don't mind me." Lydia stepped closer and whispered, "I shall attempt to have a civil conversation with your sister."

Juliet didn't hold out much hope. *Civility* was a word foreign to Hannah's vocabulary. "Then I wish you luck." She slipped her hand into the crook of Devlin's arm.

"You look exquisite tonight," he said as he led her to Lord Valentine and Lord Greystone.

Juliet met his gaze, though her stomach performed a range of somersaults. "I'm pleased you approve."

Lord Valentine kissed her hand, and while she imagined most women swooned beneath his penetrating gaze, she merely smiled and shifted her attention to Lord Greystone.

"My wife has been eager to meet the lady who saved Drake from a miserable fate." Lord Greystone inclined his head. Unlike Devlin—whose strength was evident in every bulging muscle—Lord Greystone possessed a kind, friendly countenance. But the man was skilled in the art of pugilism, had a presence that roused confidence in his ability to achieve his goals.

Juliet caught a glimpse of the baron and Hannah in the far corner. Lady Greystone had joined them, though Hannah failed to grant the lady her full attention.

"And you have Dariell to thank for your wedding band." Devlin drew Juliet to the mysterious fellow standing by the window.

Dariell bowed low. "It is a pleasure to meet you, madame. Drake, he has found someone who can smooth away his rough edges."

Devlin coughed into his fist. "You're supposed to be my friend."

"And do friends not speak the truth?"

Juliet cast the man her widest smile. There was something about the rich quality of his voice that stirred the senses. Wisdom radiated from him, warm and vibrant.

"If I may, I should like to see the ring." Dariell offered his palm and Juliet slipped her hand into his. The skin was soft, smooth, transmitted a vibrating energy that journeyed up her arm. It was nothing like the feelings of lust and love she felt for Devlin, but more the spiritual cleansing one received when touched by the hands of a priest.

Dariell closed his eyes briefly. When he opened them, he said, "You have a kind and loving heart, madame, as I undoubtedly knew you would." He ran the tip of his finger over the mystical ring and gave a hum of satisfaction. "The ring, it is a perfect fit, no?"

"Indeed. It seems you have great foresight, sir. I hope you, too, take comfort from such a gift," Juliet said, feeling energised by his touch. "May I ask if you're able to use the skill to predict your own destiny?"

Dariell raised a brow, seemingly impressed by her question. "Most people, they press me to learn what I know of their future. But you, madame, are the only person ever to consider my wants and desires."

"I must have asked you at some time," Devlin said defensively.

"No, Drake, you have not." Dariell gripped Devlin's shoulder in a gesture of friendship. "But when a man's heart is full of vengeance, he finds it difficult to think of others."

"It is not that way anymore."

"No, I can see that it is not." Dariell turned his attention back to Juliet. "And to answer your question, madame, I have had a glimpse of what life has in store for me."

"You have?" Devlin seemed surprised.

"My destiny is entwined with our good friend Lockhart's. And that is all I can say on the matter." Dariell sighed deeply. "Now, there is the matter of a mystery to solve, and I believe I am here to assist you in your endeavour."

The mere allusion to the baron's hunt for the letters drew Juliet's gaze to her father. Lady Greystone had rejoined her husband, leaving Hannah and the baron muttering quietly between themselves.

They were the last people she wanted in her home. Now that they were here, she should make every effort to uncover more clues.

"Forgive me, Mr Dariell. I shall leave you in my husband's capable hands for I must speak to my father."

"Of course, madame." He smiled. "And have no fear. A kind heart offers immunity to a viper's venom."

The comment went some way to easing Juliet's anxiety. "Even so, I shall have a care when my sister extends her fangs."

Sucking in a deep breath, and after receiving the tender touch of Devlin's hand on her arm, Juliet crossed the room to greet her father.

They finished their little tête-à-tête as soon as they witnessed her approach.

"Shouldn't you go and see what's delaying dinner?" Hannah spoke as if Juliet were still a servant in her household.

"I'm sure it won't be much longer." Noting the sour look on Hannah's face, Juliet chose to be blunt. "I'm surprised you came. No doubt you have a host of people longing for your good company tonight."

Sarcasm was lost on Hannah, but Juliet enjoyed the newfound freedom that permitted her to speak her mind.

"What? And have everyone bombard me with questions about you?" Hannah turned up her nose. "Everyone wants to know about my father's secret daughter," she said, her tone more a high-pitched screech. "Everyone wants to know about the woman Devlin Drake won in a wager."

What about me? she might have said.

"And would you not welcome the attention, Hannah?" Oh, Juliet intended to wring this conversation for everything it was worth. A kind heart only went so far. "After all, it would make a change to tell the truth for once rather than have to invent sordid stories of scandal."

A scarlet blush tainted Hannah's cheeks. "As you spent most of your time in the scullery, Juliet dear, I hardly think your opinion qualifies. And regardless of your present status, you will call me Miss Bromfield."

"Of course. And you will call me Mrs Drake."

Hannah huffed.

"Perhaps you should join Lady Greystone, Hannah. It does no harm to make yourself appear more amenable." While the baron spoke to the spiteful creature at his side, he kept his keen gaze trained on Juliet.

"But I don't want to—"

"Go," their father commanded. "I want five minutes alone with your sister."

The baron offered Juliet his arm. Once, she would have been thrilled by the prospect of walking with her father. Now, the thought filled her with dread.

"Shall we step out into the hall?" the baron continued. "I think a little privacy is called for. After all, I did not come all this way to sample Drake's best brandy."

Nerves knotted in Juliet's stomach. Oh, it was foolish to think the baron would do her harm in her own house. Not when he needed her cooperation. Besides, with a burning curiosity to discover the truth, she had no choice but to accept.

But it seemed fate had other plans.

Withers entered the drawing room to inform them that dinner was served.

The baron cursed beneath his breath. "Just find those damn letters." He tugged on her arm and drew her closer. "I know they're here. Ambrose told me so."

"Perhaps he lied."

"They're too incriminating to destroy."

The baron did not have an opportunity to say any more. Indeed, Devlin approached and did not leave her side for the rest of the evening. His friends monopolised the baron's attention until it was time to retire.

"We're sleeping together tonight," Devlin whispered in her ear as they followed their guests upstairs to bed. "Although sleep will be the last thing on our minds."

Excitement fluttered in her breast even though she knew seduction was not part of the night's agenda. No. They were to wait for Dariell, wait for information on the baron's movements during the night, wait for an opportunity to confront the devious lord and discover the reason for his duplicity.

"Is it just me, or did Mrs Barbary treat the baron with barely veiled disdain?" Juliet said as she settled into the fireside chair and cradled the glass of sherry a maid had brought to her room. "She was not as sharp with Lord Valentine, or Mr Dariell."

Devlin dropped into the seat opposite ready to join her in their nighttime vigil. "She blames him for what happened to Ambrose. Thankfully, we all ate from the same platters. Else I fear she may have laced his dinner with arsenic."

"Please tell me you're joking. While I am as eager as you to discover the truth, I'll not be an accessory to murder."

"Of course I'm joking. Cook locked the arsenic in a cupboard and wears the key tucked into the valley of her bosom. No person alive would dare venture down there."

Juliet smiled though nerves pushed to the fore when she considered what the night might bring. "Do you really believe my father will leave his chamber tonight? Do you expect to find him prowling the dark corridors?"

Devlin's mouth thinned as he stared at the amber flames. A weary sigh left his lips. "When it comes to the baron nothing surprises me. But rest assured, we will soon know the answer."

CHAPTER SIXTEEN

The faint creak of a door forced Devlin to open his eyes. While the fire still radiated a modicum of heat, the flames danced low in the grate. One glance at the stubby candle in the lamp told him the hour had long since passed the stroke of midnight.

Juliet slept in the chair opposite, a blanket draped around her shoulders.

The light pad of footsteps in the adjoining room told him to expect Dariell, but Devlin took a moment to study his wife.

A mysterious tug in his gut had prompted him to speak to her in the garden on the fateful day the baron arrived to pay his debt. The same overwhelming sense of rightness encouraged him to offer marriage. But it was her strength of character that had stolen his heart. Juliet was beautiful inside and out, and he was a better man for having met her.

Love flowed through his veins.

Love inflamed every fibre of his being.

Love held him captive.

"It is as you suspected." Dariell's soft French burr reached Devlin's ears. His friend appeared from the shadows, noted the angel sleeping in the chair and kept his voice low. "The baron, he has spent fifteen minutes in your brother's bedchamber."

"Did he see you?"

Dariell's mouth curled up in amusement. "Of course not."

"And what of Miss Bromfield?" Devlin asked, wondering if his instincts were right.

The lady had spent the evening vying for Valentine's attention, stroking her fingers seductively over her collarbone, moistening her lips, touching his arm repeatedly during dinner. The lord's lack of interest only fuelled her need to whet his appetite.

"Miss Bromfield, she left her room wearing nothing but her nightgown, crept to Lord Valentine's room and tried to gain entrance."

Devlin snorted. "Please tell me he locked the door."

"*Oui*. Of course. Valentine is no fool." Dariell shrugged. "His destiny, it lies elsewhere."

Intrigued by the comment, Devlin straightened. "And the widow, Lady Durrant, does she have a role to play in Valentine's destiny?" Hell, he hoped not. But Valentine had made a vow to marry and seemed set on the widow.

"Perhaps." Dariell's eyes gleamed with excitement, and he chuckled almost to himself. "Valentine, he has such a surprise in store." His amusement waned. "But I am here to assist you with *your* destiny, my friend, and I must tell you that the baron has just descended the grand staircase and is on the hunt."

"The conniving bastard," Devlin whispered. "The man has the devil's impudence."

"Will you confront him alone?" Dariell glanced at the beauty sleeping in the chair.

The last thing Devlin wanted was to cause Juliet more pain. But he had told her they would tackle the baron together, and he would not go back on his word.

"My wife deserves to know the truth, despite any reservations I might have."

A satisfied sigh left Dariell's lips. "You have travelled a long way to find your life's purpose, no?"

It felt as though he had spent an eternity wandering aimlessly. "The journey has been rather hazardous, treacherous in places." He glanced at Juliet. "But the discovery of a rich, new land has made every miserable moment worthwhile."

"Then all is as it should be."

"Indeed." Devlin leant forward, touched Juliet's knee and shook her gently. "Juliet. Wake up."

Her eyes fluttered beneath her lids.

"Juliet," he whispered, but she did not wake from her slumber. Devlin came to kneel beside her, took her chin gently between his fingers and pressed a tender kiss to her lips.

She sucked in a breath, and her eyes flew open. "Devlin. Has … has something happened?"

"Your father is currently prowling about downstairs. Do you wish to remain here, or shall we go and catch the blighter in the act?"

She shook her head, blinked rapidly and pushed the blanket off her shoulders. "No, we will go together." Her gaze moved languidly from Devlin's face. Her head shot back, and she gasped as she locked eyes with Dariell. "Mr Dariell, I did not see you there."

Dariell inclined his head. "Forgive me, madame. I shall return to my chamber if my services are no longer required."

Juliet stared at Dariell for a moment. "Perhaps you should accompany us." She cast Devlin a look that begged for his support. "You have a way of seeing things others do not. When it comes to my father, there is no telling what he might do."

"If that is what you wish," Dariell agreed.

"I have no objection." Devlin stood and took hold of Juliet's hand. "Let us see if the baron has had any luck finding the letters he so desperately seeks."

The long-case clock chimed three. Devlin, Juliet and Dariell all hurried down the stairs before the vibrations ceased. They had no need to hunt their prey. The faint glow of light creeping out beneath the study door alerted them to their quarry.

They tiptoed to the door and stopped outside.

Dariell clutched Devlin's arm. "I shall wait here," he mouthed silently.

Devlin nodded. He gripped Juliet's hand and waited for her nod of approval before pushing open the door gently and padding lightly into the room.

A lit candle stood in its holder on the large oak desk.

Seated in Devlin's chair while rummaging in drawers left deliberately unlocked, it wasn't until the baron heard the click of the door closing that he realised he was not alone.

Devlin smiled. "Found what you're looking for?" Arrogance dripped from every word. "Are there any cupboards you wish me to unlock? Perhaps you might like to ferret around in my wife's bedchamber, too."

The baron froze.

It took a few seconds for him to gather his composure and paste his usual arrogant smirk. "Your housekeeper refused to return those foolish letters Hannah wrote. You cannot blame a man for taking advantage of an opportunity."

"That was three years ago." It took every ounce of willpower Devlin possessed not to put an immediate end to the baron's antics. Not to end the man's life as quickly as one snuffed out a candle. "What makes you think my brother kept them?"

"Ambrose told him the letters were here," Juliet said. Her palm was hot and clammy as she gripped Devlin's hand. "And the baron told me earlier that the letters were too incriminating to destroy."

The baron slammed the desk drawer shut and sneered. "I should have known you were not to be trusted."

Devlin felt the slight tremble in Juliet's hand. Thoughts of leaping over the old desk and ramming his fist into the baron's face pushed to the fore. But for once in his life, violence would not help to solve this matter.

Unable to satisfy the ravaging hunger for revenge, Devlin opened his mouth to deliver a scathing reprimand, but Juliet spoke first.

"I am loyal to my husband, to the man who has taken better care of me than you have done these last six years." Her voice broke, but she did not shed a single tear. "I am loyal to the man who will father my children, children who will know what it means to be loved by their parents."

The words touched Devlin like nothing else before.

The image of him surrounded by little ones tugging on his hand, begging for his attention, infused his mind and body with an intense euphoria. Juliet was right. When Devlin hated he did so with a bloodthirsty hunger to rival the devil's. But when he loved, it was with a deep, abiding passion.

"What is it with the Drake men?" The baron's words dragged Devlin from his reverie. Contempt radiated from every fibre of the lord's being. "Hannah was like a dog with a bone, wouldn't let go of the notion that Ambrose might change his mind, might agree to marry her despite his thorough disrespect."

For once the baron spoke honestly about his daughter's failings. Was this really about something Miss Bromfield had written in a note? Had Biggs lied about looking for old letters merely to appease them?

"So you admit it was Ambrose who made the decision not to marry," Devlin said, his tone revealing the depth of his loathing for the gentleman currently sitting in his chair.

The sound of grinding teeth reached Devlin's ears.

"You may as well tell the truth," Juliet said. "I overheard their conversation in the garden. Hannah sobbed. Ambrose seemed composed, stoic even."

"Stoic? The heartless bastard offered to compensate her for the upset." Bromfield shot up out of the chair, braced his hands on the desk and glared at them with such menace. "As if money might mend a broken heart, might wash away the stain left by his blatant disregard."

Unperturbed by the baron's threatening countenance, Devlin straightened to his full height. "That is how things work in the *ton*." And Ambrose was a man who followed the rules, pandered to the matrons, obeyed society's edicts. "Did he not do your daughter a courtesy? Was she not permitted to say *she* ended the betrothal?"

Bromfield snorted. "Everyone knows Hannah has a lively temper. People would have drawn their own conclusions. Your brother ruined any chance she had of making a decent match."

Perhaps that was why the lady had taken to wandering the corridors in her night-rail, looking to trap a wealthy husband. The only thing the foolish chit was likely to achieve was total ruination.

"Was it your daughter's vulgar attitude that forced my brother to change his mind?" Goading the baron brought Devlin immense satisfaction. "Did he consider her unrefined manners beneath him?"

Oh, that comment certainly hit the mark.

"Beneath him!" Bromfield raged. Even in the dim light, Devlin could see that the man's cheeks burned red. "I'm a peer of the bloody realm, your brother a mere mister."

"And so Hannah wrote to him, slandered his good name," Juliet said, pressing the baron for answers, too. The tension in the air reached fever pitch. "She made up those vile stories about his preferences in the bedchamber for she hoped it might add credence to the lie that she ended the betrothal."

"Of course she made it up," Bromfield blurted. "The girl was desperate. And I supported her decision. In a society such as ours, reputation is everything."

Bile bubbled in Devlin's throat. Conflicting emotions raced through his body. Anger burned in his chest when he thought of the humiliation his brother had suffered. People in high society were too judgemental. Relief settled in his chest, too. The lewd tales were nothing but spiteful lies.

But that did not answer the question about the baron's hunt for private letters, or why Ambrose happened to be walking across the common before dawn.

"Then as a peer of the realm, I wonder what people will say when they discover you've stooped so low as to rummage in a gentleman's private desk." Devlin released Juliet's hand and stalked to meet the baron. He, too, braced his hands on the polished surface, leant forward and looked Bromfield in the eye. "You'll tell me what the hell your daughter wrote in those letters. Else I shall have no hesitation in beating the information out of you."

"You wouldn't dare." The man's nostrils flared, and his eyes bulged as he scanned the breadth of Devlin's chest.

"Wouldn't I? There are enough witnesses here to claim you provoked me. There are enough witnesses to say you were caught stealing."

The baron's lip curled up in disdain. "Your friends are heathens. There's not a gentleman in the *ton* who would believe them," he said, but his quivering chin belied his arrogant countenance.

Devlin decided to apply a little more pressure.

"Lord Valentine has an unblemished reputation," Devlin said with a wicked grin. "But you're right. I am a heathen and will think nothing of putting an end to your meddling." Devlin cast him his blackest stare. "Now tell me what the bloody hell your daughter wrote in those letters."

The baron blinked rapidly.

Devlin could feel his control slipping. He reached over the desk and grabbed the baron by his fancy cravat, ready to throttle the last breath from his lungs.

"Let go, I say." The baron clasped Devlin's hand, tried to loosen his grip. "I cannot … damn it … I cannot breathe."

"Good. Now tell me what I want to know." Devlin shook the man violently. "Tell me."

"That stupid girl mentioned the duel in the last letter she wrote to him." The words flew out of the baron's mouth, though he seemed shocked to have uttered them. As Devlin relaxed his grip, the baron closed his eyes and shook his head. "That stupid girl cannot hold her own water let alone her tongue."

The tension in the air abated as Devlin released Bromfield and the weary lord fell back into the chair.

"What duel?" Devlin asked, though one did not need Aristotle's intelligence to piece the events together.

"After your brother's dishonourable conduct, I did the only thing I could." Bromfield dragged his hand down his face and sighed. "I challenged Ambrose Drake to a duel on Wimbledon Common. It was a matter of seeking satisfaction. Of letting him know I am not a man to cross. Neither of us had any intention of firing the damn pistol."

The room seemed to sway. A cloud of confusion filled Devlin's mind. Even the most sane and logical man would struggle to make sense of the conflicting tales.

"But I was told Ambrose died from a head injury, conducive to either having fallen or being hit over the head with a heavy object." A cudgel was a footpad's weapon of choice.

An image of the scene flashed into Devlin's mind. He had spent many sleepless nights abroad punishing himself for not being there for his brother. He had imagined pools of blood. Vacant eyes staring at the heavens. A body, blue with the chill of death.

A gentle hand on his back drew Devlin to the present, and he turned to find Juliet at his side. The compassion in her eyes touched him deeply, gave him the strength to probe the baron further.

Devlin swallowed to clear the lump in his throat. "And so you want the letters your daughter wrote because they incriminate you in my brother's murder?"

The baron would have no option but to flee the country if evidence of the duel came to light. If the authorities caught him before he left London, the lord might well hang. And the discovery would lend credence should anyone suspect that it was Ambrose who chose not to marry.

The look of resignation in Bromfield's eyes told Devlin he was correct in his assumption. "The injuries suggest you did not shoot my brother. Did you lose your temper and hit him with your pistol? Did you bribe his second to keep silent?"

"Ambrose Drake was dead when we arrived. The stubborn fool refused to name a second. Had he taken a man with him no doubt he might have fought off the footpads who attacked him for his purse."

All the air in the room seemed to dissipate. He could almost feel Ambrose's presence fading as his life ebbed away. "And your second can verify this?" Devlin would have been his brother's second had he been at home.

"Mr Middle, my man of business, acted on my behalf," the baron informed.

Of course he did.

Juliet slipped her small hand into Devlin's and squeezed. "But I don't understand," she said. "A witness came forward to say he had seen Ambrose meeting a male lover on the common."

The baron grumbled under his breath. "A witness I paid in an attempt to save Hannah's reputation."

"God damn!" Devlin cried. "You've led us on a merry dance this last week. You're a conniving, devious bastard who will happily ruin another man's reputation to save your own."

Devlin thought back to the threats made by Biggs. How easy would it be to loosen a wheel, to saw through the axel on Bromfield's travelling chariot? How easy would it be to snap the baron's neck and blame it on his horse?

"You should leave this house and take Hannah with you." Juliet's calm voice broke through the chaos wreaking havoc with Devlin's mind. "Leave now, before my husband takes vengeance for the cruel way you treated his brother."

Devlin couldn't breathe.

He couldn't blink.

He could barely see a foot in front of him.

"Get out!" Juliet cried when the baron failed to respond. "And never darken our door again."

The baron rose slowly from the chair and skirted around the desk as if being careful not to disturb a deadly predator. When he reached the door, he turned back. "If you find Hannah's letters, I hope you will see fit to return them."

Good God. Were there no limits to man's effrontery?

"Get out," Devlin repeated, his tone as cold and bitter as a Siberian wind.

Still fraught with an oppressive tension, the room felt stifling. An intense relief should have settled in Devlin's bones. Now he knew what had happened to Ambrose. The consensus had always leaned to the notion that he'd been attacked by footpads. Had a vicious assault taken place? Had Ambrose fallen and hit his head? Devlin would never know. But something about the baron's story rang true.

Juliet's dainty hand came up to cup his face. "I'm so sorry, Devlin. My father is a cruel man. I only wish I could do something to make things right again."

He took her hand and pressed a kiss to her palm. "Ambrose's fate was written long before we met. There is nothing anyone can do to change that."

"No," she said in a soft whisper. Water welled in her eyes. "I hate to see you in pain. All I want for us is peace, but …" Her words faded yet he got the distinct impression there was so much more she wanted to say.

"What is it, Juliet? Tell me. Do not keep me in the dark." He would rather hear the truth than feigned words of comfort or lies.

A frustrated sigh breezed from her lips. "While I believe the baron's story about the duel, about Ambrose's fate, and the reason for telling their spiteful tales, something bothers me."

Devlin took a moment to examine his own feelings. His stomach churned. The hairs on his nape prickled with apprehension. Every instinct told him their battle was far from over.

"Do your concerns have anything to do with what we learnt from Mr Biggs?"

Her eyes widened. "Yes. How did you know?"

Devlin shrugged. "Because my heart tells me something is amiss, despite the fact my mind is trying its utmost to convince me the matter is closed."

"I saw the way Mr Biggs examined the letter. When I informed him it was a letter from Hannah to Ambrose, he screwed it up into a ball and discarded it without a second thought."

"And you're wondering why he would do that if that was the letter the baron sought?"

"Precisely."

"Then Bromfield wants letters written to my grandmother, just as Biggs suggested."

"What other explanation is there?"

Devlin considered dragging the baron back to the study, torturing him until he told them the truth. But the man was rotten to the core, and he wanted him far away from Blackwater, far away from Juliet.

"Then our search for the missing letters has only just begun."

CHAPTER SEVENTEEN

Through the window in the study, Juliet watched her father's chariot charge down the drive at breakneck speed. Behind her, Devlin sat deep in conversation with Dariell, who had witnessed the baron storm from the room and mount the stairs as if the end of the world were nigh.

For fear of what Devlin might do to the baron or Hannah should they say anything untoward, Juliet had persuaded him to remain in the study. One could not trust a word that left the baron's mouth, and so it was pointless pressing him for more information.

Even so, she believed her father had challenged Ambrose to a duel. It made perfect sense. Explained why a man of Ambrose's ilk would wander the common at an unreasonable hour.

"The baron, he is a devious character," Dariell said. "Of that, there is no doubt. But when a man lives for his reputation, he does not commit murder."

Devlin snorted. "So you believe his story, believe that Ambrose died at the hands of footpads?"

"Was his watch not recovered from the pawnbrokers? Did the trail not lead to a man suspected of a spate of thefts?"

"A man who conveniently disappeared."

"Disappeared, or fled to escape the hangman's noose?"

The tension in the air pressed down on Juliet's shoulders. It was *her* father who had unwittingly caused Ambrose's death, *her* sister's vicious lies that forced Devlin to seek revenge. She had to do something to ease her husband's pain. Dwelling on the past was of no use to anyone.

Juliet turned to Devlin. "It is easy to invent stories to account for unanswered questions. But are our efforts not better served focusing on what we can achieve now?"

"Indeed." Dariell smiled. "I could not have phrased it better, madame."

Pride filled Juliet's chest. Mr Dariell had a way of instilling confidence, of enhancing a person's sense of worth.

"Neither of us can shake the feeling that there is more to this than we first imagined." Juliet crossed the room to her husband's side and placed her hand on his shoulder. "We must look to our intuition to guide us now."

"Come. You must move your thoughts out of your head," Dariell said in the tone of a wise mystic. He beckoned her to the empty chair next to Devlin. "You must listen to your heart." He sucked in a long breath and closed his eyes. "When you breathe deeply and shift your focus, what does your heart tell you?"

Devlin glanced at Juliet and arched a brow. "Believe it or not it does work."

She shrugged in response and came to sit in the chair beside him. Holding back a chuckle, she waited for Devlin to close his eyes, for him to slow his breathing before doing the same.

It took a few attempts to ignore the voice in her head, a voice that repeated what they already knew, that seemed to take immense pleasure from confusing matters. But as she focused on her breathing, a cloak of calmness settled around her shoulders. A deeper intelligence spoke to her then, an intelligence that said but one word—*Ambrose*.

"It all comes back to your brother," she whispered. Juliet opened her eyes to find Dariell watching them, to find a tear clinging to the corner of Devlin's eye.

Devlin's eyes sprang open. He swallowed numerous times, blinked away the tear and gritted his teeth. "I felt my brother, too."

"Good." Dariell pressed his hands together in prayer. "Now, correct me if I am wrong, but this all began with an offer of marriage, no?"

"I suppose it did," Devlin replied.

"Then we must assume Ambrose had a reason to offer for Miss Bromfield. Was it for her connections, her dowry? Was it for love?"

Juliet recalled the couple's intimate encounters in the garden. They had appeared like two people in lust as opposed to love. If Ambrose had truly loved Hannah, nothing would have prevented the marriage.

"Ambrose did not need her money." Devlin sounded affronted at the prospect. "And a family with our lineage is already well connected."

Juliet couldn't help but touch her husband's arm. "And while I witnessed them locked in many passionate clinches, they did not share the soul-deep connection that speaks of true love."

As the words left her lips, it was as if her love for Devlin multiplied inside her body, pushing and pressing for freedom, until she could no longer contain the powerful sensation. Now was not the time to tell him, but the energy radiated from her, spilling out into the room.

Perhaps Devlin felt it, too, for he took her hand in his and held it as if he had no intention of ever letting go.

"So what was his reason for offering for the lady?" Dariell asked.

Silence ensued.

After a brief time, Devlin said, "Ambrose can only have

offered out of a sense of duty. He wanted sons, enough to secure the Drake name for generations. He doubted my ability to shoulder the responsibility should it fall to me."

"What?" Juliet could not contain her surprise. "But you're the most honourable man I know. I am confident you would do everything in your power to ensure the Blackwater Estate thrived in your care."

Devlin's warm eyes settled on her. "Your faith in me touches my heart."

"It is the truth," she said, choking back a sudden surge of emotion.

A look passed between them. One that needed no explanation. One that went beyond words or gestures.

"Excellent," Dariell said, breaking the spell. "And so what would have forced a man of Ambrose's integrity to break an oath?"

"Nothing." Devlin seemed most adamant.

"Nothing?" Dariell frowned. "We know that is not true. Something prompted him to change his mind. Perhaps you should ponder that thought."

The more Dariell asked his probing questions, the more confusion melted away. Why had they not spoken to him earlier?

Devlin took a moment to answer. "Perhaps Ambrose learnt something about Miss Bromfield's character, something he found unsavoury. Perhaps she was too free with her affections."

Juliet had to agree it was a possibility. When one craved attention, inevitably some men took advantage. Though Juliet had never heard talk of a scandal, and her father would have paid handsomely to silence any gossip.

"*Oui*, it is possible. Your brother, did you say he was a godly man?"

"He inherited his piety from our parents." Devlin gave a mocking snort. It told Juliet all she needed to know about his childhood. "Some of us chose not to listen."

It was not to his detriment. Juliet would not change her husband for the world. Anyone could preach of moral principles and love for all mankind. In Juliet's limited experience, those who were truly caring did not need to force their opinions on others or ensure the whole world knew of their benevolence.

Dariell fell silent for a time before asking, "And he did not write to tell you of his betrothal? He did not write to tell you why he had a change of heart?"

"No. He wrote to tell me of our grandmother's death, mentioned a few minor problems, and I never heard from him again."

Juliet wondered how he'd come to learn of his brother's demise. Was it a blunt letter from a solicitor informing him of all he had lost, all he had gained? Was it a letter from a friend expressing their deepest condolences?

"What sort of minor problems?" It was the sudden pang in Juliet's heart that made her ask, not her logical brain. Perhaps Devlin had taken his brother's words literally. She was still hoping for a clue.

"He spoke of unrest in the house amongst the servants, which is understandable considering they'd served my grandmother most of their lives. Mrs Barbary was particularly affected by her death. Ambrose spouted something religious as a means of dealing with the matter."

Devlin rose from the chair. He crossed the room to the drinks tray, poured brandy into a crystal tumbler and swallowed the contents without pause. Juliet and Dariell declined his offer of refreshment, and so Devlin returned to his seat.

Dariell gave a curious hum. "And what were these pious words?"

"I cannot recall exactly." Devlin closed his eyes and pinched the bridge of his nose. The action seemed to prompt his memory. "Something about trusting in the will of God, that under his watchful eye the truth prevails. It was the same speech my parents recited during difficult times."

Dariell came to his feet and wandered over to the window. He stared out into the darkness. The soft glow of candlelight cast his reflection in the glass and Juliet could see him tapping his finger to his lips in thoughtful contemplation.

Devlin took the opportunity to capture her hand and bring it to his lips. His touch was warm, comforting. "I'm glad you're here," he whispered.

"I'm glad I'm here, too." There was nowhere in the world she would rather be.

Dariell muttered to himself—a host of incoherent questions judging by the tone—but then he asked, "And where is God's watchful eye?"

Juliet wasn't sure if it was a rhetorical question or if he required an answer.

"It is ... it is everywhere," she stuttered.

"*Oui.*" Dariell swung around, his eyes wide, sparkling, like a sergeant from Bow Street having stumbled upon a vital clue. "While it is my humble opinion that we are closest to the Lord in times of servitude, there is a place where we feel at one with his presence?"

"You mean in church," Devlin said.

"There is a private chapel here on the grounds is there not?" The Frenchman was already at the door before he stopped and glanced back over his shoulder. "Well, are you coming?"

Devlin rose slowly to his feet. "Coming where?"

"To church, of course."

The wind howled through the ancient building. Dark shadows danced on the stone walls. The glass in the windows looked dull, the night having swallowed the vibrant colours seen vividly during the day. It was as if God had fallen into a deep slumber and the devil had invaded his house, determined to cause mischief. A bitter chill hung in the air, biting, clawing at one's cheeks. They had left the house in a hurry, not bothering with the layers of clothing needed to keep out the cold, to protect them from the harsh elements.

"Are you going to tell me what we're doing here?" Devlin said though he did not doubt his friend's logic. Not for a second.

"Did you not listen to what I said?" Dariell sounded amused.

During the short walk from the house, a walk that saw them jog to outrun the arctic breeze that tried to catch them with its frigid fingers, Dariell had repeated his mantra.

Go where your heart leads you.

"What am I supposed to do?" Devlin shrugged. "Wander around until I receive an epiphany?"

"You must look to your heart, for there you will find your brother." Dariell clasped his hands behind his back as he examined the centuries-old flagstones. "Take a moment."

Devlin glanced at Juliet, who placed the lamp on the stone altar and held her hands in front of the flame. She must be frozen to her bones, and the thought forced him to concentrate on the task.

Devlin paced back and forth along the aisle. Various thoughts entered his head. The fact his wife might catch her death if they did not hurry back to the house being the most prominent. What he would do to the baron if murder were no longer a crime being another example.

"You're thinking, my friend." Dariell's words cut through the silence. "That is not how this works."

There was no logical explanation for the things Dariell knew. Perhaps the Lord spoke to him in a series of dreams. Perhaps he was skilled in reading people's minds, the unique language of their bodies. Perhaps everyone's destiny was written, and he was but one of the few privileged people to have viewed the book.

Juliet approached.

She placed her hand on his arm. "When would Ambrose come here? Only on Sundays? Only when he had something to confess?"

"The answer is I don't know." For most of their adult lives, they had lived on different continents. Blood bound them together. Their ancestral name gave them a joint purpose. Their parents had instilled the need for family loyalty, but as to the character of the real man behind the name, behind the position, Devlin could only guess.

An image entered Devlin's head, of a lonely man burdened with responsibility, with no one to share in his troubles. Did Ambrose kneel at the altar and pray for a good harvest? Did he beg the Lord to send him someone to love, someone to share in his triumphs and woes?

Someone like Juliet.

Overcome with a sudden surge of gratitude, of respect, of love, he drew his wife into his arms and kissed her so deeply he hoped she could taste the passion pumping through his veins.

"Your lips are cold," he said before kissing her softly one last time. "Let me carry you back to the house where it is warm."

She smiled. "Like you did on our wedding day. Except then it was because I couldn't keep up with your long strides."

It seemed like a lifetime ago. So much had happened. So much had changed. How was it his life was so blessed while Ambrose had suffered so miserably?

"That was simply an excuse to hold you close." The sudden realisation that he could never be without her sent his heart pounding against his ribs.

"And I would love nothing more than to rest my head on your shoulder again, but we must try to focus on the reason we're here."

"We're wasting our time," he whispered in the hope Dariell

wouldn't hear him, but the fellow was standing before the altar staring up at the scene portrayed by the stained glass.

When one has a moral dilemma, let God decide the outcome.

Ambrose had written that in his letter, too, but Devlin had dismissed it as just another opportunity for his pious parents to preach from beyond the grave.

Devlin wrapped his arm around Juliet's shoulder. "Come. If we're to remain here a moment longer at least stand before the candle lamp."

He drew her down the aisle to the altar, just as he had done on their wedding day, on the day she had put her trust in him. The urge to drop down onto the red velvet kneeler and give thanks came upon him once again.

Then a fierce gale blew the chapel door open, sending it smashing against the stonework. The blast of wind tore through the small building. The candle flickered in the lamp. Outside the trees creaked and groaned under the pressure. Rain pelted the tiny diamond-shaped panes.

Dariell opened the glass door on the lamp and blew out the flame. "The reverend, he has left the linen cloths draped across the altar. We cannot risk the lamp toppling over and starting a fire."

Another howling gust sent Juliet teetering backwards—from fright more than the power of the storm. Devlin stumbled back, eager to stop her falling, but caught the heel of his boot on the kneeler and almost brought them both crashing to the floor.

"Damnation." How he kept them upright he would never know. "Are you all right?"

"Yes." Juliet put her hand to her heart. "Oh, close the door, Devlin, before we're taken clean off our feet."

Devlin was more concerned his wife might catch her death, but he raced down the aisle, slammed the wooden door shut and turned the key in the lock.

"We daren't risk walking back to the house in this," he said as he strode back towards them.

Dariell had removed a linen cloth from the altar and draped it around Juliet's shoulders. "It should keep the cold out."

"Thank you, Mr Dariell."

As Devlin moved to step over the kneeler, he noticed he had ripped the velvet cushion from its wooden plinth as he'd fallen back. He crouched down to secure the padding back in place. Should Juliet trip over it in the dark she would likely twist her ankle.

"Is there something wrong?" Juliet asked when he failed to stand, when he remained rooted to the spot.

Devlin held the loose cushion in one hand while he studied the contents buried in the hollow space carved into the wood beneath. Blood surged through his veins sending his pulse racing. It wasn't the fact that the kneeler had come apart so easily. It wasn't the fact that godly intervention had led him to make the discovery. It was the fact that after searching every inch of the house in vain he had finally found a thin bundle of letters.

It didn't matter that it was dark. The smell of musty paper wafted up to his nostrils. The length of pink ribbon securing the package spoke of a feminine hand. Devlin ran the tips of his fingers over the brown spots marring the paper, marks that spoke of age, of decay.

Juliet came to stand at his side. Her sudden gasp echoed his sense of shock.

Dariell was too busy rummaging around in the oak cupboard behind the pulpit to make any comment.

"Do you think they're the letters from Hannah?" Juliet knelt down beside him. "From first glance, I am more inclined to believe they belonged to your grandmother."

The crashing of flint against steel caught their attention, and Dariell came to join them a few moments later carrying the glowing lamp.

"If a man cannot light a candle in church then there is something amiss, no?" Dariell placed the lamp on the stone floor beside them. "Well, my friend, do you intend to sit here all night, or will you examine the contents of these precious documents?"

While everyone longed to hear the truth, sometimes it brought pain, it brought problems, it brought havoc to people's lives. Devlin was the happiest he had ever been, and he couldn't help but feel some reservation.

Devlin snorted. "The selfish part of me would prefer to remain ignorant."

"But you're a man who respects honesty," Juliet said, "a man who prefers the truth to a pack of lies."

"Indeed." Devlin's fingers shook as he reached down into the small space and retrieved the letters. The same trembling fingers tugged on the bow, unravelled the ribbon and placed the pile on the floor.

"May I?" Juliet said when Devlin could do nothing but stare.

"Be my guest."

Juliet turned over the letter on top of the pile. It bore his grandmother's name, the Blackwater address scrawled in the hand of someone unused to writing letters. The childlike strokes screamed of inexperience.

"Read it," Devlin said, his tone harder than he intended. "I cannot."

Juliet took the letter and examined the broken wax seal. "It bears no significant markings, though it is impossible to distinguish minute detail in this light."

Devlin held his breath when she peeled back the folds. An eternity passed while she read silently. His heartbeat drummed in his ears in time with the frantic voice in his head that warned him to expect the worst. Whatever was written on the fragile pieces of paper, the words would be powerful.

Juliet slapped her hand over her mouth as she read. Devlin

could tell from the exposed whites of her eyes that the news was as damning as he suspected.

"Tell me," he commanded, not knowing what the hell to think.

"In a moment."

Juliet picked up the pile of letters, flicked to the one at the bottom and read that, too.

She read another and another.

While Dariell sat patiently in the box pew and watched with interest, Devlin thought his head might explode from the frustration that came with waiting.

Eventually, Juliet looked up at him, confusion swimming in her eyes. "I need to reread them to gain a better understanding of the situation. Some are written to your grandmother by her maid. One is a letter written by your grandmother but never sent. It reads like a confession, a confession to God."

"Juliet, please, put me out of my misery and tell me what the hell this is all about."

She swallowed and sucked in a breath. "It appears that my father is ... my father is illegitimate. It appears that my father is the son of your grandmother's maid."

CHAPTER EIGHTEEN

"Baron Bromfield's mother was a maid?" Devlin repeated for the third time. During those few minutes he had sat patiently waiting for Juliet to finish reading the missives, he knew to expect something shocking. But not this. "How is that possible? How is it no one knows the truth?"

The baron knew the truth. How else would Biggs have known about the old letters?

"I need to reread them, but I suspect your grandmother kept them as a form of penance." Juliet picked a letter from those she had laid out on the flagstone floor. After one quick look at the words hidden beneath the folds, she handed it to Devlin. "Read this one."

Dariell cleared his throat and stood. "There is no respite from this terrible weather." He cocked his head and stared at nothing in particular. The brief moment of silence was broken by the patter of rain hitting the windowpane. "But I must venture back to the house. I must leave you to study these new revelations. Valentine, he wishes us to depart before noon tomorrow, and the need for sleep calls me to my bed."

Still clutching the letter, Devlin came to his feet. He placed a hand on his friend's shoulder. "We would not have found the letters without your intervention. Had you not asked probing questions, we would still be clambering about in the dark."

Dariell's lips twitched in amusement. "This is true. Did you think I came only to sample your fine port and meet your delightful wife?"

"I would not presume to understand your mysterious motives." The letter in Devlin's hand burned for his attention. Curiosity forced him to embrace his friend and bid him goodnight. "Will you join us for breakfast in the morning?"

"Of course."

Juliet rushed to her feet and hugged the Frenchman. "Thank you, Mr Dariell. You truly are a wonder."

Dariell embraced Juliet as a father would a beloved child. In such a way that the connection went beyond the physical. In such a way that he seemed blessed to have met her. "You are everything I imagined you to be," he said cryptically before bidding them goodnight and leaving them alone in the church.

"We will stay for ten minutes, no more." Devlin scooped up the letters. "It's too cold to sit on the floor. Come."

He led her into one of the box pews, spread the letters out on the wooden shelf meant for prayer books and hymnals. "We should place them in chronological order."

"They are all dated, so the task should not be too difficult."

There were seven letters in total—six from the maid named Susan and one from Charlotte Drake. Devlin had no idea how long they spent reading each one, but an hour slipped away from them. He held Juliet close to his chest as she read them aloud for a final time.

"Evidently, the baron inherited his cold heart from his father," Juliet said with an air of melancholy. "What sort of man takes advantage of a young girl?"

Juliet referred to her father as the baron more so these last few days. Her tone contained an air of detachment when she spoke his name. Yet Devlin knew that the baron's lack of devotion caused her great pain.

"The sort of man who married a barren woman yet desperately craved a son. The sort who placed society's expectations over his love and loyalty to his wife."

The sort who saw servants as commodities, not people.

Juliet squinted at the letter in her hand. "Susan's writing is poor, but you can feel her distress leaping off the page."

Devlin focused on the letter that mattered most to him—Charlotte Drake's confession. The one placed in the kneeler so that the Lord might acknowledge the dreadful part she had played, so that the Lord might offer his forgiveness.

"During her time as mistress of Blackwater, my grandmother hired a tutor to teach the servants to read and write. My mother told me that Charlotte sought to improve the lives of those in her service." Devlin could picture the beaming look of pride on his mother's face when she spoke of the lady's altruism. "Only now do we discover that the woman was a damn hypocrite."

Juliet pursed her lips. Compassion swam in her green eyes. "Perhaps *misguided* is a more appropriate word. In encouraging Susan to carry Bromfield's child, perhaps she hoped to improve the girl's life. We know nothing of Susan's background. She might have had an ailing mother in need of medicine. There could well have been five hungry mouths to feed at home. The Bromfields might have paid her handsomely for the child."

For the first time since meeting her, Juliet's words lacked conviction. As always, she looked for the good not the corrupt. But one damning piece of information conveyed the reality of the situation.

"Juliet, the girl did not want to give up her child and begged my grandmother for her assistance."

Devlin blinked to clear the image of a frail girl sent away

from Blackwater to live with her abusers. A girl frightened and alone and left with those who cared only for the unborn babe.

"I know." Juliet sighed.

"She feared for her life," Devlin persisted, angry that a relation of his could behave so cruelly. "Someone must have taken pity on her there, for how else would she have had the means to send these letters?"

"It's clear the Bromfields trusted your grandmother. No doubt they hoped she would write to the maid, make her see that her child would have a better life."

Devlin dragged his hand down his face. Now he knew why the baron risked everything to ensure no one discovered the truth. But there were still too many questions. Questions he wasn't sure he wanted to ask. Questions that would bring unwelcome answers.

Juliet shivered at his side. She wrapped the altar cloth firmly about her shoulders.

"Let us return to the house," he said, gathering up the letters. "We can discuss the matter further while nestled beneath the coverlet."

Juliet's eyes brightened. "And how might we do that from separate rooms?" Her teasing tone sent his heart pounding.

"I thought that because it's so cold out, and because I fear the baron might return, that we could sleep together tonight." He intended to sleep with her every night and hoped she would have no complaint.

"You're frightened?" She raised a mocking brow. "Frightened of the baron?"

"Of course not. I'm frightened of leaving you alone, of not being there should anything untoward happen."

I'm frightened of losing you.

"And it would give us an opportunity to discuss the letters," he added in a logical tone, "an opportunity to *converse* privately."

A smile touched her lips. "An opportunity to converse, or an opportunity to dance?"

"Both."

"Both? But it will soon be dawn."

Devlin shrugged. Some things were more important than sleep. "After what we've learnt, I doubt either of us will sleep tonight."

"Then let us make haste." Juliet stood. "You want to talk and dance, and I want you to make love to me again."

Blood pooled heavy in his loins at the prospect. Her honesty fed his desire. Oh, his wife had a way of making him forget everything else in the world existed.

Devlin stood, too. He took hold of her chin and kissed her once on the mouth. "Do you like the feel of me pushing inside you, Juliet?" After a night of lies and deceit, he needed to hear the truth. He needed the only thing in his life that was real.

"Like it?" she said, a little breathless. "Devlin, I have never felt more complete." She cupped his cheek. "Surely by now you know what you mean to me." After swallowing deeply, she gazed into his eyes for the longest time. "I love you."

The sudden rush of emotion almost choked him.

The power of it almost knocked him off his feet.

How had this magical thing happened?

They should have been wrong for each other in so many ways, yet everything about their relationship felt right—felt perfect.

Devlin kissed her then, with a passion that he'd spent a life-time saving just for her. "You're the love I never thought to find. You're the love I thought denied me. You're everything to me, Juliet. Everything."

"Then take me home and show me all that is in your heart."

Juliet pushed the thin bundle of letters down between her chemise and stays. They hurried back to the house. The rain pelted their faces. The wind whipped at their clothes. The cold air nipped at their cheeks. But still, they stopped on the stone bridge and kissed each other until they were panting, until he could think of nothing other than filling her full.

After hiding the letters under the mattress in her room, they stripped naked and slipped into bed. Devlin covered her body, and she wrapped her lithe legs around him.

"Don't wait," Juliet whispered. "I need to join with you now."

Making love to her had a new meaning tonight. While lust raged through his veins, wild and hot and rampant, his heart swelled to the point it might burst from his chest. The urge to make her understand the depth of his emotions, to speak the truth plainly, pushed to the fore.

"I am in love with you, Juliet." He came up on one elbow for fear of squashing her. "You captured my heart, took me as your prisoner the moment we met."

The smile that warmed her face this time was brighter than any he had ever seen. Happiness swam in her eyes. "And despite being intimidated by your size, you intrigued me, Mr Drake."

"Do I intrigue you now?" he drawled as his hard cock pressed against her thigh.

"More than you know."

"I love you, Juliet." Oh, it felt so good to say it.

"I love you, Devlin Drake." She stretched her hands down to his buttocks, dug her nails into his flesh, urged him to hurry. "Show me."

A wave of ecstasy swept through him as he entered her body in one long, deep thrust. He had everything he'd ever wanted. The only thing he needed. Her body was used to him now, accepted him with ease.

"Tell me you'll sleep with me every night," he said as he withdrew only to enter her again in a slow, sensual slide.

"Oh, I want ... I want nothing more than to lie in your arms each night," she panted.

"No one will ever come between us." He pushed deeper this

time. Harder. "No one will ever tear us apart." He would throttle the baron if he tried.

"Yes … we will …we will always be together."

"Always," he said, trying to ignore the sudden pang in his chest that said their troubles were far from over.

CHAPTER NINETEEN

"You must promise to visit us soon." Lydia took hold of Juliet's hands as they stood in the entrance hall. "Having lived with each other for the last five years, it does the men good to spend time together." Lydia smiled. "And it would give us time to converse privately."

"I would love to see the old stone circle you mentioned." At dinner, Juliet had been fascinated to learn of the ancient monument. "It makes one think of druid rituals and dancing naked in the moonlight with flowers in one's hair."

Lydia chuckled. "Well, it can be a little cold to bare all in November. Perhaps it is something we can do when spring comes again." Drawing Juliet into an embrace, she whispered, "Take care of Devlin. You love him, don't you?"

"Is it so obvious?"

"The love that radiates from both of you is blinding." Lydia straightened. "Well, we must be on our way. We have left Ada to train the new maids, and lord knows what chaos we will find on our return."

"Devlin told me you hired staff without experience or references." Juliet admired anyone willing to help those in need, anyone willing to give the downtrodden a chance.

It drew her thoughts back to Charlotte Drake. After studying her letter again this morning, it was clear the woman felt remorse, shame even, for having coerced her maid to give up her child.

What happened to Susan?

She did not return to work at Blackwater, and there were no letters to offer clues as to the poor girl's fate. Juliet had taken the opportunity before breakfast to ask Mrs Barbary if she knew of the maid whose position she had taken. As always, the house-keeper gave the impression she had better things to do with her time than gossip about the past. But she did recall the mistress mentioning the girl's name on occasion.

"Greystone is a rather unconventional man," Lydia said, drag-ging Juliet out of her reverie. Love for her husband radiated from every aspect of her countenance, too. "He likes to help the disad-vantaged and relies more on instinct than references when it comes to such matters. As I'm sure they all do."

One did not need to be a wise scholar to know from where the men took their guidance. "Mr Dariell is an influential friend and confidant. One with a surprising level of insight, and remarkable intellect."

"Indeed." Lydia rubbed Juliet's arm. "Write to me and let me know when you might visit."

Again, the comment drew Juliet's thoughts back to the letters. An urgency to make sense of it all held her in its grip. Devlin was of a similar mind too, for no sooner had they waved goodbye to their guests than her husband suggested returning to her bedchamber.

"I must take Rufus out at noon," she said, glancing at the long-case clock and realising she had half an hour until she needed to be in the stables. "You know as well as I that disturbing his routine will set me back days in his training regime."

Devlin raised an arrogant brow and smiled. "Will you not surrender to me, my love? Will you not admit that I have won this wager? The dog is wild. Under no circumstances will I let him run amok in this house."

Juliet would not be deterred. "Rufus knows I come for him at noon and I shall not disappoint."

"Not even to spend time alone with your husband?"

"Do not try to persuade me to break my oath, Devlin." She straightened her back. "You must know that when I make a promise, I keep it. Is integrity not one of the qualities you require in a wife?"

"It is one of the many qualities I admire in you." He captured her chin between his fingers and pressed his lips to hers. Though chaste in its delivery, she felt the tingles all the way to her toes.

"Come," she said, fighting the temptation to straddle him and soothe away all his woes. "We have half an hour to discuss our theories regarding the letters."

"A discussion in your bedchamber is exactly what I need," he teased.

Oh, the thought of slipping into bed next to him sent her pulse racing, but there would be time for amorous activities later. "We must decide what to do with the letters."

"I've thought long and hard about that. We will use them to bribe your father." The razor-sharp edge to his tone said he was serious. "I'll not have him interfering in our lives, threatening you. Nor will I tolerate your sister's vicious tongue a moment longer."

Juliet glimpsed the dark devil men feared.

"But should we not return them to the church, honour your grandmother's wishes?" She thought to suggest they burn them, but she could not interfere with his grandmother's quest for forgiveness. Clearly, Charlotte Drake had kept the letters for a reason.

Then a terrible thought struck her as she recalled her father's earlier comment.

"Devlin, when I spoke to my father before dinner he said the letters contained incriminating evidence, that Ambrose had confirmed they were in his possession. I assumed he referred to the duel."

"And now you think he was referring to his illegitimacy?"

Juliet had worn *her* illegitimacy like a noose around her neck. Over the years, she had learnt to breathe a little despite the constrictions. She knew her place, how many steps she could take before the rope grew taut and rubbed painful welts into her skin.

The baron would never cope with the restrictions, with the direct cuts, with the disdain directed his way. No wonder the lord had taken extreme measures to ensure the truth remained hidden.

"A man with my father's power and position might escape punishment for partaking in a duel, especially when Ambrose died from an injury to his head." Juliet took a step closer to her husband and placed her hand on his arm. Touching him banished any anxiety. "But he would suffer greatly if anyone discovered he was the son of a maid."

A brief silence ensued.

Devlin stared at a nondescript point on the tiled floor as he considered her comment. When he eventually looked up to meet her gaze, she saw sorrow lingering in his obsidian eyes.

"Then in a random twist of fate," he began with an air of melancholy, "my grandmother's letters led to Ambrose's death. I am convinced that news of the baron's illegitimacy caused him to end his betrothal to your sister."

"And consequently, led to the duel that brought your brother to the common at dawn."

"Indeed."

Fate could be cruel as well as kind—she knew that.

But what should they do with the information? Would her

father ever give up his search for the evidence that would ruin his beloved reputation?

"I should take Rufus out," Juliet said in the hope the cold air might clear the cloud of confusion. "While I'm gone, think about your need for vengeance. Decide whether you truly want to approach my father and tell him what we have discovered."

Devlin pursed his lips. "I shall be in the study, and will—"

The creak of a hinge drew their attention to the closed door at the end of the hall. Perhaps Juliet imagined hearing the doorknob rattle, imagined the faint patter of footsteps echoing down the stone staircase that led to the servants' quarters.

"We will discuss the matter upon your return," Devlin continued. "Somewhere that guarantees privacy." The beginnings of a wicked grin graced his lips. "Somewhere quiet. Somewhere secluded."

The tug deep in her core almost forced her to cancel Rufus' daily outing. But there was nothing like the thrum of anticipation to heat the blood.

Placing her palms on her husband's impressive chest, Juliet came up on her tiptoes and kissed him once on the mouth.

"I shall not be long. Pray that Rufus doesn't run away, else I shall have to spend the afternoon looking for him."

"Trust me. That dog will feel the devil's wrath if you're not back here in an hour."

With a light heart and a skip in her step, Juliet led Rufus from the stables and out along the path that ran parallel to the manicured lawns. She would take him over the stone bridge to the open fields where he could run to his heart's content. The gardeners forever complained about him digging in the rose beds or watering the shrubs.

The nip in the air stung her cheeks. After cold hours spent in the church the previous evening, she was thankful for the thick travelling cloak draped around her shoulders. Besides, chasing after Rufus would soon warm her bones.

"Rufus!" Juliet stopped walking and waited for the hound to turn and look at her. "Sit, Rufus," she said, holding her hand aloft as a signal of intention.

For once, the dog did exactly as he was told, and Juliet rewarded him with a pat on the head and a small chunk of dried beef she'd saved from last night's dinner.

Despite all that had happened with the baron, happiness swelled inside. She wanted to shout, to stand on the stone bridge and tell the world she loved Devlin Drake. Her husband stimulated her mind, invaded her thoughts, her heart, her body. He soothed and excited with his commanding presence, a presence that was as potent as any drug.

She craved his company, his voice, his mouth, his touch.

Oh, Lord!

With a quick shake of the head, she forced herself from her musings.

Poor Rufus. He deserved her undivided attention. How else was she to train the hound and win the wager? Sinful thoughts flooded her mind. What would she ask of her husband should she succeed in her task?

How ironic that fate chose that moment to show her how far she was from achieving her goal.

Nose to the ground, Rufus had sniffed out a scent. He bounded over to the rhododendrons, chewed on something he'd found hidden there before darting off on the hunt. Juliet chased after him, calling his name and issuing commands, but he refused to listen and charged about as merry as a march hare.

"Rufus!"

The hound disappeared from sight.

Oh, the devil!

She had promised Devlin she would be but an hour.

Juliet hurried across the lawn, caught sight of Rufus shooting down the narrow flight of steps leading into the icehouse. There could only be one reason why he would venture in there—the daft dog was chasing a rabbit.

"Rufus!"

The iron gate leading into the icehouse was wide open.

How odd.

With a clawing sense of trepidation, Juliet descended the worn stone steps. One look at the dark, dank tunnel beyond the gate and her stomach quivered. A strange whirring sound sent her nerves scattering. But then hadn't Devlin said something about it being an unusual design, that a large wooden wheel assisted with drainage?

The dog's bark echoed through the chambers.

"Rufus! Come here." Juliet waited, then stepped over the threshold.

An earthy tang invaded her nostrils. The temperature plummeted. Every hair on her arms stood to attention. When she exhaled, puffs of white mist penetrated the darkness, swirling into the atmosphere like a ghostly apparition.

"Rufus!"

With her hands braced on the wall for support, she edged forward, past the first chamber piled with straw that acted as insulation. A sliver of daylight in the middle chamber drew her to the room with a mound of ice in one corner. The groundsmen were waiting for the first hard frost of winter to replenish supplies. The fast-flowing water from the stream powered the giant wheel, the race serving as a means of draining the water should the temperature rise and the ice melt.

Juliet pushed at the iron railings leading into the chamber and stepped into the room. Worried that Rufus had fallen into the water channel, she shuffled closer to the wheel. Fear crept across her scalp. She could feel someone watching, their beady eyes boring into her back.

Then she heard Rufus charging along the tunnel behind her, heard the iron gate slam shut and the clunk of a latch sliding into the lock. Juliet swung around, noted a hooded figure on the opposite side of the iron bars.

"Wait!" Juliet called. Panic rose like a wave in her stomach. "Don't leave me in here."

Had the groundsman not seen her?

She darted forward, her legs moving before her mind could form a thought, her heartbeat pounding in her ears.

Disturbed by her sudden movement, the figure shrank back against the corridor wall, back into the shadows.

"Open the door," Juliet demanded, though the nervous thread in her voice made her sound desperate. Weak. "Can you hear me?"

Silence breezed cold through the tunnel to prickle the hairs on her nape. Silence loud enough to overshadow the creaking of the wooden wheel or the rush of running water.

A blast of breath left the figure's mouth in a puff of white smoke.

"What do you want?" Juliet kept her voice calm. It suddenly occurred to her that the clawing fear in the air was not her own.

A croak left her captor's mouth. "Tell me where I can find the letters."

Juliet considered the slender silhouette, the feminine ring to her tone despite the woman's desperate attempt to disguise her voice. Hannah would not hide in the darkness. She would confront her quarry, ready to parry swords, ready for battle.

"Tell me where I can find the letters," the woman repeated, "and you can leave here unharmed."

"Letters? You will need to be specific." Juliet's mind whirred quicker than the wheel. Each time she came to the same conclusion. She recognised the harsh edge to the woman's voice. "But I think you need to explain why they are so important you would lock your mistress in the icehouse, Mrs Barbary."

Silence ensued.

Juliet could feel the uncertainty, the confusion, filling the space between them. Perhaps it was foolish of her to speak the housekeeper's name aloud. Perhaps the woman's only dilemma now was how to dispose of her mistress and make it appear as a terrible accident.

"Explain why you want them, and I shall tell you what you need to know," Juliet said, offering an olive branch. "I trust you speak of the letters written to Charlotte Drake."

Mrs Barbary took a step forward. A sliver of daylight streaming down from the round hole in the ceiling caught the side of her face. The hard, disapproving stare Juliet had witnessed too many times to mention was replaced by one of panic, of pain.

"Are you trying to protect your mistress?" Juliet said, aware that Charlotte Drake had encouraged her maid to give up her child. "Is it that you do not wish for others to learn of her dealings with the Bromfields?"

"The Bromfields." Mrs Barbary almost spat the bitter words from her mouth. "You're all the same. Evil is in your blood."

"And I do not disagree with your assessment." How could she after all she had learnt about her father, about her grandparents? "But I am not a Bromfield. I am a Duval, now a Drake. If you open the door, we can discuss this problem in a rational manner."

The tip of Juliet's nose was numb, her fingers, too, despite the fact she wore gloves. The thought of spending any more time in the icehouse chilled her to her bones.

"It's too late for that."

"It is never too late."

Mrs Barbary shuffled on the spot. The longer she stood there, the more agitated she became. "Just tell me where I might find the letters. I know you have them. Three years, three long years I've searched the house."

Three years?

Had Charlotte Drake confessed hours before her death? Had she asked Mrs Barbary to destroy the letters but died before she told her where to find them?

But there was more to the story than that. There had to be.

Mrs Barbary's actions would see her swing from the gallows. Did Charlotte Drake's reputation mean so much that the woman would risk her life?

"You were Charlotte's maid once," Juliet said. "Did she teach you to read and write? Was she kind and loving? I'm told she cared for her staff." No doubt that was her penance after the abominable way she had treated her maid Susan. "I need to know that Charlotte trusted you before I can tell you anything."

Mrs Barbary took another step forward. The woman seemed changed. The solid shell had cracked to reveal a trembling wreck hidden beneath. But fear and frenzy went hand in hand just like night and day. And it was plain to see that a catalogue of emotions battled beneath the surface.

"Charlotte loved you like a daughter," Juliet said, hoping to prompt the woman to speak, to confirm or deny the statement. "You must have been close, considering the time you've spent at Blackwater."

A sob caught in the back of the woman's throat, but she fought to keep it at bay. "It was all a lie. An ugly lie that tainted every happy memory."

"Did Charlotte tell you something before she died? Did she make her last confession, to you her trusted confidante?"

Had Charlotte shattered the illusion?

"Trusted confidante?" Mrs Barbary blurted. "The woman lied to me for fifty years."

Lord, they were going around in circles. Frustration wrung tight in her chest. Juliet could not reveal a family secret to a servant. The only way to gain any ground was to incite the woman to speak.

Juliet gripped the iron bars and squeezed in the hope of getting the blood flowing to her fingers. "Charlotte was everything a mistress should aspire to be," she said in a tone the housekeeper often used to show her disdain. "I cannot believe a lady of her standing would lie to anyone. I can only assume that you have committed a great sin and that the evidence of it is written somewhere amongst the missives."

Juliet stamped her foot—not for effect but because her feet were as frozen as the blocks of ice stored in the underground room.

"Oh, you would not say that if you knew how she spoke about your family." Her thin mouth twisted in contempt. "She would never have permitted her grandson to marry Bromfield's bastard."

The words hit like a stone to the throat—hard, stealing her breath, leaving an uncomfortable pain that made it hard to swallow. The urge to shrink within herself, to hide, to know her place, left her shoulders slumped, her head bowed.

The wheel churned in the water, creaking, groaning, taunting, the sound growing as loud as Hannah's mocking jeers.

You're no good. You don't belong here. You don't belong anywhere.

"You would never have been mistress of this house if Charlotte Drake were alive." Mrs Barbary's blunt tone sliced through the air, intending to maim.

"Then clearly you do not know your new master very well," Juliet heard herself say. "No one tells Devlin Drake what to do." Devlin was a man who cared nothing for propriety, for other people's opinions.

You're the love I never thought to find. You're the love I thought denied me.

Devlin's words bulled into her mind, knocking away all doubts.

Then a thought struck her. The baron's illegitimacy affected Hannah, too.

"Did Charlotte disapprove of Ambrose's ch-choice of bride?" Juliet's teeth chattered. "Did she force him to end his betrothal to Miss Bromfield?"

"Of course she disapproved." Mrs Barbary snorted. "I was there that night, hiding in the shadows during their heated argument. She told him all about the baron's tainted bloodlines, about the role she played in ruining her young maid's life."

Mrs Barbary knew everything.

So why did she need the letters?

"Ambrose did not strike me as a man who would condone her behaviour." But from what Devlin had said, a pure bloodline was on Ambrose's list of criteria he looked for in a bride, along with wealth and reputation.

Mrs Barbary shook her head. "Ambrose was furious. Ashamed of what she had done. But still, he did his grandmother's bidding."

And in doing so, he brought about his own demise.

Perhaps the arctic chill in the chamber made it difficult to think clearly. Perhaps there were so many conflicting tales, Juliet didn't know what to believe.

"And so you despise the Bromfields for what happened to Ambrose." Juliet was only repeating what Devlin had told her. "You despise the Bromfields for corrupting your beloved mistress. And the fact she kept the secret causes you pain."

It was the only logical explanation.

A growl resonated from the back of Mrs Barbary's throat. Fire flashed in her hard eyes. Anger—hot and volatile—collided with the frigid air.

"You're all the same," Mrs Barbary raged. "Poor Charlotte. Poor Ambrose. What about Susan? No one mentioned Susan. No one mentioned the girl abused by those in a position to know better." Now the housekeeper had started ranting she didn't stop. "No one mentioned me. A girl taken from her home at the age of twelve. A girl who believed her mistress cared for her when all the time her love and devotion served her own ends."

Juliet simply stared and tried to absorb the constant stream of information.

"For fifty years I've lived a lie. She took me in to repay a debt." Mrs Barbary swiped the air. "I had to hide in the dressing room and listen to her tell her grandson how she had done her duty by me to make amends for what she had done to my sister, Susan."

Susan? Susan was Mrs Barbary's sister?

Heavens above!

"And all these years I thought my sister died from a fever while serving at the Bromfields' house. Yet she died giving birth to that bastard's by-blow. And it was Charlotte Drake who condemned her to death."

Ice-cold fingers crept up Juliet's back. She shivered. Tried to stop the morbid thought entering her head, but it swept through her like a bitter wind, leaving her trembling inside.

"How did Charlotte Drake die?" Juliet asked in so quiet a voice it was barely audible.

Mrs Barbary's vacant stare was unnerving. "She breathed her last breath as I smothered her with a pillow," the housekeeper said in a tone that would keep the blocks of ice in the corner frozen for months. "It was only fitting that she died in her bed, too."

The blood drained from Juliet's face. She felt sick to her stomach.

But it was not pity for Charlotte Drake that brought the tears to her eyes. It was the realisation that she knew too much now. That this woman had murdered once and would easily do so again.

"Now tell me where I might find the letters," Mrs Barbary said in the tone that always sent the maids scurrying.

"So you might shame the baron?"

"So I can destroy them and protect my sister's memory."

They were not Juliet's letters to give away.

It was not her decision to make.

"I cannot tell you what you want to know."

Mrs Barbary pressed her sallow face to the bars. "Then I shall return in an hour. Let's see how you fare once the cold bites your bones."

CHAPTER TWENTY

Devlin stared at the array of letters spread over his desk. He had retrieved them from beneath the mattress in Juliet's bedchamber intending to reread them. But somehow it did not seem important, and he couldn't quite rouse the enthusiasm.

The baron's version of the events surrounding Ambrose's death rang true. All evidence pointed to Ambrose being attacked with a cudgel by footpads. Even so, Devlin struggled with the fact a man of Ambrose's intelligence could be so foolish.

But Devlin had come home to restore his brother's reputation, to punish Miss Bromfield for her wicked lies and tales. The letters gave him the leverage needed to succeed in the task. The Bromfields would pay. But another powerful emotion replaced the vengeance that once burned in Devlin's veins.

Love.

Every nerve, every fibre of his body thrummed with this new sensation.

He could not keep his hands off his wife. Indeed, when she returned, he would lock the study door and take comfort in her sweet voice, in the potent scent that clung to her skin. He would tell her again what she meant to him, that she had saved a devil of a man from a life in hell. He would make love to her, show her the depth of his passion.

Lord, he was working his way through every room in the house, replacing a miserable memory for one that heated his blood. In the dining room, Juliet made him forget about the raps on the knuckles with the cutlery, the taunts that clumsy boys must learn obedience. In the ballroom, he forgot that a beast looked ugly seated on the bench, that a man his size lacked the skill to compose music. And when he made love to his wife on the desk in the study, he would forget the lecture that said he was too wild and unpredictable to be the master of Blackwater.

Devlin glanced at the mantel clock.

A fire in his chest ignited when he imagined Juliet bursting in through the door, her cheeks rosy, a beaming smile illuminating her face.

He waited. Ten minutes felt like an hour.

Where the hell had she got to?

Another twenty minutes passed.

The clock chimed two.

Frustration itched beneath his skin. Devlin stood, stared out of the window for a time.

An uneasy sense of foreboding overcame him, forced him to wind the bell on the wall behind and ring for Withers.

A light rap on the door signalled the butler. "You rang, sir?"

What was he supposed to say? Where the hell is my wife?

"I want you to check with the stable hands and see if Mrs Drake has returned with Rufus."

No doubt the hound had taken to his heels again. And Juliet would not return without him. The air outside was glacial. A raw, biting wind meant it was too cold to spend more than an hour outdoors. Was this what his life had come to? Worrying about the wind, the rain, about anything that might see his happiness dragged from underneath him?

"I shall visit the stables at once, sir." Withers inclined his head, turned in the slow, methodical way that was supposed to instill calm and confidence but in this instance did the opposite.

"Never mind, Withers, I shall go myself."

The voice in Devlin's head shouted for him not to overreact. The crippling ache in his heart made him dart through the corridors as if the barn was on fire.

Rufus was not in the stables.

"I saw Mrs Barbary chasing after him some time ago," a groom shouted. "I expect he ran away from Mrs Drake again." But Devlin was already racing back to the house.

Devlin found Mrs Barbary in his study, gaping at the letters on the desk. Her face was ashen. Perhaps seeing his grandmother's name on the missives brought back memories of the past.

"Oh, Mr Drake." The housekeeper jumped to attention. She seemed unsettled. "I came looking for you. I came to—"

"Yes. I know. Rufus is up to his tricks again and has run away from his mistress."

Mrs Barbary nodded. "He came bounding across the lawn. I tried to catch him, but the beast is too quick for a woman of my age."

"And where is Mrs Drake?" Impatience rang in every word.

"Mrs Drake?" The housekeeper glanced at the letters again. "I've not seen Mrs Drake since she took Rufus for a walk."

"And where does she usually take him?" A gnawing feeling of dread settled around him when the long-case clock struck the half hour.

After the incident in the brook, the hours spent in the church last night and now the lengthy time spent out of doors, Juliet would be lucky if she caught just a chill.

"Mrs Drake takes him far from the house so that he might run and expend his energy."

God damn, she could be anywhere.

He dragged his hand down his face and sighed. "Have a hot bath drawn in her chamber. Have Tilly warm her bed with a pan. And ask Cook to make a tisane. I shall see if I can find her."

There was no time to wait for the housekeeper's reply. Indeed, he was at the study door before a prickle of awareness forced him back to the desk. He gathered the letters together and stuffed them into the inside pocket of his coat.

Mrs Barbary watched his every move.

Devlin was already out past the orchard, staring at the vast expanse of fields when he decided the search would be easier on horseback.

Then another thought struck him.

Would Juliet have ventured so far after what happened with Biggs? The blackguard had not returned to Blackwater and was probably hundreds of miles away by now. Still, would she have taken the risk?

The icy wind whipped at his hair and stung his cheeks to remind him that time was precious, and he could not linger about too long.

Heading back through the orchard, he took the shortest route via the walled garden. As he passed the potting sheds, he heard scratching and whining. Sad eyes and a slobbering mouth met him as he stared in through the small window. Rufus! No doubt the wayward dog had darted into the shed, and the door had closed behind him.

"You have a lot to answer for," Devlin said as he turned the knob.

The door was locked.

He looked around, hoped to glimpse one of the many gardeners or groundsmen who serviced the estate, but to no avail.

Rufus barked. The hound scratched at the door as if the air was swiftly diminishing and he couldn't catch his breath. In the end, Devlin had no choice but to barge the door with his shoulder until it burst open and almost came clean off its hinges.

As soon as the dog was free of his prison, he bounded off towards the gravel path that snaked around the grounds.

Devlin cursed the damn animal. He took a moment to ensure Juliet was not trapped inside the shed and then he broke into a run, chased Rufus as far as the manicured lawns.

The dog stopped and waited.

Was this just a game?

Did he take pleasure in running his master and mistress around ragged?

No sooner had Devlin reached the dog than he ran off again. This time, Devlin refused to follow, but the hound returned to bite and tug his coattails.

"What is it?"

Was Rufus trying to tell him something?

Would he lead Devlin to Juliet?

Devlin swallowed his annoyance. "Then take me to her. Show me where she is."

He curbed his temper when the dog bolted towards the icehouse, ignored the urge to shout when Rufus flew down the stone steps and sat patiently in front of the iron gate.

The day was already bitter. If Rufus thought to take him into the underground chamber, he could think again. But when Devlin failed to open the gate, Rufus pawed the ground as if he intended to dig his way under.

The gate was unlocked.

The hinges groaned as Devlin yanked it open.

Rufus pushed through the gap and darted into the dark corridor. Devlin followed. It had been fifteen years or more since he had been in the storage room, was just a boy when he and his brother used to hide and play tricks.

God's teeth, it was cold.

A shiver ran the length of his spine.

The whirring of the old wheel and Rufus' loud bark drew him

towards the large chamber. Daylight shone through the delivery hole in the ceiling, illuminating the strange scene within.

With his teeth bared and a vibrating growl rattling in his throat, Rufus stood before a cloaked figure, ready to pounce.

The person was too tall to be Juliet.

"Get away from me." The woman's voice echoed through the stone room. She shuffled back towards the narrow channel sunken into the floor.

Rufus prowled forward.

"Who are you? What the hell are you doing down here?" Devlin entered the chamber, noted another figure curled into a ball on the floor near the ice pile and knew it was Juliet. He was at her side in seconds. "Juliet? Can you hear me?" He took hold of her shoulders and turned her onto her back.

Good God, her lips were blue, her cheeks a pale shade of grey. Fear held him in a vice-like grip, dragging his breath from his lungs in ragged pants.

"Speak to me," he begged. "Juliet."

He needed to get her outside, into the house, somewhere warm.

Devlin stripped off his coat and draped it over her frozen frame, then he scooped her up into his arms. Panic took him again when he failed to feel any heat from her body.

"Did you do this?" he snapped, hugging his wife close to his chest. "Do you work for the baron? Did Biggs send you?"

The woman tried to skirt around Rufus, but he jumped and bounded until she had no choice but to take another step back. The hood of her cloak fell down to reveal a familiar face.

"Mrs Barbary?" Shock prevented him from forming another word.

"Shame on you," she cried, clearly distraught. "Shame on all of you."

Her final step sent her tumbling into the frigid water in the channel. Perhaps she thought to swim the length, that the water had to go somewhere and it was her only means of escape. But the sodden ends of her cloak got caught in the wooden structure, dragging her beneath the water, trapping her beneath the wheel.

Cradling his wife in his arms, Devlin rushed to the edge. Juliet was still breathing, but if he left the chamber Mrs Barbary would surely drown. The woman had served his family faithfully for years. And yet she had lied to him when he had asked her about Juliet.

He touched Juliet's cheek. "Stay with me, love. I shall soon have you warm again."

Her eyes fluttered open, and she whispered, "Devlin. You came."

Torn between his heart and his conscience, he did the only thing he could. "Rufus will sit with you for a minute or two and then I shall take you home."

Placing Juliet down gently on the stone floor, he summoned Rufus. "Lie down." Devlin pointed to a spot next to his wife's body. Surprisingly, the dog did as he was told. He settled beside Juliet, so close she was bound to feel the heat radiating from his large body.

Devlin wasted no time. He lay on the floor and reached down beneath the wheel. His fingers brushed the sodden fabric of Mrs Barbary's cloak, and with two hands he grabbed and tugged as hard as he could.

After numerous failed attempts, he finally found the strength to drag her out, to heave her up onto the floor of the chamber. Finding her unresponsive, he turned her head to one side and pumped her chest, waiting for her to cough, to spew the water in her lungs. With no sign of a pulse, he spent another minute trying to rouse her, but it was hopeless.

Failure weighed heavy in his heart, but Juliet was his priority now.

"Perhaps you're not daft after all," he said as he patted Rufus on the head.

Hauling Juliet into his arms, Devlin raced to the house. Rufus ran, too, barking to alert the servants of their approach.

Juliet's eyes flickered open. "Hold me … hold me close, Devlin. I'm so cold."

The pain in his chest—fear of losing her, fear of how he might function without Juliet at his side—rose to his throat. "Stay with me." *Never leave me.* "Don't think of the cold. Think about what you want as your prize now you have won the wager."

A weak smile touched her lips, and his heart ached at the sight. "I did? But how? Rufus is like a disobedient child who doesn't do a thing I say."

"Rufus may be a disobedient child, but he loves you."

She smiled again, closed her eyes and curled into his chest.

Devlin pressed a kiss to her forehead and whispered, "No one loves you as much as I do."

Juliet was dreaming, dreaming of lying on a picnic blanket on the lawn, the sun beating down, Devlin leaning over her, all dark and handsome. He kissed her deeply, with a passion that stole her breath. Happiness flowed from her toes to the tips of her fingers, warming her body, soothing her soul.

The image faded and then she felt something wet against her cheek.

Her eyes shot open.

The large figure sprawled beside her in bed was not her husband.

"Rufus." She couldn't help but giggle. "You're not supposed to be here. Who let you in?"

"I did." Devlin's voice drifted over her, soft and smooth and caressing. "We fought for the coveted position on the bed. Rufus won."

Devlin sat in the chair beside her. A lock of ebony hair hung over his brow. The dark shadows across his jaw and the creases in his shirt told her he'd been there for some time.

"Rufus won?" She doubted that.

"I let him win. He deserves a reward for leading me to the icehouse, for leading me to you." A smile touched his lips, but she could hear the distress in his voice.

"I'm thankful you came when you did. Lord, I've never felt so cold."

She could not remember much after leaving the chamber. A flurry of activity. The doctor forcing her to swallow a vile-tasting liquid. Devlin pacing the floor in her bedchamber. Devlin insisting that she drink the tisane. Devlin drawing the coverlet up to her chin and kissing her goodnight.

"Dr Hughes said you should rest for a day or two. That we're to contact him at the first signs of a chill or fever."

She saw it then, the look of terror swimming in his eyes, the cracks in the dam struggling to keep a wealth of emotion at bay.

"I feel perfectly fine."

"Still, it is wise to heed his words."

Juliet nodded, and that seemed to bring him some comfort. "What time is it?"

Devlin shrugged. "The clock chimed three the last time I heard."

The faint hum of activity downstairs and the slivers of daylight streaming in through the curtains told her she had slept for a whole day. She glanced around the dreary room, suddenly recalled she lay in the bed where Charlotte Drake took her last breath. The image of Mrs Barbary looming over the bed made her heart skip a beat.

"What happened to Mrs Barbary?" She had a faint recollection of her falling into the water channel.

Devlin lowered his gaze and shook his head. "The magistrate and the coroner have been this morning. We've had to leave her in the icehouse until the jury attends later today. The inquest is tomorrow."

Inquest? How were they to explain the nature of the woman's death? "There is something I must tell you, about the letters, about Mrs Barbary's involvement." She tried to sit up.

"I know." Devlin leant forward and placed a comforting hand on her arm. "You told me last night while I lay with you on the bed. At first, I thought you were delirious but the more I thought about it the more it made sense."

"My grandmother was your grandmother's maid."

"Yes," he said in a hushed voice. "And I hope that wherever she is, she takes comfort from the fact that her granddaughter is an angel here on earth. That her granddaughter is the mistress of Blackwater and will see to it that her children treat others with the love and respect they deserve."

The notion touched her in a way she had not thought possible. She would do everything in her power to ensure Susan's sacrifice was not in vain.

"That makes Mrs Barbary my great-aunt." Juliet tried to swallow past the lump in her throat. "She saw me as a Bromfield, as a member of the vile family who ruined her sister's life. If only she would have embraced me."

"The woman could not see past her bitterness."

"She blamed your grandmother, too, for lying to her all those years." As Juliet had no memory of telling Devlin anything about Mrs Barbary's confession, she told him everything again from the beginning. "Do you think Mrs Barbary took her own life? Her death means we must tell the magistrate about my father's illegitimacy."

A brief silence ensued before Devlin said, "I told the magistrate a variation of the truth. Yesterday, Mrs Barbary informed Cook that the icehouse was unsafe and that until she had inspected the problem, no one was to venture down there."

"Is that true?"

"It is. Cook verified that the conversation had taken place as she had wanted ice to make sorbets."

"But how did you account for me being there?"

"I told them the housekeeper lured you down there on false pretences. That she harboured resentment over the death of my grandmother and Ambrose and blamed you, a Bromfield, for what had happened. Tilly and the other maids corroborated her open hatred of Hannah and the baron."

"I see."

Why had he not told the whole truth?

It was an opportunity to get his revenge on the Bromfields, too.

"Everything else I told them was the truth," Devlin continued. "I explained that I went out to find you and Rufus, that the dog led me to the icehouse. I told them how she tried to make her escape and got caught under the wheel."

A shiver crept down Juliet's back like the trace of frosty fingers. The memory of being locked in that frigid room would haunt her forever.

"Did they believe you?"

Devlin raised an arrogant brow. "Love, I could sell rosary beads to the devil. Besides, there are no wounds or signs of violence on the body. And the doctor has confirmed that your symptoms are conducive with being in the cold for a considerable amount of time."

A wave of relief rippled across her shoulders. But still, she had some compassion for Mrs Barbary. Hurt and disappointment had made her do dreadful things.

"But if you had told them about Susan, you would have hurt my father and Hannah, as you have wanted to do for so long."

Devlin sighed. He came to sit on the side of the bed, captured her hand and brought it to his lips. Those dark, mysterious eyes she loved searched her face. "And for every stone I throw at your father I now throw at you, at our unborn children, at the hopes for the future."

Love for her husband swelled in her chest. He had promised to protect her from the baron and not once had he faltered. "But I have suffered disgrace my whole life. I would welcome it gladly if I thought it might bring you peace."

"But you would not wish to hurt our children."

"We must hope they are strong enough of character to cope with anything that comes their way."

"And they will be." He bent his head and kissed her. "How can they not with you as their mother?" A mischievous smile formed. "Besides, we have the letters. We have the proof your father fought so desperately to find. We will use them to our advantage. Shall we go to London? Shall we visit your father and tell him of our lucky discovery?"

The thought of forcing the baron to acknowledge his hypocrisy caused a knot in her stomach. "Yes, though I doubt the meeting will be pleasant. And then promise me we can forget all about the letters." She sat up, though the task was made more difficult by the mounds of blankets on the bed. Then she realised she was naked. "Good Lord."

"You refused to wear one of the nightgowns purchased from the modiste." Devlin's gaze slid across her bare shoulders, igniting a fire in her belly. "I have had a hell of a night trying to keep you warm."

"A hell of a night?" she teased. "What about today? I feel cold to my bones and Rufus is of no use."

The hound opened one eye upon hearing his name but then fell back to sleep.

"What would you have me do?" Devlin said with a grin. "Stoke the fire? Fetch another blanket?"

He was the only thing she needed. "Body heat is supposed to be the best way to warm the blood."

A wicked glint flashed in his obsidian eyes. "As I have a

rather large body, I should be able to heat you quite quickly." Devlin stood. He strode over to the door and called Rufus. "I shall take him down to the stables and let a groom take him out."

Rufus jumped off the bed and came to heel at Devlin's side. Juliet could hear him talking to Rufus as they headed out of the door and down the stairs.

In a matter of minutes, her husband returned. He locked the door, stripped off his clothing and slipped into bed beside her. "Now, where would you like me to start?"

CHAPTER TWENTY-ONE

"If you have come to berate me over my conduct the other day, then you can save your breath." The baron stood before the fire in the drawing room, his hands clasped behind his back. He wielded his arrogance like a shield, but Devlin had the one weapon capable of cleaving it in two. "I assume it's just a matter of time before you find an excuse to call me out."

Devlin relaxed back in the sofa while Juliet sat comfortably at his side.

"And I don't know why I must be party to this ridiculous conversation," Miss Bromfield complained from the chair opposite. "So I wrote to tell Ambrose he was a fool. So I told a few tales, cast aspersions on his character. I was upset. Do I not have the right to voice my opinion?"

"You have no right to spread malicious lies," Juliet said with a level of confidence Devlin had not seen when she stood outside his house in Wimpole Street, nibbling her bottom lip. "You have no right to slander a gentleman's good name just to bolster your own sense of worth."

Miss Bromfield tutted. "He's dead. What does it matter?"

"It matters to me." Devlin cast the chit his hardest stare, took pleasure in her nervous gulp. He glanced at the baron. "We thought you might like to know that we found the letters you seek."

Miss Bromfield sat forward. "You mean Ambrose kept them?" With hope in her eyes, she looked up at her father. "Well, surely that means he cared something for me."

Devlin held the next sentence in his mouth for a few seconds as one would a fine wine. He savoured the taste, anticipated the way its potency would relax his shoulders, would send a wave of satisfaction surging through his veins.

"I am not speaking of the letters sent to Ambrose," he said, relishing every word. "I speak of the letters written to my grandmother, to Charlotte Drake. Letters written by her maid Susan while she attended your parents, Baron."

All life drained from the baron's face. He reached for the mantel and gripped the wood. "You found them? You've … you've read them?"

"Numerous times."

The baron gulped. With trembling fingers he reached into his coat pocket, withdrew a handkerchief and used it to mop the beads of sweat from his brow.

"Papa? Is everything all right?" For once, Miss Bromfield sounded anxious.

The baron could not find his voice and simply shook his head. The action sent Miss Bromfield into a tizzy. Still looking confused and bewildered, she jumped up and assisted her father into a seat.

"What is it, Papa?" She turned to Juliet and scowled. "What have you done?"

"It is not a case of what we have done," Devlin said, unable to suppress his jubilation. "But more a case of what your grandfather did."

The baron's complexion turned grey, sallow. He swayed in the chair, looked ready to cast up his accounts. "Leave us, Hannah. I'll not have you party to this conversation."

"Miss Bromfield stays," Devlin said, his tone hard and unforgiving. The witch would hear everything he had to say. "She stays. Else you leave me no option but to put the evidence in print. Some magazines thrive on gossip."

"You wouldn't dare."

"It would be a fitting retribution, do you not think?"

Miss Bromfield braced her hands on her hips and glared. "I do not know what game you're playing here but say what you must and then leave. You should be grateful I have not thrown you out already."

The baron squirmed in his chair. "I beg you. Spare the dear girl. My daughter has suffered enough heartache."

Miss Bromfield? Suffered? What about Juliet?

Devlin's blood boiled. The man could not have said anything more damning. It took every ounce of willpower he possessed not to—

Damn it.

Devlin shot out of his seat. He crossed the room, grabbed the lord by his cravat and hauled him to his feet. "If you were twenty years younger, I would beat you black and blue."

"Do it, if it means you'll keep this from Hannah."

"From Hannah?" God's teeth, Devlin's hands throbbed with the need to punish this man. He took one look at Juliet's face, noted there wasn't a glimmer of pain in her eyes and it brought him back to his senses. "Do you see the lady before you?"

The baron turned to look at Miss Bromfield.

"I speak of Juliet, you fool. I speak of the only person in this room who possesses an ounce of integrity. I speak of a woman who puts every highborn lady to shame." Devlin forced the baron to look at Juliet. "She is the only decent member of this family. And still, your thoughts are with the daughter whose vile tongue has cost you everything."

Devlin threw the baron down into the chair and returned to the sofa.

"Do you feel better now?" Juliet whispered as Devlin settled beside her.

"Considerably so." He tugged at the ends of his coat sleeves.

"Then I'm pleased." Juliet gave him a beaming smile and then she straightened. "What my husband is trying to say, dear Miss Bromfield, is that we have evidence to prove that our father is illegitimate, too. Indeed, it means you are the granddaughter of a maid."

A deathly silence ensued.

Miss Bromfield snorted. "I have never heard anything so preposterous."

"Oh, it's true," Devlin replied. "Your father is the son of a maid. It is the reason he was rummaging in my desk at three in the morning. The reason you were torn from your bed in your nightrail and forced to make a hasty retreat."

Miss Bromfield turned to the baron who sat with his head hung low and did not meet her gaze. "Papa? Tell them. Tell them to stop spouting nonsense." Deep furrows lined her brow. "Papa?" After a long, drawn-out silence, she said. "Is it true? Was your mother a m-maid?"

"I believe so," came the baron's hushed reply.

"Brace yourself," Juliet warned.

"Why?" Devlin glanced at Miss Bromfield's stone-like expression. "What will she do?"

"You'll see."

It started as a squeak in the back of Miss Bromfield's throat. Like a bubbling pot, the sound grew progressively louder as the chit started shaking. The high-pitched wail reverberated off the walls. And then she tore around the room in a frenzy, knocking over the table, smashing the vase. With gritted teeth she clawed at the cushion, sending feathers flying into the air.

"Do something," Devlin shouted to the baron, who sat dumb-founded. "The girl will do herself an injury."

Juliet stood calmly. She strode over to Miss Bromfield, who had taken to ripping apart another cushion, and slapped her hard across the face. "Stop it, Hannah. Stop it now."

Miss Bromfield blinked. She put her hand to her flaming cheek and then crumpled into floods of tears.

Juliet caught her sister and held her in an embrace. "It is better you know the truth."

"I'm the granddaughter of a maid," she sobbed, her shoulders shaking with the force. "I'm ruined. Ruined. Ruined. Ruined."

"Pull yourself together," Juliet snapped. "I am the daughter of an actress though am more ashamed to say I'm the daughter of Baron Bromfield."

"Now listen here," the baron began. "Just because—"

"Be quiet," Juliet interjected. "After the way you have behaved do not dare chastise me now." She gripped Miss Brom-field by the upper arms and guided her into the chair. "Now, dry your eyes and listen to what my husband has to say."

Devlin's gaze never left Juliet, even when she returned to her seat. Pride swelled in his chest, along with respect and love and a host of other emotions he could not even begin to explain.

"Well?" Miss Bromfield sniffed. "Will you make court jesters out of us, Mr Drake? Are we to be paraded around like the fools of the fair?"

Devlin suppressed a smirk. The thought was tempting. "Rest assured. The letters will remain hidden on the proviso you both do exactly as I say."

The baron snorted. "You want money. Is that it?"

"I would not take your money if I was begging in the gutter. But you will both work to ensure you clear my brother's name. You will do everything in your power to restore his reputation. By whatever means necessary. Do this, and we shall not reveal the contents of the letters written to Charlotte Drake."

The tension in the air was palpable.

"And that is all you seek?" the baron said, his beady eyes narrowed.

Juliet tapped Devlin's leg and turned to whisper in his ear.

"My wife has a few stipulations of her own."

Juliet inclined her head to him and then turned to face the Bromfields. "We find ourselves in the unfortunate position of being without a housekeeper. I would like to employ Mrs Wendell if she is happy to move to Blackwater."

"Mrs Wendell?" The baron's cheeks ballooned. "But she has worked in this house for years."

"Then perhaps she needs a change of scenery. I would also like to take Nora as my lady's maid." Juliet gave a satisfied sigh.

A sob choked in the back of Miss Bromfield's throat. "Take the furniture. Take the silver. I don't care what you take just as long as you keep our secret."

The baron's shoulders sagged in resignation. "Take them. Take the whole damn house if you must."

"Then I shall go and break the good news. Mr Drake can finish with the proceedings here." Juliet rose from her seat with the grace of a duchess. She left the room without a backwards glance.

"So what do you really want, Drake?" the baron said in a tone reeking of suspicion.

"Only that which we have already stipulated. You have a month to correct public opinion regarding my brother." Devlin wondered if they knew what that meant. It meant Miss Bromfield would look foolish, would appear inferior to those gentlemen looking to make a decent match. Miss Bromfield's foolish tongue would cost her dearly.

"And how can I trust you to keep your end of the bargain?" the baron said.

"You can't. And you will never find the letters." Devlin had returned them to their hiding place beneath the velvet kneeler. All but one which he retrieved from his pocket and handed to the baron. "This is an example of what I have hidden away. Keep it. Should any further attempts be made to recover the letters, I shall have no option but to reveal all I know."

Miss Bromfield whimpered. "We will do everything you ask, Mr Drake. Rest assured. The last thing I want is for people to discover I am related to the hired help."

"Excellent. I am glad we understand one another."

A host of other questions bombarded Devlin's mind. He would have answers for those, too, before he left the baron to deal with the volatile lady at his side.

"Might I ask if you've heard from Mr Biggs? He was alive when we parted company though I have not seen him of late."

The baron scoffed. "Then you're the reason the rogue robbed Mr Middle's office and caught the mail coach north."

"Someone had to make the fellow see sense." Now to return to the matter of his brother. "Did Ambrose tell you how he came by the letters? The ones written by the maid we now know to be your mother."

An agonising groan left Miss Bromfield's lips.

"Your grandmother gave them to Ambrose when she persuaded him to break his oath to my daughter."

Miss Bromfield's sudden gasp revealed her surprise. "What! So it's all your fault." Tears trickled down her face. "Ambrose would have married me were you not your father's by-blow."

"Shut up, Hannah, before the servants hear."

It occurred to Devlin that the baron's motives for the duel stemmed from more than just the disrespect shown to his daughter. Would the baron have fired if given a chance? Would the baron have murdered Ambrose to keep his secret safe?

Either way, it didn't matter now.

Ambrose was dead, and Devlin had his own reasons for not revealing the truth.

"I shall return for Mrs Wendell and Nora first thing in the

morning." Devlin stood and strode to the door. As his fingers settled around the handle, he stopped and turned to face the sorry pair. "One more thing before I go."

"What now?" The baron huffed. "I knew there would be something."

"Should either one of you do anything to hurt my wife, I shall steal into this house at night and take you both hostage. Indeed, you might find yourselves smuggled onto a stinking hulk, might wake on a cramped ship bound for the Americas." He cast a wicked grin. "Good day to you."

The argument in the drawing room started as soon as Devlin closed the door. Miss Bromfield shouted and screamed. The crashing of glass reached Devlin's ears along with the baron's cries and protests.

Not wishing to be a witness to a murder, Devlin chose to wait outside. After a minute or so, Juliet appeared at the door and hurried down the steps. Her wide smile told him they had just hired a new housekeeper and maid.

"Oh, I cannot wait for Mrs Wendell and Nora to see Blackwater." Excitement radiated. Juliet looked happy. "Did you see Hannah's face when she learnt of her imperfect bloodline?"

"It was priceless."

"I shouldn't gloat, but I cannot help it."

Devlin stepped aside as the groom opened the carriage door and lowered the steps. Devlin took Juliet's hand, assisted her into their conveyance and followed closely behind. They settled into opposite seats, simply because he liked to gaze upon her during their journey.

"Your sister's temper is likely to land her in Newgate," Devlin said as the carriage rattled along the busy street.

"At least she had something to be cross about this time. Usually, she flies into a rage at the mere sight of the dinner menu."

Was the lady's volatile nature the real reason Ambrose decided to—

Enough.

Devlin had spent three years thinking about Ambrose. Now it was time to think about his own future. "On the subject of dinner," he said, "I thought we might stay in Wimpole Street tonight rather than travel to Blackwater."

Besides the need to collect their new housekeeper and maid, there was another reason he wanted to remain in town. The shocking note had arrived just before they had left for London.

Valentine was to fight a duel at dawn.

Devlin had meant to tell Juliet on the journey but wanted to deal with the baron first. He would tell her later this evening when they were nestled in bed, else she would only worry that he might act as Valentine's second. Dariell had accepted the role. Valentine was perhaps the greatest shot in all of England, so the Frenchman had nothing to fear.

Valentine, he has such a surprise in store.

Dariell's words drifted through Devlin's mind. Strangely, he did not feel a sense of foreboding. How could he when this was Valentine's destiny?

"I was going to suggest we stay in town tonight." Juliet's sweet voice dragged Devlin from his reverie.

"You were?" Devlin raised a curious brow. "Why? Has it something to do with the fact that we have made love in every room in Blackwater?"

"Most rooms," she corrected, moistening her lips. "But it's not so much about the place as it is about the person."

That told him.

Devlin smiled. "Your honesty is perhaps your greatest asset, Mrs Drake. Along with your incredible stamina and your ability to tame wild beasts."

Juliet raised her chin. "You must admit I did an excellent job with Rufus."

"You did indeed, which is why I intend to reward you with whatever your heart desires."

Her jade green eyes softened. Love lingered there. He knew the emotion by sight now. "You have already given me everything I want. What could I possibly ask for that I don't—" She stopped abruptly and sucked in a breath. "Oh, I know exactly what I want."

"You do?" Did she mean children? At the rate they made love, she could well be with child. The thought found him in the grip of another powerful emotion. The need to protect his family raged like a fire within.

"I would like a mate—"

"A mate!"

"For Rufus."

"You want to lumber us with another uncontrollable beast?"

"A mate might calm him down."

"I highly doubt it."

Juliet chuckled. "Why? It worked for *you*."

Devlin laughed then. "You have a valid point. But I'll not have two dogs in the house."

"Not even if I can train them to behave?" She arched a brow by way of a challenge.

"Are you suggesting we make another wager, Mrs Drake?"

"Not at all. The pressure to win is far too great." She crossed the carriage, fell into his lap and pressed a soft kiss to his lips. "Are you sure there is nothing I can do to change your mind?"

The minx!

She only had to look at him with those mesmerising green eyes, and he was a slave to her wants and whims.

"It will take an awful lot of work to persuade me," Devlin teased as he tugged down the window blind to his left. "And you know I'm stubborn. You know I am the beast most men fear."

Juliet twined her hands around his neck as he leant forward

and lowered the other blind, too. "You're not a beast. You're just a very large man."

"Do you think you have what it takes to manage me?"

"Yes, Mr Drake," she breathed as she rained kisses along his jaw. "I believe I might manage you very well."

The End

Thank you!

Thank you for reading *A Wicked Wager.*

What surprise awaits Valentine at his dawn appointment?

Find out in *Valentine's Vow*
Avenging Lords Series Book 3

Coming soon!
Valentine's Vow

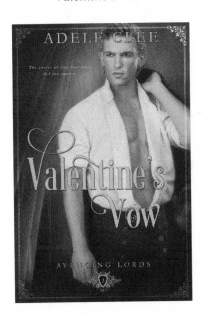

Made in the USA
Columbia, SC
26 August 2020

17499492R00145